Finally

Ruth Smith

Copyright © 2014 Ruth Smith
All rights reserved.

ISBN: 1482513099
ISBN 13: 9781482513097
Library of Congress Control Number: 2013914639
CreateSpace Independent Publishing Platform
North Charleston, South Carolina

Acknowledgments

First and foremost, I want to thank my Lord and Savior, Jesus Christ, because with him, all things are possible. To my late brother, Court: thanks for telling me that I could do or be anything I wanted to be. To the kids at school who asked me what I was waiting for: I thank you with all my heart. Your words truly inspired me to get writing! To the love of my life, Russell: thank you for listening to me read and talk about my book, over and over again! You are a trooper! To Mrs. Miller: thank you for your help and inspiration. You have truly been an angel! What would I have done without you? To my family and friends: thank you for your support and believing in me. Special thanks to my sister, Laurel, for her support and encouragement. To Buddy and Shadow, my beloved pups: thank you for your inspiration, protection, and for loving me unconditionally. I will be loving and missing you always. And to my readers, some finallys are but a moment and others are life changing. It is my prayer that all of your finallys will be blessed. Thank you so very much for reading my story.

Chapter 1

"Hey, what are you doing sneaking out already?" Dr. Ray called out when he looked up from the nurse's station and noticed Annie heading out the back door.

"Well, for starters, I was hoping no one would see me!" Annie replied.

A warm smile replaced the tired lines on his face as he walked to meet her in the hall. "Even though, you were just going to take off and leave me, I wanted you to know that I couldn't let you leave without wishing you a happy birthday!"

Annie turned back around and hurried to give her friend a hug. "You are such a sweetheart to always remember my birthday."

Dr. Ray and his wife, Sue, had been close friends of Annie's family for as long as she could remember. Annie believed she owed the career of her dreams to Dr. Ray. However, he would always disagree and say that there had been only one reason Annie had gone to nursing school with a full scholarship: and that was because of her exceptional ability.

Still holding on to Annie's hands, Dr. Ray stepped back, let out a chuckle, and said, "I couldn't help overhearing your conversation with Dr. Stevens, and I'm quite sure that I heard you tell him today was your twenty-fifth birthday. Young lady, if my memory serves me correctly, your twenty-fifth birthday was ten years ago! I remember that day well because that was the year that you and Alex met your parents and Sue and I down at Lake Powell. You know, Annie, there is just no way that I could ever forget that day. Maybe it was the beautiful birthday cake Alex made you. It's kind of hard to forget a catfish-shaped birthday cake that's decorated with twenty-five sardines."

"Oh, I remember that day, too!" Annie added. "Alex didn't waste a minute! As soon as I blew out the candles, he hurried and gathered up those sardines so we could use them for bait! Even so, it sure turned out to be a great trip."

"It sure did." Dr. Ray chuckled again. "We had more fish than we could use. Those fish took to the sardines but oh my, those stinky little fish didn't do too much for the flavor of the icing!"

By then Annie was giggling. "No, they didn't, but Alex was so proud of his cake decorating. He always comes up with something to make my birthdays memorable! In fact, that's what he's doing at this very moment. He and the kids took a quick trip over to Cedar City to do some shopping. They wouldn't give me any details, but then, knowing Alex as I do, I know it will be great! It's kind of silly, but I get so excited waiting to see what he's going to do. It makes me feel like a big kid!"

Dr. Ray smiled with a twinkle in his eye and said, "What do you mean, Annie? You're still a kid to me!"

"Oh sure, I guess that's why you just reminded me that my twenty-fifth birthday was ten years ago, and I'm sure you're going to enjoy setting the record straight with Dr. Stevens. But you know what? It's OK, because I'm going to go home and celebrate my birthday with my adorable family, and you, my dear friend, are going to spend the rest of the night working."

Unfortunately, their conversation had to end when they heard the front desk page Dr. Ray. After a quick good-bye, Annie turned and headed back to the exit. As she was pushing the door open, she happened to notice her watch and was thrilled to see that it was only 6:30. Usually, it was 7:00 or later before she finished up her paperwork and gave the report to the oncoming shift. As she made her way across the parking lot, she thought about what she had just said to Dr. Ray. It was so true—she couldn't wait to see what Alex had planned for her birthday.

Alex and Annie had grown up together in the small town of Milford, Utah. Only a few months separated their birthdays, and because their parents had been and were still very close friends, their friendship had begun when they were just babies. They had played in the same neighborhood. They had gone to school together and even attended the same church.

Finally

Annie's first vivid memory of Alex was when he and his best friend, Jake Whittaker, had decided to glue her beautiful new, Easter dress to her chair during Sunday school. The whole incident began when Alex spotted a tube of super glue sitting on the kitchen counter as he was eating breakfast that morning. For some unknown reason, he put the glue in his pocket, and he didn't even remember it until he got a little bored during the Sunday school lesson. After a sneaky discussion, Alex and Jake, who was also having trouble listening to the teacher, thought it would be interesting to see if super glue really was as strong as the TV commercial said it was. They devised a plan and decided that Annie would be their test subject since they were sitting directly behind her. The two boys lowered their heads and pretended to listen to the teacher, and then Jake carefully lifted one of the lacy layers of Annie's dress so that Alex could squirt a line of glue along the backside of the metal seat. After, they carefully patted the material to the chair to make sure it made contact with the glue. Annie had been totally oblivious to their antics, as she had been listening to the teacher's lesson about Easter.

Even though Alex and Jake had doubted that the dress would actually stick to the chair, they decided they would stay to see what happened. As soon as the class finished the closing prayer, Annie stood up and waited patiently in front of her chair for the other children to finish saying their good-byes before she said her own to Mrs. Anderson.

The boys' hearts began to pound, and their eyes grew large with anticipation as they peered down at the ruffled edge of Annie's dress, which was still draped across the chair. They didn't even hear the conversation between Annie and their teacher, because they were busy waiting for the result of their experiment. Then it happened! Annie only had to take three small steps before the commotion. As soon as she took her third step, the chair followed and crashed into the back of her legs. The unexpected force caught her little body off guard and caused her to tumble across the room. Her face hit the floor first, and then the chair, with the skirt of the dress still glued to the seat, smacked into the back of her head before it landed on top of her body.

The bewildered Mrs. Anderson started to scream as she ran across the room to help Annie, and she screamed even louder when she saw that Annie's face was covered with blood. Needless to say, the next few moments were more chaotic and irreverent than usual in the quiet little church. Everyone came running, and it didn't take the adults long to figure out what had happened.

Thankfully, Annie's only injury was a bloody nose, and she didn't even cry until she had to watch her mother cut her beautiful, new Easter dress loose from the chair. Alex and Jake got a scolding they never forgot—from the pastor, their teacher, their parents, their grandparents, and quite a few members of the fellowship. As the years passed, the event actually worked in Annie's favor. When she needed to give Alex a hard time, she would bring up the story and then remind him that he had cried more than she had! Annie always said Alex had cried because of the scoldings but Alex knew he had cried because he had made Annie cry. It was the only time Annie could remember that Alex had intentionally been hurtful toward her.

If you were to asked Annie when it was that she fell in love with her husband, she couldn't exactly tell you, but she knew without a doubt that she was still madly in love with him. And if you were to ask Alex the same question, he would have told you it was the day he made her cry.

Finally, Annie was headed for home. As she steered the truck down Main Street, she thought about the events of the day. There hadn't been too much time for celebrating, considering the fact that there had been five emergencies, seven acute patients and the delivery of one new baby. She hadn't even had time to stop for lunch, but that was OK because she couldn't wait to tell the kids that their Sunday school teacher, Mrs. Miller, had delivered her baby girl on her birthday! Annie cherished the time she worked in the OB. Each new little baby brought so much hope and promise to the world. She believed that it was a privilege to be present when patients took their first breath of life as well as when they took their last. Working in the healthcare profession had taught Annie many things, but the one lesson she tried never to forget was that life was precious and that every single moment of it counted!

As she continued down Main Street, it seemed like it was only yesterday that she and Alex were welcoming their own children into the world. It was almost impossible to believe that today was her thirty-fifth birthday. She thought about how cute the kids had looked that morning when she'd walked in the kitchen. The three of them had been sitting together at the kitchen bar, munching down their favorite cold cereals. With that thought, a stab of guilt jabbed at her heart.

Finally

She felt bad that the kids had to eat cereal every morning, but there just wasn't time for anything else.

Guilt had descended upon her shortly after the birth of her first child. She felt guilty if she let her baby's diapers get too wet or if he rolled too far and bumped his head. It had seemed to her that every bad thing that happened to Jack was her fault! Finally, one day in desperation, Annie had turned to her mother, hoping that she would have an explanation for her feelings. She had been somewhat disappointed when her mother had only looked at her and nonchalantly said, "You know, honey, I still suffer from the same condition. I still feel guilty if you have a bad day. I'll get to thinking that there must have been something that I could have done to help you. Come to think about it, my condition has only gotten worse. Now, I feel guilty about things that happen to my grandkids."

When her mother had finished with her confession, she and Annie had laughed until they cried. After their uncontrolled laughter, Lil had taken her daughter's hand and said. "Sweetie, Jack's blessed to have been born to a momma who cares about him so much. You just keep doing what you're doing, and everything will work itself out."

What her mother had said was so true, because things always seemed to work out. After all, Jack was now half grown. Annie had to chuckle out loud as she continued down the street. She thought about Jack and how he'd consumed three bowls of cereal before his sisters had even sat down to eat their bowls of cereal. He'd grown over a foot in less than a year and a half, and he was constantly looking for something to eat. For their own protection, Kara and Molly had gotten into the habit of hiding their favorite snacks because Jack seemed to eat everything in the house.

Jack, who was now thirteen, resembled Annie more than Alex. His hair was just about the same shade of blond, and he had the same deep blue velvet eyes. Jack was already a very handsome young man, and thanks to his good looks, every other little girl in town had a crush on him. At least twice a week, a little girl would call the house and ask if he was home, but, before you could tell Jack that he was wanted on the phone, he would disappear. He'd announced more than once that he didn't have time to waste on girls because his true love was football!

Annie couldn't believe how grownup Jack had looked that morning. He had worn his favorite football jersey. The jersey had been the only thing that he had wanted for his birthday. It was a jersey just like the one his favorite football player wore. After hours of surfing on the web, Alex was able to find an authentic team jersey and an autographed poster. Football had never appealed much to Annie, but she was trying her best to learn the game, and she loved watching Jack play. She remembered him eating breakfast that morning, a spoon in one hand and a football in the other. He was always ready for the game.

Her thoughts went back to a few months before, when they had celebrated Alex and Jack's birthdays. They had spent the entire day celebrating with the annual Davis family barbeque/birthday party. The annual event had all started when Jack had decided to come two weeks earlier than his original due date and was born on Alex's birthday. The first birthday party that Annie had for Alex and Jack had been small and simple compared to the large party that it had become. Now, it took Annie weeks of planning and preparing, but it was always worth it when she watched Alex and Jack enjoy their special day together.

This year, they had added to the celebration by inviting Jack's closest friends for a sleepover after the barbeque. Annie and Alex couldn't believe how much pizza, chips and ice cream the boys had consumed, especially when they considered how many hotdogs and hamburgers they had eaten just hours before. After all those carbohydrates, the boys had run wild in the backyard and golf course far into the early morning hours, but that had been OK. After all, how many times in your life do you get to celebrate your son's first day of becoming a teenager!

It had always touched Annie's heart deeply how proud Alex was that his firstborn son had been given to him on his own birthday, and every year, just like the first, when Annie would ask Alex what he wanted for his birthday, he would say: "I told you the day Jack was born. He was the best birthday present I ever got, and he's the only one that I'll ever need, unless, you want to have another baby on my birthday!"

As she continued driving down main, Annie's thoughts drifted to Kara. Her sweet little face had taken on quite a scowl of disgust as she had watched her big, brother gulp down the milk from his fourth bowl of cereal after she had announced that she was glad her favorite cereal wasn't the same as Jack's. She giggled at her brother when he belched in reply. Then she had continued

Finally

to smile and eat the rest of her breakfast. Kara's beautiful little face was shaped like a heart, and she had big, brown eyes, topped off with long, dark eyelashes and long, brown hair that cascaded halfway down her back. Friends and family were always telling Annie and Alex that if Alex had been born a female, he would have looked just like Kara. Her beauty continued through to the inside. Sometimes, it was hard to believe that she was only ten years old. Kara was very compassionate, caring, and constantly on the lookout to help others. Just yesterday, she had turned down an offer to go roller-skating with her friends and instead chose to help Mr. and Mrs. Evans rake their fall leaves.

Annie smiled as she thought of the homemade birthday card that she had found leaning against the tea canister that morning. She pictured Kara tiptoeing through the house after everyone had gone to bed to deliver the card. And it was Kara who had led the family in a chorus of *Happy Birthday* as soon as everyone had gathered in the kitchen. The little girl never seemed to stop thinking of what she could do for others.

Next, Annie thought of her baby, Molly, and how she had started to tremble with excitement the moment she heard the word, "birthday." She had trembled so much that she had almost toppled from her chair. After settling back down, Molly had tried to spill the beans about a big birthday surprise but was ambushed by her siblings and father. Annie had thought the whole situation was unfair and had quickly come to Molly's rescue. Annie lifted Molly high above the angry crowd and carried her through the kitchen. Before leaving the room she had turned and said, "I can't believe that you guys are picking on my precious baby girl. Mommy will save you, and now I think we had better get you ready for the day before I have to leave for work."

After leaving the kitchen, they had walked hand in hand to the bathroom. Molly had looked at Annie with her big brown eyes and said, "Mommy, we have to fix my hair extra special, because today's your birthday! Right, Mommy?"

Molly had been dubbed the drama queen when she was just weeks old. Starting with a little squeak, she would look to see if she had anyone's attention. If the squeak didn't do the trick, she would begin to squeal and wouldn't stop until she had the entire family's attention. After reeling them in, she would start with a small grin, which most always grew into a contagious giggle that spread throughout the family. With her first steps, she had danced; with her first words, she had sung; and like every true entertainer, Molly had loved the full attention of her audience. In fact, most of the time she commanded it, and with all the commanding she did, Annie and Alex were often amazed at the patience that her brother and sister had for their little sister.

Molly had the same color of brown eyes as Kara, and her hair was the exact color of Annie's and Jack's. The big difference in their hair was that Jack and Annie had straighter-than-straight hair, and Molly had out-of-control extra curly hair. Sometimes she looked like Alex; sometimes she looked like Annie. And for some reason, it seemed like everyone thought it was necessary to figure out just who it was she resembled. After listening to all the observations and comments, Annie would tactfully share her own opinion: she thought Molly looked exactly like herself. Molly's blessings of beauty and charm won her the hearts of her family and friends, as well as strangers. Quite often, someone would say to them, "You ought to take Molly to Hollywood; that little girl could be a star." But Annie and Alex thought Molly was fine right where she was, and besides, she already was their little star.

Mornings passed far too quickly. After finishing Molly's hair, Annie dashed back to the kitchen and circled the table quickly to give everyone a kiss goodbye. When Annie reached to give Alex a kiss, he playfully grabbed her arm and pulled her back. "Come here, Birthday Girl," he said and softly spanked her rear end. Before giving his wife a second kiss, he winked and added, "You know, I'm hoping that we can work on the project tonight."

"Mmm sounds good to me," Annie answered with a smile and a wink of her own before heading toward the door.

"The project" was Annie's and Alex's code for new baby. They had always planned on having four children, but after Molly had been born, they had felt complete. That was until early last summer, when Alex confessed to Annie that he really wanted to have another child. Annie herself had been feeling baby hungry too, and so it was an easy decision for them to make. However, when you got right down to it, the idea had probably been Molly's, because when Annie and Alex had asked her what she wanted for her third birthday, she had innocently answered, "Daddy and Mommy, I want a new baby brudder or sister."

Although she didn't seem to mind that she didn't get a new sibling for her birthday, she did remind Alex and Annie daily that she still wanted a new baby! Both Alex and Annie knew that Jack and Kara would be happy with a new

Finally

addition to the family, but they had decided that they wouldn't say anything to the kids until something happened. They didn't want them to be disappointed.

After leaving the house, Annie hurried across town to the hospital. She had always liked the fact that in Milford, it only took you five minutes to get anywhere you wanted or needed to go. Annie was so grateful that she didn't have to worry about the kids. On the days she worked, Alex took Molly to preschool, Kara to the grade school, and now that Jack was in the seventh grade, he and Alex both went to the high school. Because Milford was such a small town, the junior and senior high schools were combined. After school, Alex would pick up Molly at one of their parents' homes and then make sure that the kids got to their afternoon activities. On the days they weren't busy, the kids would hang out with their dad while he finished up his school day, or Jack and Kara would take Molly home and baby-sit her. Annie had been a working mother since Jack was two months old, and she had always been grateful that Alex was such an active and involved dad. She didn't know how single moms ever survived, and she couldn't even think about what she would do without Alex.

Annie had never figured out what she had done to deserve Alex. He treated her like a queen, and not a day passed that he didn't remind her of his love. He was passionate and tender. He helped whenever he could around the house. He never forgot special occasions, and he sent flowers "just because." He was the kind of man most women could only dream about.

As she continued to reminisce, Annie thought about the time that she and Alex had graduated from college. Months before Alex graduated; he had applied to over a dozen schools in and out of Utah. In the end, two schools offered him a teaching position. One of the offers came from a very prestigious private high school in Salt Lake City, and it included an unbelievable salary for a first-year teacher. The other offer was from their old alma mater, Milford High School. If the difference in the salary didn't help them make up their minds, knowing that Annie might not be able to work full-time for years, because of the limited number of staff at Milford's small hospital, should have. But it really didn't take them long to decide, because both Alex and Annie knew that deep in their hearts, no amount of money could compare with going home.

Remembering that she needed to pick up the mail, Annie steered the truck into the first parking spot on Main Street that she could find. Before opening the door, Annie rested her hands on the steering wheel and took a moment to sum up all of her thoughts. It was then she realized that her life was everything she had ever hoped for: all of her dreams had come true.

Main Street ran north to south and consisted of two lanes. Annie had always liked the unique, old buildings that lined both sides of the road. Not long ago, she had heard talk that the city was going to demolish all of the buildings on the east side of the street so that they could widen the road and have more room for parking. She wasn't too excited about the whole idea, but she hadn't spent too much time worrying about it, because she knew change was slow to happen in a small town like Milford, and that was just one more reason why she loved living there.

Back in the 1800s, Milford had got its start as a mining town, and it still resembled many old mining towns. The stores all had adjoining walls, and the homes were built on very small lots. The old town was a symbol of the old west, and it held memories and secrets of the past. On the hill above Main Street stood a silver water tower. And just one street east of Main, was the Union Pacific Railroad Depot and its train tracks. Each of these landmarks had been so important to the little town's birth and survival.

Stepping out of the truck, the crisp breeze caused the trees' leaves to dance and Annie to shiver. She took a moment, as she walked from her truck to the post office, to admire the trees that Doc Symonds had planted years ago. It was amazing, how much the trees decorated the old street. Looking up past the tops of the trees and to the sky, Annie noticed that there were thick, dark, rain clouds moving in from the south. The mixture of the dark sky, crisp air, and the leaves only reinforced the thought that fall was coming and fall had always been her favorite time of year. Annie looked up at the clouds one more time, and hoped that they would move in and spill some of their moisture. Rain was always welcomed in this little desert town, located in Southwestern Utah. But the small town was far more famous for its wind than the rain. Picking up her pace, Annie quickly stepped into the post office, grabbed her mail, and began to file through the stack of envelopes. As she headed back to her truck, she was surprised when she heard a familiar voice call out.

"Happy birthday," Karen shouted as she hurried out of her car to catch up with Annie. "Well, have you had a good day? Did you get your flowers? Is there time for me to stop by tonight?" Karen asked excitedly.

Finally

"It's been a great day. The flowers are beautiful, thank you. And I always have time for you," Annie answered as she hugged her best friend.

Annie and Karen had been best friends forever. They had grown up in houses across the street from each other and had spent countless hours playing and growing up together. New acquaintances often mistook them for sisters, and they had stopped counting how many times people had asked them if they were twins. It was easy to see why people might think they were related. Annie and Karen both had blonde hair and blue eyes, and they were similar in size and had many of the same body and facial characteristics.

Their years of friendship had never been dull. Since they had grown up without computers, satellite TV, and cell phones, they had flourished on imagination and mischief. Once pretending to be disc jockeys from a local radio station, Karen and Annie decided to make a few phone calls to the good citizens of Milford. After a short introduction, the pretend disc jockeys would ask the innocents to sing a jingle from a well-known TV commercial. If the caller could sing the jingle word for word, Karen and Annie promised them a free case of that very product. Each time, as Karen and Annie would listen to the hopeful crooners; they would cover the phone's receiver with their hands and roll on the floor with silent laughter. Karen and Annie decided to take their mischievous gag one step further and informed the would-be winners that they could pick up their prizes at the local grocery store on Saturday morning at ten o'clock sharp.

Annie and Karen never thought that so many people would actually buy into their silliness, but they had. The following Saturday morning, there were over twenty very angry people at the grocery store, demanding to know who was behind the dastardly deed. The outrageous gag put the whole town in quite an uproar, and the local sheriff was called to investigate! The sheriff told the local paper that he would not rest until he found those who were responsible for the outlandish act. In the end, both of the girls had felt awful, though, neither one felt bad enough to confess, especially after they overheard their mothers discussing the news with several other mothers, who had congregated on Karen's front porch. They felt terrible as they listened to their mothers proudly announce to everyone how thankful they were that their children would never be a part of such a devilish prank. As soon as Annie and Karen were alone, they made a vow never to tell another soul of their transgression and swore that they would be good girls from that moment on, or at least they would try to be.

"What do Alex and the kids have planned for tonight?" Karen asked as they began walking back to their cars.

"I'm not sure. They were being very secretive when I kissed them good-bye this morning," Annie answered.

Looking down at her watch, Karen asked, "Can I come over in about forty-five minutes? I'm going to run home, get dinner taken care of, and then I can head over about seven-thirty."

"That sounds good! Hey, I think I know why Alex went to Cedar," Annie said with a mischievous grin. "He gave in and gave me one clue last night! He said that my present was black. Do you remember that cute leather jacket we saw when we took the kids school shopping? I'm pretty sure that's what it is!"

"Oh yeah, we found it at Style's. Wow, I loved that jacket, and it looked so cute on you. You know, I just might have to borrow it," Karen called out as she crossed the street to her car.

As soon as Annie opened the garage door, she was surprised by a banner that had been tacked up across the wall. The words she read brought tears to her eyes: "Happy birthday, Mom! We Love You, Alex, Jack, Kara, and Molly." Annie was searching for a tissue, but before she could find one, her cell phone rang. The caller ID said that it was Alex. She hurried to answer it and said in a silly voice, "Yo, Momma speaking!"

"More like my crazy Momma," Jack answered back with a chuckle. "Hey Mom, Dad wants me to tell you that we will be home in about an hour."

"OK, I'm glad you let me know. Oh, and I hope that Style's wasn't too busy today. Sometimes that place is such a mad house!"

"Good try, Mom! Dad figured you'd try and get something out of me about your present. He said all I can tell you is that we're bringing home two pizzas, a box of breadsticks, and a German chocolate birthday cake. Oh yeah, and Dad let us get two new movies. And since it's your birthday and Friday night, he said that we can stay up late and watch both of them!"

"Sounds great, and I can't wait to eat! I'm so glad you got pizza. I have been craving it all day!" Annie answered, and then even though she knew the answer to her question, she asked, "Hey, do you guys have your seatbelts on?" Alex was the all-time overprotective father and a very careful driver. He had a firm rule that the car would not move until the seatbelts were buckled. Annie didn't have to worry about him driving too fast either, because he always stayed within five miles of the speed limit. Actually, she was the one who was guilty of driving with a lead foot.

Annie could imagine Jack's expression when she heard him say, "Mom, you know you don't have to worry about that!"

"Oh, I know. It's just the mom in me! Hey, you guys be careful, and I'll see you all in about an hour," Annie answered and then added, "Jack, I love you. Will you do me a favor and hold the phone out so I can tell the rest of them that I love them too?"

There was a pause before Jack whispered back, "Yes, I will. And Mom, I love you too."

It had been a while since she'd heard Jack say the words "I love you." He was a sweet boy, but Annie had come to accept that the little boy who used to tell her that he loved her at least twenty times a day was now a teenager, and telling his mother that he loved her was no longer a priority.

Before heading in the house, Annie slipped off her shoes in the garage and paused for a moment after she had hung her sweater on one of the coat hooks in the washroom. The only sound she heard was the hum of an empty house. Oh, how she hated that noise! Most mothers would have loved a few moments to themselves, but not Annie. After growing up as an only child, she had grown to love the noise and confusion that her family made.

From her earliest memory, Annie knew she was the center of her parents' world, and they could not have loved her more, but she had always longed to have a sister or brother. That longing eased when Karen came into her life, and she treasured every moment that she spent with Karen and her siblings. She loved the commotion and excitement of a big family, and Karen enjoyed the tranquility of Annie's house. Together, they had the best of both worlds.

Annie's parents had loved it when Annie and Alex started dating, and it didn't take them very long to realize that Alex was the son that they had always prayed for. When the grandchildren joined the family, it was as if Alex and Annie had given her parents the world. Finally, they had their big family.

As Annie started down the hall, a familiar emotion of accomplishment and pride circled her heart. It had taken her and Alex almost a full year of doing whatever they could to keep costs down so that they could make their dreams of owning their own home come true. Walking through the house, Annie pulled the blinds and turned on a few lamps. She thought about the day they'd moved in. It had been December 17. The moment the papers were signed, they returned to their apartment, loaded up their belongings, and started moving. That night they had slept in sleeping bags by the fireplace. Jack and Kara had a blast. It turned out that it was a great night for everyone, including Annie and Alex, because it was the night that Molly was conceived. The next few days were very busy. The whole family had worked side by side to get things organized while at the same time, decorated for the holidays. Their hard work paid off, and by Christmas Eve, they were pretty much settled in.

Their house was located on the outskirts of Milford, and if you walked out the back gate, you would find yourself on the number four fairway of the little town's famous five-hole golf course, dubbed the "Windy Five." The kids loved hunting for lizards, searching for treasures, and building huts among the sagebrush in the warm weather months. When the weather turned cold, the abandoned golf course became their very own winter kingdom. They spent hours building snow forts, having snowball fights, and using the small-sloped hills for sledding. As excited as Jack and Kara had been about the play area of their new home, they were overjoyed with the fact that they both got their own bedrooms. And after years of living in a one-bathroom, two-bedroom apartment, everyone was thrilled to have three bathrooms.

Before heading to the tub, Annie decided she had better add a load of clothes to the washer and tidy up the house a bit. In just seconds, her arms were filled with treasures. She found three of Molly's dolls on the couch. In a corner by the front door, she picked up Jack's football shoes and a pile of three book bags and jackets. Many times, if Annie had to pick up the house after a long day at work, she would use one of her, I deserve the right to get angry speeches, but, not tonight. With her arms full, she went upstairs and returned the kids' belongings to their bedrooms. Then she closed a few more blinds and turned on a couple more lamps before she hurried and hopped in the tub. Annie figured she had time for a twenty-minute soak, and then she would throw on a pair of sweats and head back downstairs to wait for Karen.

Just as planned, the doorbell rang at seven-thirty. When Annie opened the door, Karen greeted her with two sodas and a lovely basket that was filled to the brim with all of her favorite things: bubble bath, a new pair of pajamas, and several boxes of her favorite tea and cookies.

"Shall we open a box of those cookies to help us wash down our sodas?" Karen asked as she headed for the couch.

"Sounds wonderful," Annie answered.

It had always made perfectly good sense to Annie and Karen to drink diet soda so that they could save their calories for the important things like cookies, candy, and anything that was made with cream cheese!

Facing each other on the couch, Karen was the first to speak, "Alex and the kids must not be home yet; it's too quiet here. I'll bet that your mom got you that cute scarecrow on the porch. I love it! Where did she get it? Did I tell you about poor old Jan? Oh, and before I forget, I told Betty that we would be in charge of Kara and Holly's class Halloween Party. Do you have any good ideas? Matt just got home, so I don't have to worry whether or not I'll still have a house when I get home, so before Alex and the kids get home, we had better hurry and catch up, because we haven't talked for days!"

After taking another swallow of her soda to help wash down the cookie that she had just devoured, Annie replied, "No, they're not home yet. They called a little bit ago and said they'd be home in about an hour. Yep, I love it, too! I'm thinking that Mom ordered it. No, but, Sarah, told me that Jan hadn't been feeling well. I hope she feels better soon. I would love to help with the party and I will start looking for some cute ideas. And to clarify your last comment, it's been a week!"

Whenever Annie had a bad day, Alex would say, "Why don't you call Karen?" Or he might suggest, "You'd better go get Karen and go for a ride or a walk." No matter how large or small the problem was, after the two friends had talked things always seemed to be better. Alex always claimed that Karen was a lot cheaper than a therapist. And each time he made his claim, Annie would remind him that she would make sure to spend the money that Karen was saving them the next time she went shopping! It was strange how the two friends could talk to each other, often times without even finishing a complete sentence. Even stranger, was that they could both totally comprehended what they had said to each other without even finishing their sentences. Their husbands had never figured out how they did it, but both men understood just how much the two friends meant to each other.

It was about 7:55 when Annie realized that Alex and the kids weren't home yet. She tried calling Alex's cell phone, but there was no answer. Karen reminded her how often the signal was bad through the Minersville pass and said that they probably stopped to get her another birthday present.

Annie knew that what she was really saying was, "Don't worry; they're on their way."

The two women tried to carry on with their chatting, but it was only moments later that Annie's worrying got the best of her. Walking over to the south window, she looked in the direction of the highway and said, "It's just so unusual for Alex not to call, especially when he had Jack call and tell me that they'd be home in an hour." Looking out the window, she could see that there were quite a few sets of headlights shining from the cars making their way into town. With a worried voice she added, "Oh, I'm sure they'll be coming." She was too worried to sit back down, so she continued to stand at the window and stare at the highway, praying to God that he would bring her family home safely.

Karen was totally sympathetic to her friend's worry and joined Annie at the window. As they watched, the drizzle turned into a down pour. Karen's concerns for Annie's family deepened. "Why don't you try calling them again? Maybe the cell phone has service now?"

Annie rang the number twice, but there was no answer.

"The battery must have died, or maybe they turned off the phone by accident. Knowing Alex, he's probably driving ten miles an hour in this rain," Karen added, trying to provide Annie with an explanation for her family's absence.

Looking up at the clock, which now read 9:00 p.m., Annie knew that something was wrong. Karen felt it too! This just wasn't like Alex. They both knew that he would have called. It was only seconds later that they noticed headlights coming up the road.

"Thank goodness. They probably had a flat tire or something like that," Annie said while thinking that she needed to stop worrying so much about everything.

Both women let out a sigh of relief as they turned and noticed the lights of the car had stopped in the front of the house.

"I guess they want to make a grand entrance through the front door," Annie laughed, and then she and Karen hurried to the front door.

Finally

When Annie opened the door, she and Karen were both surprised to see that the car out front was one of the local police trucks, and Deputy Dan Jones was walking up the path toward the door.

Dan had been a neighbor of Alex and Annie's when they had lived in the apartments. They couldn't have asked for better neighbors. Annie and Alex thought the world of Dan and his wife.

Why in the world is Dan here? Annie and Karen thought to themselves.

With his head down, Dan reached for the doorbell. He didn't even notice that Karen and Annie had already opened the screen door.

"Dan, are you OK?" Karen asked as she reached to open the door wider.

The two women noticed that Dan seemed shaken. When he looked up, they noticed that he was as white as a ghost.

Dan looked at Annie and then at Karen. With a low voice, he said, "I'm really glad you're here."

Then for a few moments, he seemed to be in some sort of a trance. Several times he turned to face Annie but then he would turn back to look at Karen. Each time, he'd clear his throat as if he was getting ready to speak, but nothing came out.

After watching him repeat this process several times, Karen couldn't take it anymore. "What is it, Dan?" As soon as the words had left her lips, she regretted them.

"Annie, Karen, I think you had better sit down," Dan answered as he led the two women into the front room.

Karen didn't know why, but she reached and took a hold of Annie's arm. They were sitting side by side when Dan knelt down in front of them. Annie had worked as a nurse long enough to know the look on Dan's face. Suddenly, she started asking him questions. She wanted to know how his wife and baby were. She had heard he was in line for a promotion and she wanted to know how that was going.

Annie stood up from the couch and began nervously pacing the floor. She continued to ask Dan questions; the strange part about the conversation was she wouldn't give him time to answer. She simply asked question after question: "Do you and your family enjoy living in your new home? I haven't seen Dixie for ages. Why don't we all get together and go out for dinner, real soon? You know, catch up on all that's been going on."

Patiently, Dan and Karen listened to Annie as she subconsciously avoided what Dan had to say. And then she stopped and stood completely still in the center of the room. For a moment, there was an eerie silence. One was afraid of what he had to say, and the other two were afraid of what they would hear.

Annie walked back to the couch, sat down, and looked directly into Dan's eyes and asked? "What is it Dan?"

Dan tried to swallow, but his mouth was so dry. "Annie" His voice cracked. "There was an accident."

"Oh, God in heaven, where are they? Did you take them back to Cedar, or are they here?" Annie asked, leaping from the couch.

"Annie." Dan's voice became stronger as he grabbed her by the arm and gently pulled her back down to the couch. Tears began to fall from his eyes. "Annie, they didn't make it. They didn't make it!" he repeated, trying hard to choke back the tears. What kind of police officer was he? He wanted to be strong for this poor woman, but he couldn't. This was too much!

"No, there's been a mistake. No, no. They went to Cedar. They went to get me a present for my birthday," Annie said calmly. For a second, she stared at the wall as she tried to take in what Dan had just told her. Still staring at the wall, Annie said, "I really didn't think they needed to go. I told Alex not to worry about my birthday. I told him that he had enough to do. They just went to Cedar, Dan. In fact, I just talked to Jack, and he said that they were bringing pizza and movies home. We're going to celebrate my birthday tonight! They just went to Cedar, and everyone comes home from Cedar." Annie's voice started to quiver. "Right, Karen?"

In total numbness, Karen put her arm around her friend. *This can't possibly be happening.* Karen thought to herself.

Dan was at a loss for words. He had worked on the force for ten years, and nothing compared to what he had witnessed tonight. He didn't know how to tell this sweet lady how her entire family had just been killed, but somehow the words came out. It felt as if something or someone had taken control of his voice. The tone of his voice was still low, and very slowly, he began to tell her what had happened. He didn't know which was worse—the look on her face or the scene of the accident that he had just witnessed. One thing was for certain; as long as he lived, he knew that he would never forget either.

Finally

"Annie, there was a semi. It was heading south toward Cedar. The driver lost control. As of this moment, we think the weight of the load shifted and caused the driver to lose control. He just couldn't control the truck. The truck swerved into the northbound lane." Dan's voice cracked. He cleared his throat, but it felt like something was choking him.

Annie's body collapsed as her mind began to absorb Dan's words. Dan and Karen reached for her as she crumbled to the ground.

"No! No! No! Please, God, no! Please, Dan! No, no, no," Annie wailed through trembling lips.

"Annie, I know this sounds so ignorant," Dan said as he tried to speak through his own tears. "It appears they were all killed instantly, including the driver of the semi. No one suffered." After hearing his own words, Dan was sickened even more. *Why did I just say that?* He asked himself. Quickly he was summoned back to reality when he heard her cry.

The cry came from so deep within her. It was as though Annie's very soul was being ripped from her body, right before their very eyes. Struggling with her own shock and disbelief, Karen continued to hold her friend, rocking her like a baby, knowing there was nothing she could say or do to help.

"I'm so sorry. I'm so sorry, Annie," Dan said as he lifted her broken body back to the couch.

After what seemed an eternity, Annie drew in several breaths and asked Dan to repeat what he had told her. She needed to hear it one more time. She listened, only this time without a sound. In her mind, she was trying to grasp onto the reality of what had happened. She gazed at the portrait of her family that hung above the fireplace.

As Dan repeated the story, she kept telling herself, *they're gone. My life is gone.*

Dan stayed as long as he could, but he knew he had to get back to the other officers, and then he had to finish his reports.

"Can I call someone for you, Annie?" He asked.

Karen was the first one to speak. "I'll take care of things, Dan."

Dan wrapped his arms around Annie once again. "I'm so sorry. Annie, if there is anything my family or I can do for you, please call us. I mean it, Annie—anything."

Annie tried to respond, but it was as if her body had separated from her voice. As Dan walked to the front door, he looked back at the two women sitting on the couch, and then he let himself out. He took in a deep breath and let the raindrops splash against his cheeks, hoping they would wake him from this living nightmare. He couldn't even imagine what that poor woman was feeling or how she was ever going to get through a tragedy such as this. As he drove away, he consciously made a quick right and steered the car toward home. He needed to hold his wife and kiss his children goodnight before he went back to finish the job that lay ahead of him.

Chapter 2

Annie pulled away from the comfort of her friend's embrace and tried to wipe away some of her tears with the back of her hand. Brokenhearted and confused, she looked at her best friend and said, "This is so totally unbelievable! I just don't understand why God has done this."

"I don't know, sweetie," Karen answered as she reached and gently wiped more tears from Annie's cheeks. She didn't know what to say because she'd been asking herself the same question, along with so many others. Karen just couldn't begin to comprehend why God would let this happen to Annie and Alex. They were the most loving and kind people on this earth. They were good people. They were the cutest couple she'd ever known. They had fun together. They really and truly loved each other. They loved their parents; they were good parents; they were good friends; they loved their jobs; they loved life. So why, why, why did this have to happen? Why did God let this happen? A deep fear raced through Karen's soul. If this event had caused her to question her faith in God's will, what living hell was her sweet Annie going through?

Still shaken beyond description and in shock, Annie and Karen sat side by side in total silence, until Karen realized that someone needed to tell Annie's and Alex's parents about the accident. Out of sheer nervousness, Karen cleared her throat several times and then with a raspy voice said, "We need to call your parents. I can call them if you want me to. I think they need to be told, you know, before the news spreads."

Even in their state of distress, both women knew that once the news about Alex and the children's death was found out, it would spread though the little town of Milford faster than a wildfire. Shaking her head, Annie answered, "No, I have to do this. I need to be the one to tell them." As she made her way to the phone, she said aloud, "Why has this happened? I don't understand. I just don't understand! I will never understand this!" And each word that Annie spoke confirmed Karen's fear for her dear friend's faith.

Both calls were the same. Her voice was slow and methodical as she tried to explain to her parents what had happened. And just like Annie, they were confused, which made it all the harder on Annie because she had to repeat the terrible news several times before they were able to comprehend what she was saying.

Finally, Annie put down the receiver. "They're coming," she said softly. She was still standing by the phone when they heard the doorbell ring.

Karen quickly stood up from the couch and hurried to the front door. Before she turned the doorknob, she was filled with a strong need to take care of Annie. There was no way that Annie was ready to deal with a bunch of people, and Karen wasn't about to let her!

"I can't do this!" Annie whispered.

"Don't worry, sweetie. I'll take care of you," Karen said reassuringly as she pulled the door open.

Both Annie and Karen were somewhat puzzled to see that it was Dan again, and this time, he was holding some type of a box with a handle. They were more than surprised when they saw that the box was an animal carrier. Annie became confused, and Karen became irritated.

"Dan, Annie doesn't have a pet!" Karen whispered as he stood on the porch.

He looked at Karen, nodded his head to signal he knew what he was doing. Then without waiting to be invited in, he walked in and went straight to the couch. He gently sat the carrier down and made a motion with his hands for the ladies to come and join him.

"When I left here, I needed to stop by my house for a minute. That's where Steve found me. We didn't know what to do with him, so I hope that I've made the right choice." Dan paused for a second then added, "The puppy was thrown from the car, but the walls of the carrier must have protected him. I had Steve take the little guy over to Doc Turner's, you know, to make sure that he was OK. He said that the puppy is real shaken, but he's fine." Then Dan opened the door of the carrier, reached in, and took out a little ball of black fur. "He sure is a little cutie!"

Karen had placed herself on the arm of the couch right next to Annie. She couldn't believe Dan's lack of consideration toward her friend, and she was just about to remind Dan once more that Annie didn't have a dog and that it would probably be best if he took the puppy and left, but in the same instant, Annie noticed a blue bow around the puppy's neck and realized that her suspicions about Alex's gift had been wrong. It wasn't a black leather jacket; it was a little black puppy. Instinctively, she reached for the shaken puppy, took him in her arms, and then fell back against the couch. She pulled him next to her chest and gently stroked his soft fur. With a reassuring voice, she promised to take care of him. Instantly, the puppy burrowed his little body against her breast. To their surprise, they noticed that he'd stopped shaking.

Dan was amazed. "Wow! Look how he just settled right down. Doc told me that after all he'd been through, the little dog would shake for days!"

To get a better look at the pup, Karen moved from the arm of the chair and joined Dan, who was kneeling in front of the couch. That's when she noticed a small scroll tied to the puppy's bow. She gave the paper a gentle tug, and it fell softly into the palm of her hand. As soon as Annie saw the small piece of paper, she gently lowered the puppy to her lap and reached for it with trembling hands. Annie looked to Karen, who gave a reassuring smile and nod that silently told her friend that it was OK to continue.

At first, Annie's voice quivered when she read the introduction that Jack had written, "Hey Mom." Then she nervously cleared her throat and proceeded to read the note. Here is your present! Sorry we couldn't wrap it. All of us decided that you needed something to keep you company when we're not home, because we all know you don't like to be alone, and we sure don't want you to be lonely. We thought about a cat but decided to get a dog. Mom, don't panic! We all promised Dad that we'll help feed him, take him for walks, and we double promised to take care of his messes. Molly said that he could be her baby brother until you get her a real one! And by the way, me and Kara are starting to wonder if there is something more to her obsession about a new baby! We'll ask you later! His name is Buddy. We hope you don't mind that we named him. It just seemed to fit when Kara said, "Here little Buddy!" He came right to her. I think he's real smart, and I just know you are going to love him.

Dad told us that dogs grow up faster than kids, so when Buddy gets bigger and heads out to chase a few rabbits, and I'm out playing football, and the girls are out doing girl stuff, whatever that is, and dad is out doing dad stuff, he got you something real special. He said that it's to remind you that you're never really alone because we'll always be close to your heart! Hint: look under the ribbon!

    Hope you have the best birthday ever, Love Ya Forever,

    Your Fam

P.S. This is pretty mushy stuff for me to be writing, but it's OK because Dad made me write it, and I didn't mind, 'cause I got the best mom ever!

After she had finished reading the note, Annie happened to catch a glimpse of a silver chain which was hidden by the puppy's fur and discovered that the chain held a beautiful heart pendant. Its design had been made from etching together the initials A, A, J, K, M, and B, which encircled the words, "Love ya forever."

Karen broke the silence when she placed her hand on Annie's arm and said, "It's beautiful!"

Annie smiled at Karen and then moved returned her gaze to the small heart. She thoughtfully ran her fingertips over the etching several times before she realized that the pendant was actually a locket. Inside the locket was a miniature photo of her family. "I've never seen this picture!" Annie said softly and then added, "They must have had it taken today." More tears began to fall from her cheek as she lifted the chain to her neck.

Instinctively, Karen reached over and helped her to close the clasp.

Seconds later, the front door opened. Annie's parents, Barney and Lil, arrived first, followed by Alex's parents, Joe and Gladys. They all rushed to Annie's side and throughout the coming hours, the details of the tragic events were repeated over and over, in conversation and in their individual minds. Annie and Alex's pastors, a married couple who shared the title and duties of the church, were among the first to come and offer their condolences and support. Upon their arrival, someone had asked them if they would lead the family in prayer. Annie sat quietly while everyone circled around her. After her pastors anointed her head with holy oil, she listened as they asked the Lord to bless her with strength and courage, and for her to be comforted with the understanding

Finally

of his will through her trials. Alone in her thoughts, Annie decided that she had not been blessed with strength or courage, and she already knew that she would never understand why this had to happen to her family.

Somehow the night had turned into morning, and after hours of refusing to rest, Annie gave in and went to her room. Her mother and Karen walked with her to the bedroom, tucked her in bed like she was a child, and then left, hoping that Annie would be able to sleep. Lying in the bed with the little puppy snuggled closely to her breast, Annie watched him sleep and wished that she could close her eyes and find slumber as easily as he did. Over and over, she tried closing her eyes, but as much as her body needed rest, her mind would not allow it. The past hours raced through her mind with the same scene playing over and over, like a DVD player that was stuck on replay. She could see the facial expressions of each family member and friend as they rushed to comfort her. Most of them had come hoping the story had gotten mixed up and that somehow, when they walked through the door, they would see Alex and the children unharmed and alive.

Even more haunting were the images of her family driving home from Cedar City. First, a familiar and comforting scene, Alex was in the driver's seat with his hands griping the wheel at two and ten. Jack was in the passenger seat; Kara was in the backseat behind Alex; and Molly was in her car seat behind Jack. Alex carefully maneuvered the curves of the Minersville Pass, and then, out of nowhere, a roaring semi appeared, thundering its way through the turns, and then the fatal collision flashed through her mind. She heard her family's cries of terror!

The restlessness of her body matched that of her mind. Annie wanted to get off the bed, but she didn't want to disturb Buddy. Her restlessness proved stronger than her consideration for Buddy, and each time she moved, he would open his eyes long enough to make sure she was still there, and then he would drift back to sleep. She knew the poor little pup was exhausted from the trauma that he'd endured. Annie thought how hard it must have been for him to have been separated from his mother. Then she thought of her own children being separated from their mother, and a stabbing pain ripped through her heart.

"Did they cry? Did my babies cry for me?" Annie whispered out loud as she lay curled up in the fetal position. Her hand reached for the locket, and she slowly moved her fingertip across the etching, tracing each initial. She could hear Jack's voice say, "You're never really alone because we'll always be close to your heart!"

Annie was startled and pulled from her thoughts when Karen entered the room carrying a mug of hot tea followed by her mom who was carrying a plate of toast.

"We thought maybe you could use something to eat," Karen said as she sat the mug on the nightstand. "I also have a prescription from Dr. Ray. He thought you might need something to help you rest. He feels really bad. He wanted to talk to you himself, but they needed him at the hospital. I guess they had an emergency. Dr. Ray said that he would come as soon as he could."

Without saying a word, Annie sat up and took the pill from Karen and then reached for the tea. The hot liquid burned the inside of her mouth and the back of her throat, but she didn't care. She just wanted the medicine to work quickly. She wanted to go away from the pain, even if the relief was only temporary.

Lil sat down on the bed, next to her daughter. With her hand, she reached and gently stroked Annie's tearstained cheeks. With their faces only inches apart, Annie sobbed, "Oh, Momma, what am I going to do?"

Annie's mother reached for her only child and held her close to her breast. As she rocked Annie in her arms, Lil felt utterly hopeless. She didn't know what to say; she didn't know what to do. How could she possibly give anything to her daughter when she was feeling as though her own world had come crashing to a complete stop?

After Annie fell asleep, Lil and Karen thought that Annie would be able to rest better if they took Buddy with them, but when Karen tried to pick him up he started to growl and wiggled free from her grasp.

Karen looked toward Lil and said, "I guess Buddy doesn't want to go with us!"

The little dog backed up next to Annie and took a protective stance at her side. With his chest puffed out and his eyes fixed with a glare, he watched the two women as they spoke.

"This little puppy is amazing. I think he knows exactly why he's here," Karen whispered.

Lil nodded her head in agreement as she replied, "I think you're right!"

As they left the room, they looked back to check on Annie, and they couldn't believe the little dog hadn't changed his position. He didn't move until they closed the door. Once he felt sure that no one was going to take him away from his new master, Buddy nuzzled his way back into the comfort of her arms, closed his eyes, and fell asleep.

Sleep wasn't the escape Annie had thought it would be. She dreamed that Jack, Kara, and Molly were crying for her and she was searching for them, but no matter how hard she tried, she couldn't find them. She dreamed Alex was reaching for her, but as soon as he was able to grasp her hand, he would slowly let go. She could only watch him fall away from her as his body gently tumbled down a dark tunnel toward a light. She heard him calling her name. His voice would start out loudly, and then it would grow softer the farther he fell from her.

When Annie woke up, she was soaking wet, and her heart was pounding. Because she was a nurse, she figured she'd had some type of panic attack, which was a very common reaction for someone who had been through trauma. She had seen many patients have panic attacks, never thinking she would have one herself. Sitting up in the bed, she closed her eyes again and took in several long, deep breaths. Then she opened her eyes and looked around the room. Every moment of the past few hours came back clearly into her mind. The moment Buddy felt Annie stir; he quickly stood up and tried patiently to wait for her to notice him. After a few minutes, he decided that he'd have to do something to get her attention. Buddy laid his little head on Annie's lap, looked up at her with his big puppy eyes, and then let out his very best whimper. His plan worked. Annie reached down and gently picked up the puppy and nuzzled her nose to his neck.

Her voice was still raspy from sleep when she looked at Buddy and said, "I don't know what to do, little guy. I really need Alex. You see, when we decided to get married, we made a deal with each other that we'd always talk about things and that we wouldn't make important plans and decisions without each other."

After speaking, Annie realized that her mouth and lips were dry; in fact, her entire body felt dehydrated. She knew that she needed a drink, but she knew that she wasn't ready to leave the sanctuary of the bedroom just yet. She was grateful when she looked over at the nightstand and saw that the tea and toast were still there. The cold tea did the trick, and after eating a few bites of the toast, Annie was more than happy to share the rest with Buddy.

Sitting alone in the middle of the bed, she tried to think what she should do, but the biggest decision she could make was that she needed to get dressed. The tub was half full when Annie noticed that someone had set the basket Karen had given to her on the bathroom counter. She reached for the bottle of bubble bath and poured a generous amount into the tub.

Annie laid her head on a folded towel and then propped her feet near the faucet to let a small stream of very hot water run down her leg. Her only constructive thought was that she hoped no one had heard the water running. She just wasn't ready to talk to anyone, and she still needed more time to think. Annie had always been famous for loving a long hot bath, but this time, she wasn't even sure how long she had soaked. She was only aware that her body was way past the wrinkled prune stage.

After drying off, Annie opened the closet doors to look for something to wear but only found herself staring at Alex's side of the closet. Her eyes moved slowly along the bar. All of his suits were hung with a matching shirt and tie, and all of his slacks had matching shirts. Then she lowered her gaze to his shelves. One shelf was for old Levis; one shelf was for new Levis; and three shelves were for T-shirts. One was full of colored T-shirts, and the other two were filled with his beloved white T-shirts.

As she looked at Alex's clothes, Annie smiled and thought back to their first days together as newlyweds, living on their own in Salt Lake City. After hurrying home from a short honeymoon, they had packed all their belongings in the back of a pickup truck and moved to Salt Lake City. They moved into their apartment on Thursday and started college the following Monday. Even though they were very busy, they were incredibly happy. There had only been one problem, and it wasn't even a very big problem. Annie had worried that she was doing something wrong as she watched Alex go from a guy who dressed smart to borderline geek! The first week, she had thought that maybe it was because they hadn't had time to do the laundry and Alex was just being nice wearing whatever he could find. The second week, Annie thought she would be a good wife and make sure that Alex's clothes were washed and ready to go. But by the third week, when she watched him head out the door for an important job interview that would give them some extra income, wearing a bright red shirt with a pair of green slacks, topped off with a light blue jacket. She panicked and called Gladys.

Still convinced that she must have done something wrong, Annie cried her heart out to her new mother-in-law. After Gladys had finished laughing, she told Annie that she had been expecting her call. Then she confessed that Alex had made Gladys promise not to tell that he had a terrible case of color blindness. Annie was flabbergasted! She couldn't understand why a level-headed guy like Alex would think that she would think anything about it. But it did help her to understand why he had always colored such funky pictures in grade school. Gladys calmed Annie down and explained to her that it was just a guy thing; Alex's father had the same problem, and she'd had this same talk with his mother. Then she told Annie how to arrange Alex's clothes and gave her some advice: "Just make sure you're with Alex whenever he buys his clothes, or, better yet, pick them out yourself. Believe me! You'll be glad you did!"

Coming back from her thoughts, Annie put on a pair of jeans and a white tank. Then thinking she needed something warmer, she thought she would put on one of Alex's flannel shirts. Instead of getting a clean one from the closet, she turned around and walked over to the dirty laundry basket. As she buttoned up the shirt, she thought about how Alex had always teased her about wearing his shirts and how he had told her a million times that she wore them more than he did. Annie lifted her arm and breathed in. She could smell him, and oh, how she wanted to smell him. She needed to smell him.

With her face pressed against her arm, she pleaded, "Help me, Alex. Somehow, someway, baby, please help me!"

Buddy had followed Annie into the bathroom and for a while kept himself occupied by sniffing everything in sight. When he reached the closet, he discovered one of Alex's old tennis shoes. It took him several minutes of tugging and pulling to drag the shoe to a spot in the middle of the bathroom floor. Then like a conquering hero, he climbed on top of the shoe and gave a little bark of victory before he settled down to gnaw on the shoelace. When Annie noticed that Buddy had one of Alex's shoes, her first instinct was to take it away, but after seeing how happy an old shoe made him, she decided to let him keep it.

Annie mechanically brushed her teeth and pulled her hair back into a ponytail. Buddy waited patiently by her feet, but his instinct to go outside became stronger than his will to protect Annie. He let out a whimper, tugged gently at her pants, and Annie got the message. Annie carried the little ball of black fur out to the deck and down the stairs. As she waited for Buddy to do his thing, she thought about when she and Alex had built the house. She remembered how she had disagreed with him about his idea to have an outside door from their bedroom to the deck. She had tried to argue that it was just an unnecessary expense, but he had insisted that they would need a door and a deck for the hot tub he'd planned to buy one day. Annie was so glad Alex hadn't listened to her. They had used the door for many late-night escapes. After making sure the kids were asleep, they would head out to the backyard and cuddle up together in a blanket. They enjoyed watching the magnificent night skies filled with millions of twinkling stars, but their favorite thing to watch was a lightning show from a passing summer night's storm. Now, not only was Annie grateful for the time they had spent together, but today she was grateful that Alex had insisted on the door, because today it gave her a little more time to herself.

Annie wanted to give Buddy a moment to run around the yard, but she didn't want to stand where someone might see her, so she hurried under the deck and leaned against the wall of the house. Thinking she was alone, Annie was quite surprised to see her father walk around the corner of the house and was even more surprised to see that he was smoking a cigarette. She cleared her throat so that he wouldn't be startled.

She and her father had always enjoyed jesting with each other, and even though it was the darkest of times, it was just a natural reaction for her to give him a hard time about smoking. She tried to sound like her mother when she said, "Barney, you said you quit smoking!"

The warning she'd intended to give him had not been successful, and he jumped at the first sound of her voice. It took him several seconds to find her. When he spotted Annie under the deck, all he could do was give her an apologetic look and say, "I did."

Annie even found a little smile when she saw the expression on his face. Her father looked like a child who'd just gotten caught dipping his hands into a cookie jar.

Barney took one last drag of the cigarette before he tossed the butt to the ground and then added, "Please, just don't tell your mother. You know how upset she gets."

As he looked at his beautiful daughter, Barney couldn't even begin to understand why this had happened to her. If there was one person on this earth who didn't deserve this, it was his little girl. She was the kindest, most loving person he'd ever known.

"How are you doing, sweetheart?" He asked but then wished he could take back what he'd said. "That was a stupid thing to say."

Annie looked into her father's sad eyes and answered, "No, it wasn't."

Standing side by side with their arms around each other, they watched Buddy as he played with one of Jack's old baseballs.

"Why didn't we get a dog sooner?" Annie asked.

"At this minute, I'm asking myself why I didn't do a lot of things," her father said as he choked back his tears.

Annie couldn't believe that her father had even said such a thing. "Oh, please don't say that, Dad. My kids couldn't have a better grandpa. They adore you."

In silence, they continued to look at the little pup as he pushed the ball around in a circle with his little nose.

"Annie, I don't know how to say this except to just say it. The mortuary called, and they said that when you were able, they needed to know what to do. You know, about, about the arrangements." Barney's voice had started out strong but had weakened as he fought through his tears. He was barely able to finish his next sentence. "Annie, they said that if you wanted to see them, it would be possible."

Annie's heart broke even more as she watched her father's sturdy frame crumble with uncontrollable sobs. She turned and took hold of her father, knowing he needed this time to grieve.

"I'm so sorry. I wanted to be strong for you. It's my job to take care of you. I'll take care of everything. Oh God in Heaven, you shouldn't have to go through this, not you," he whispered.

Annie's hold around her father tightened. "Oh, Daddy, I love you so much."

Chapter 3

After the funeral services, all of Annie's family and friends gathered in the church meeting hall for a luncheon. The mood of the crowd had lightened, and everyone seemed to relax and appreciate being together as they ate. Annie sat quietly at the table that she shared with Alex's sister's family. She thought of Alex as she played with the food on her plate and how he had always called the food at funerals, "comfort food." She thought about the last few days, and she couldn't believe how much love and support the community had shown to her and her family. She felt that the services had gone well. Her pastors had conducted the services, and Annie had been the main speaker. When they had planned the service, everyone had worried it would be too hard for her but she knew, there was no one else, who knew Alex and the children like she did.

Annie had stood as solid as a rock as she shared special memories of her husband and children's lives. Now thinking to herself, she could only hope that she had given them the honor that they had deserved. When they were planning the service, Annie remembered that Alex had once said to her that if he were to go first, he wanted his favorite song played at his funeral, and, of course she honored his request.

Now the words of the song kept mixing in with her thoughts: *"Lord, I give you my life because you sacrificed your life for me."* Each time she heard the words, she responded with lyrics of her own: "I don't want to give you anything! I want my family back!"

Annie was brought back from her thoughts when several of her friends from work came to tell her good-bye, and it wasn't long after that the rest of the crowd followed their lead. Once everyone left, the hall was quiet except for the sounds of a few close family members and women from the church, who were cleaning up. Thinking she should probably get up and help, Annie tried, but she couldn't find the strength. She was glad she didn't have to worry about Buddy, because her father had volunteered to take him outside. He had insisted that the little puppy had sat still long enough, but Annie knew that her father probably needed an excuse to find a quiet place to have a cigarette. It would have been easy to want to join him, if only she had enjoyed the nasty habit. Knowing she had to move, Annie reached deep within and found the strength to stand. As she walked across the floor, the heels of her shoes made a soft clicking sound against the hardwood floor. It was so bizarre how many insignificant sounds she had heard in the last few days.

She walked over to the table where her mother and Karen were packing up the scrapbooks and photos and carefully placing them into the boxes to take back home. The scrapbooks had been placed on a table for everyone to look at, along with the recent photos of Alex, the kids, and Buddy. The photos had miraculously been recovered from the accident site. Annie looked at the scrapbooks and thought of all the hours she had spent making them. Never in a million years had she thought that she would be the one left with recorded history of her children's lives. She had made the scrapbooks so that her children could remember their childhood and accomplishments after she and Alex were gone. She had wanted the books to be shared with her grandchildren and great-grandchildren. In silence, she helped her mother and Karen finish. When they were done, everyone went back to Annie's house.

Back at the house, Annie found Karen in the kitchen trying to figure out where she could put all the leftover food. She was having quite a time, due to the fact that the refrigerator was already bursting with the food that people had brought to the house over the past few days.

"Why don't you take most of that home to Matt and the kids?" Annie suggested.

"OK, if that's what you want me to do," Karen answered, knowing there was no way that Annie was going to be able to eat all of it.

Finally

"You know, I couldn't have made it through these past few days without you," Annie said, fighting more tears.

"I know that you would have done the same for me," Karen said, reaching to put her arm around her friend.

"Will you do me one more favor?" Annie asked.

"Anything," Karen answered.

"I'm OK. I want you to go home and be with your family. The kids were having a real tough time today. And when you get there, I want you to grab hold of the kids and Matt and just hold them, and then hold them for me, too," Annie said, trying to smile through her tears.

Karen nodded her head. "I will, but you have to promise me that you will call me if you need anything."

"I promise," Annie replied.

Not many words passed between Karen and Annie as they busied themselves and made boxes for Karen's family, Annie's parents, and Alex's parents and sisters. Even after sharing the food, Annie figured that she had more than enough to last for weeks. She had only gone through the motion of keeping some of the food for herself, so that her mother wouldn't worry. Annie knew she wouldn't be able to eat much of it. Food hadn't sat well with her since the accident.

After they finished in the kitchen, Annie helped Karen out to the car with the boxes. Before she left, Karen gave Annie a big hug and said, "The only thing I can think to say is I love you."

"That's always a good thing to say. Thank you so much for everything," Annie replied. As she walked back to the house, she thought she'd better see how Buddy was doing. He'd fallen asleep in her arms on the way home from the church, and she had laid him on the couch. In the meantime, Buddy had woke up and must have been thinking he needed to check on Annie, because as soon as she opened the door, he was there to greet her. He surprised Annie, but what surprised her even more was that he wasn't alone. Her father, mother, Joe, and Gladys were right behind him, and she could tell by the looks on their faces that they had something to say to her. The expression on her father's face told her they had picked straws to see who would do the talking. Obviously, her father had lost.

"Annie, we need to speak to you. Now, I'm not going to beat around the bush. We don't want you to be alone, and so we've decided that we're all going to take turns staying with you for a while." He had done his best to sound firm, while his partners in crime nodded their heads in unison to show that they agreed completely with the plan.

Annie had anticipated that they would want to do something like this, and so she gave them her somewhat rehearsed reply. "I love you all so much. Alex and the kids loved you so much. No; what I meant to say is that they still love you. They will always love you." Before she could continue, she had to pause and clear her throat. Her voice was a bit stronger when she added, "It's just so hard to believe that they're really gone. The last few days have been a horrible living hell for all of us and this hell is far from over. I know you're all worried about me, but I'm just as worried about you. So, I'm hoping that you'll all be able to accept what I'm going to say next. We're all exhausted. I want you to all go home, get in your own beds, and try to get a good night's rest. I'm going to be really honest: I really think that I need to be alone. I'll be OK."

For a few seconds Annie was met with dead silence, and then she watched four heads shake in expressions of disagreement. But then, she was totally taken aback when Gladys said, "Honey, if you're absolutely sure that's what you want, then I think we should respect your wishes. And you know, all you have to do is call, and we'll come right back."

Annie had always loved her mother-in-law, but at that moment, she didn't think she could ever love her more. After they said their goodnights at the front door, Annie stood still at the front door and didn't close the door until both cars had driven away. Once they were gone, she closed the door slowly and then rested her face against the door's hard wood. With her hand still holding onto the doorknob, she took a long, deep breath and it was at that moment that reality hit. It roared through her soul like a fast train, barreling down the tracks, screaming to her again and again that she was alone! Her body started to tremble with fear.

"You said that you'd be all right. You said you needed to be alone," she reminded herself in a strong voice, but her strength quickly weakened, and she sounded more like a frightened child. Overcome with emotion and confusion, she cried, "Oh why did I tell them to go? Daddy, I've changed my mind!" And then with anger she screamed, "This isn't the way it's supposed to be! I want my babies. I want my husband back!"

Annie sobbed as her trembling body fell slowly to the floor and folded into the fetal position. Even though Buddy was just a baby, he knew that she needed him. Sitting next to her, he watched over her for almost two hours and he wouldn't have disturbed her then, but once more his body's need to go outside became stronger than his love and loyalty to his master. To get Annie's attention, Buddy whimpered softly and gently nudged his little nose against her hand. His touch drew Annie from the dark and lonely place she had gone. When she was able to look up, the first thing she noticed was the clock. She couldn't believe that is was almost midnight. As her head became clearer, she realized that Buddy was trying to tell her that he needed to go outside.

Out of concern for Buddy, Annie hurried to get the door open, and as soon as the space was wide enough, he had scurried out the door and on to the front lawn. Annie followed close behind. As she stood alone in the middle of the front lawn, she couldn't believe how incredibly quiet the night was. Staring up at the night sky, she tried to imagine that she could see past the stars and see the doorway to heaven, just like she had done the night her grandma had passed away. Sadly, all she could see then and now was a solar system. She remembered how she had worried about how to break the news about grandma to Jack and Kara.

But she shouldn't have worried, because when she told the kids that grandma had gone to heaven to live with Jesus, Kara had just smiled her sweet little smile and said, "Momma, if Great-Grandma is with Jesus, you and Grandma don't need to worry about her no more!"

And then Jack had added, "And she's happy now that she doesn't have to hurt no more!"

Annie wished she still possessed that innocence. It wasn't that she didn't believe that her family was with God. That wasn't the problem. She just didn't want anything to do with a God who had stolen her family from her. It had always been a comfort to her knowing that God's word taught her that "His Will" would be done. If she had a problem accepting something that had happened, the first thing she would do was pray to the Lord, but not now. She didn't want to talk to him.

As soon as she and Buddy walked back in the house, Annie hurried and turned on the gas fireplace.

"That ought to help warm us up, little guy," she said as she headed to the kitchen to fix herself a cup of tea and get Buddy a doggie treat. Annie had to smile when she opened the pantry and saw the shelf that her big-hearted father had filled with dog food, dog treats, and every kind of dog toy and supply that he could find at the local grocery store.

As soon as the tea was done, Annie hurried and turned on the TV to give the room some noise. She couldn't stand the quiet any longer. With Buddy next to her on the couch, she surfed through the channels at least four times and then settled on an old movie that she had watched at least ten times. It took her several minutes of staring at the screen before she realized that she couldn't hear what they were saying. She tried turning up the volume, but it didn't seem to make much of a difference because no matter how hard she tried, she just couldn't seem to focus. Annie looked down at Buddy who was looking back at her. He wiggled his tail and yapped softly at her. Unable to resist his sweetness, she lifted him until they were nose to nose.

Annie chuckled as she watched the little pup tilt his head from side to side. "You are cute! You know, you look like a little, furry, baby pig, but I'm guessing you're a Schnauzer." She nuzzled her nose in his neck and then set him back down in her lap and scratched his neck. "I wonder where they got you. You've been through a lot yourself, haven't you, sweetheart? Oh, I'm so sorry, Buddy. I'm just so sorry that you only got to spend a few hours with them." When she thought about what she'd said, Annie couldn't stop her tears. She picked up the little pup and held him to her chest, and then, lovingly, Buddy lifted his paws to her shoulders and burrowed his little face next to her neck.

She was exhausted, but she knew she wouldn't sleep. She reached for the bottle of sleeping pills and then tried to get comfortable on the couch as she covered herself with two of her mother's handmade afghans. With reluctance, she closed her eyes and waited for the pill to work. She thought of all the times she'd tucked an afghan around her babies and told them that when they were covered with one of grandma's afghans, they were covered with a hug! Now, she couldn't think of a time when she had needed a hug more. Once she was settled, Buddy made his way back into her arms, and together they drifted off to sleep while the TV rambled on into the night.

Chapter 4

Annie knew she would have to keep herself busy, and it was just days after the funeral that she decided to take on the task of writing thank you notes. Even though she had many offers from family members and friends who wanted to help, Annie declined their offers and tried gracefully to explain that she wanted and needed to write them herself.

To ease some of their worries, Barney, Lil, Joe, Gladys, and Karen created a schedule of visits throughout the day. It was during one of Karen's scheduled visits that Annie confessed that she had figured out what was going on. At first, Karen had tried to act like she didn't know what Annie was talking about, but she couldn't do it, because they had never kept anything from each other.

During another one of Karen's visits, out of the blue, Annie looked at her and said, "You know, Alex and I talked a few times about what the other should do if one of us passed away. I guess we just thought it would happen when we were old." She paused for a moment, moved her gaze from Karen to the kitchen window, and then stared out across the valley. "I think Mom and Dad are worried that I might try to harm myself, but they don't need to worry about that. Do you remember the night that Jim Anderson's wife committed suicide? Poor woman, she just couldn't take it after Jim died. It was all so tragic, and her poor parents, they never got over it, did they?"

Even though Annie was asking questions, Karen knew she didn't want any answers. She just wanted someone to listen.

"It all seems so ironic now, but we actually promised each other that if something happened to one of us, the other would go on. Come to think about it, Alex was the one who came up with the promise." Annie paused again. This time she moved her eyes and looked at the pile of scrapbooks that were sitting on the table. Then she looked at Karen and added, "I can't help it. I just keep wondering why I wasn't with them."

As Karen listened, she wished she had some profound words to say to Annie that would take some of this horrible pain from her, but she didn't have any. She didn't know if she ever would, but she hoped that talking would help Annie to work through some of her grief. Karen had felt comforted when she heard her friend say the words, "I made a promise."

When Annie finally looked over and noticed the expression on Karen's face, she slapped her on the knee and said, "You old dog, you've been thinking the same thing as my mom and dad!"

Karen swallowed hard and tried to fight the urge to giggle. There was nothing funny about this situation, but she couldn't control herself and burst out laughing. Seconds later, Annie joined her.

"This isn't funny!" Karen spat out in between laughs.

"No, but it feels good to laugh, even if it isn't funny!" Annie replied as she reached to wipe the tears from the corners of her eyes.

It took Annie several weeks to finish the thank you cards. After, she tried to take back some kind of routine and decided to start by doing the laundry. After the accident, family and friends had tried to take her laundry away, but she had demanded that she wanted everything to be left as it was. As she carefully folded each piece of clothing, she couldn't help but think of all the times she'd complained about doing laundry. Now if she could only have them back, she would promise never to complain about anything. She would wash the dirtiest laundry all day long, and she'd clean the bathrooms without ever saying a word about how gross they were. Unfortunately, she knew all the promises in the world weren't going to change things.

As she sorted the dirty laundry, she couldn't bring herself to wash Alex's flannel shirt that he'd worn or the kids' pajamas that they had worn the night before the accident. Treating each item of clothing like they were precious gems, she carefully folded them and thoughtfully placed the children's pajamas in the top drawer of their dressers and hung Alex's shirt next to his others in their closet. The next morning Annie decided to clean house, and it turned out to be a full-scale operation that went on for days. She worked hard scrubbing,

Finally

wiping, and dusting everything in the house that was cleanable, but she was always mindful to put everything back in its place.

As the days wore on, her friends and family's worries grew. They felt Annie was carrying on as if Alex had taken the kids on a vacation and was using the time to get caught up around the house while they were gone. On the other hand, Annie did her best not to get frustrated when they fussed over her. She knew it was because they loved her, and she was thankful that so many people cared about her, but sometimes it was hard because someone wanted to help with everything she did. Over and over, Annie had to explain that she appreciated that they wanted to help, but she was fine, and she was doing what she needed to do.

Even though Annie had decided to keep herself busy, she knew she wasn't ready to go back to work. In fact at that point, she wasn't sure if she'd ever be able to go back to work. Just the thought of leaving the sanctuary of her home was frightening. She was thankful that Alex had always insisted on having life insurance. Annie knew she'd be more than OK financially for the rest of her life if she decided to use the money from the trucking company's settlement.

Annie wanted to scream every time she thought about her meeting with the trucking company owners and their lawyers. Her family hadn't even been buried a week when they had called and insisted on having plenty of life insurance, because at least she had the comfort of not worrying about how she was going to live. Even if Alex hadn't insisted on the asked if they could meet with her. Her father had argued that she needed to get a lawyer, but, Annie said that she would go to the meeting first and then decide whether or not she would get a lawyer. Truthfully, she didn't care about the money, because there was no monetary figure that could represent the lost of her family.

Annie had wanted to throw up on the cherry wood boardroom table when the pasty faced lawyer had looked at her and said, "Mrs. Davis, I think you'll see that our offer is more than fair!" It made her blood boil every time she thought about his choice of words. Annie kept asking herself what had been fair about the situation. To Annie, "fair" was what guilty parties said when they weren't big enough to say, "Sorry, we messed up." Still, when they revealed the dollar amount of the settlement, Annie was overwhelmed. More than anything, she had came to that meeting hoping someone would apologize to her and promise her that they would never let anything like this happen again, but they didn't. Even though, she was angry for their lack of sympathy, she knew that she didn't want to go through the mess of getting a lawyer and enduring a trial. With a sick and heavy heart, she accepted the settlement and signed the papers. As soon as she was finished, she went straight to a bank and deposited the money.

Everything about the money seemed so ironic when Annie thought of all the years that she and Alex had worked so hard to stay ahead. All they had ever wanted was to be able to live comfortably and make sure that they were able to give their kids a good life. Alex's biggest wish for his family was that his kids would be able to attend college and that he and Annie would be financially secure when they retired. And now, here she was, with more than what Alex thought he'd always wanted, and it meant absolutely nothing!

Annie's pastors stopped by to check on her every Sunday afternoon, and each time they would let her know that the congregation had missed her at church and that the fellowship was continuing to hold her up in prayer. Annie hadn't gone to church since the accident, and she had no intention of ever going again. There was nothing more she needed to learn about God.

The pastors began each visit with the usual small talk about the weather, and then they would share some uninteresting news with Annie about what was going at church. Then they would ask Annie if they could pray together. Annie didn't want to be hurtful to Dan and Carol. It wasn't their fault. Out of respect for them, she would bow her head and pretend to listen, but in her mind she would scream silently to herself so that she couldn't hear what they were saying.

Dan and Carol understood that Annie was struggling with her faith, and it broke their hearts to watch such a beautiful soul turn her back on God. But they wouldn't give up. They loved her too much, and they knew God loved her even more. On one of their Sunday visits, Carol asked Annie if she had ever thought about going to a grief support group. Carol even offered to drive and attend the meeting with Annie, since the group was located in Cedar City. Annie told them she would think about it, but deep down she knew she had no intention of going. Besides, she knew that there wasn't going to be anyone there who would understand what she was going through. There would be a few people there who had lost a spouse or a child, or maybe there would be someone who had lost two children. She might find someone there who had lost a spouse and a child, but she was sure that she wouldn't find anyone who had lost his or her entire family in a single moment! Annie just couldn't see how sitting in a circle with a bunch of brokenhearted people was going to help her, and there was nothing she could possibly do or say to help someone else. Besides, she knew if she went, she'd only end up being the person the rest of the group would look at and think, "I guess it could have been worse."

Before the accident, Annie was the kind of person who said yes to anything, especially if it meant helping someone. But now, things were different, and she was a different person. Deep down, there was even a small part of her that wished she didn't have to feel like she did. In fact, if she were to be honest with herself, she'd have to admit that she hated the way she felt and the way she was behaving, but it wasn't her fault; it was God's fault. He had caused her to change.

One Sunday visit, Annie noticed that Dave and Carol had left several books on the table in the entry. As she carried them into the kitchen, she read the titles out loud to Buddy. "Let's see, there's, *How to Cope with the Death of Your Spouse*; *How Do I live without My Child*, and finally there's *Finding God Again*. Well Bud, I really don't think these books deal with my problems." With Buddy close behind, Annie walked straight to the trash and began dropping the books in, one by one. As she did, she pretended to read them again, only this time she made up her own titles. Her voice was filled with bitterness as she spoke, "*What Do You Do When God Steals Your Family? Once You Were Happy, Now You Are Not,*" and how about this one called, *Because of Stupid Mistakes, My Family Is Dead.*"

She was just about to toss the last book in the trash when she noticed the bookmark in it. Out of sheer curiosity, Annie pulled it from the book. As she did, she handled it as if she were removing a dead mouse from a trap. Then continuing to act as though the bookmark was a threat, she held it at a distance and read each word slowly and deliberately.

Romans 8:26
"And we know that in all things God works for the good of those who love him, who have been called according to his purpose."

Annie's body started to shake with frustration, and her voice was filled with bitterness and fury as she tore the bookmark to shreds and shouted, "God, where is the good in this and for what purpose have you done this to me?"

Along with worrying about Annie's spirituality, everyone worried about her health. Someone was always commenting about how much weight she had lost. Since everyone seemed so worried, Annie hadn't dared to tell anyone about her constant stomachaches and her fatigue since the accident. When someone asked her about her weight, she'd try to wash it off and say that it was just stress and that in time her body would get back to normal. She didn't want people to worry about her more than they already were.

Even though two months had passed, Barney and Lil continued to keep a close eye on Annie, and it was during one of their afternoon visits that they became alarmed when they couldn't find her after searching through her house. On Lil's second search through the kitchen, she happened to catch a glimpse of Annie through the kitchen window. She saw Annie sitting in the backyard swing.

"Found her!" Lil called out to Barney, who rushed to the kitchen when he heard his wife call out.

They were both filled with relief and concern as they hurried to the back door.

As Barney reached for the door handle, he looked at his wife and asked, "Don't you think it's kind of strange that she's outside in the swing? It's chilly, and she doesn't even have a jacket on."

Lil didn't answer, and Barney was not offended. They just wanted to get to their daughter as quickly as they could and find out if she was OK.

"Hello," they called to signal their arrival, but Annie was so deep in her in own thoughts that she didn't hear them.

"Annie, sweetheart, are you OK?" Barney asked with a gentle voice as he tapped his daughter softly on her shoulder to get her attention.

Annie had no idea that her parents were standing behind her and was startled when she felt her father's hand touch her shoulder. She jumped and cried out, "Oh my gosh Dad, you scared me!"

Rather curious to know what his daughter was thinking about, Barney asked, "Well my goodness, Annie, where were you just then?"

Lil and Barney were both surprised to hear what she had to say. "Well, you both know that I have lost weight, and you both know that I haven't felt well. I really thought it was just all the stress and stuff. Anyway, earlier, when I came out here to let Buddy run for a bit. I sat down and I got thinking about stuff, and that's when I remembered that I haven't had a period since the accident. And there's something else that I haven't told you guys. Alex and I were trying to have another baby before the accident!"

At first, her words seemed jumbled, and then her mother put it all together. "Oh sweetie, oh, Annie, that would be so wonderful for you, for all of us." With tears of joy, streaming from her eyes, Lil hurried to embrace her daughter.

Annie wouldn't accept the embrace and turned away from her mother. Annie stared across the valley again. Barney and Lil looked at each other and then back at Annie, each sensing that something wasn't quite right. When Annie spoke again, she didn't even sound like herself. "I have three pregnancy tests up in bathroom. I brought them home from work last summer, when Alex and I first started trying. I really don't need to take a test, because I know that I'm pregnant!" The tone of her voice changed. It was loud and full of anger. "I know why, too. It's because they weren't supposed to die! But God can't bring them back now. He just can't do that. So he's trying to make it up to me. That's why he's giving me this baby. God's trying to tell me that he's so sorry that he screwed up!"

Overcome with emotion, Lil shouted, "Annie, don't talk like that!"

Annie broke from her stare and turned to face her mother. Lil was about to say more, but Barney knew he needed to do something quickly to defuse the situation. He hurried and stepped between his daughter and wife, and as he did, he reached for his wife's hand. Then he knelt down and placed his other hand on Annie's lap.

"Come on, girls! Come on now! Why don't we just take a second and calm down. And then, Annie, you could go in the house and take one of those tests. You know, just to make sure, and then we'll all go out and celebrate with a Chinese dinner at the Station Restaurant. If you want, we could call and invite Joe and Gladys, and their family, and Karen and her family to go with us. This is such wonderful news, I would invite the entire town to come and celebrate with us." Barney didn't move until he felt both of his girls had calmed down.

It didn't take Annie long to stand up from the swing and hold her arms out for her mother. "I'm so sorry, Mom!"

"I'm sorry, too!" Lil answered back, reaching to put her arms around her daughter. "It's all forgotten. This is going to be a good day! Come on, let's go into the house."

Annie and her parents walked back to the house, arm and arm, and it felt good for them to feel something other than sorrow. It was the first feeling of hope they had felt since the accident.

Karen had stopped by and found Barney, Lil, and Buddy waiting patiently on the couch.

"Where's Annie?" Karen asked as she made herself comfortable on a chair.

Lil and Barney were more than happy to tell her the good news, but as soon as they said the word, "celebrate," they heard a heartbreaking scream and a loud crashing sound. Instantly, everyone ran for the staircase. As they hurried up the steps, they could hear the sounds of glass crashing against the tiled floor. Buddy and Karen were the first to reach the bathroom door. Karen hurried to open it but found it was locked. Knowing something was terribly wrong, Buddy began barking anxiously at the closed door.

"Annie, let me in. Let me in," Karen screamed.

As soon as Lil and Barney had caught up to Karen, the three started pounding at the door, begging Annie to open the door, but the only response they heard was the sound of more glass breaking. Thinking of how she could help, Lil remembered where the emergency key was and ran to get it. As she ran, she thought of the time that she had been told of its whereabouts in case of an emergency. It was the first year the kids had moved into the house. She and Barney had come over to spend the night with the grandchildren. Annie and Alex were going out to celebrate the New Year with Karen and Matt. Her daughter had looked so beautiful that night in the light blue sweater that she had gotten her for Christmas. Lil prayed silently as she ran back to the bathroom door, "Please God, let my daughter be OK, please, oh, please."

"Here, get that door open," Lil shouted as she handed the key to her husband.

As soon as they heard the lock click, Barney pushed the door open. All of their hearts felt like someone had ripped them from their bodies when they saw Annie's crumpled body sitting in a sea of liquid and broken glass.

"Why? Why is God doing this to me?" Annie sobbed. "All I wanted was a baby, just one baby. Why does God hate me so much?"

Together, Lil and Barney quickly gathered their daughter in their arms and held on to her with every ounce of strength they had left.

"I don't want to be here anymore. It's too hard, Mom!" Annie cried.

"No, Annie! No, sweetie, don't say that! You're all we have. Please baby, please don't say that," Barney pleaded through his tears.

This time, it was Lil who found the courage for all of them. Her voice was strong when she said, "I won't let you go, Annie. I will not lose you too! Now, I want you to let your father and I help you get up." Lil looked toward her husband and motioned for him to follow her lead. When they got Annie to her feet, she used her strong voice again and added, "OK now, let's go downstairs. Come on, Annie, you can do this."

Karen intentionally hung back and decided that she could be of more help if she stayed upstairs and tried to clean up the bathroom. As she began to pick up the hundreds of shards of broken glass, Karen was glad that she was alone because she knew at that moment she really couldn't help anyone. She couldn't stop herself from crying about how sad her dear friend's life had become.

Annie was shaking and totally oblivious to the fact her parents had helped her back down the stairs to the couch. She was grateful to have her parents' arms around her and to hear the soothing sounds of their voices, but when she saw the weary look on their faces, she became angry at herself. "Dad, Mom, I'm sorry! I'm so sorry! I shouldn't have acted like that! How could I have put you through that?"

Barney lifted his hand and gently traced the profile of his daughter's face. His voice was filled with compassion when he answered, "I think you had some kind of a breakdown or anxiety attack. You weren't yourself. You don't have to be sorry about anything, little girl. You've been through so much, but your mother and I need to know if you need help. I need you to tell me the truth. Would you hurt yourself? Do you need help?"

Annie took a deep breath and then confessed her feelings to her parents. "No, but I think you're right, Dad. I think I had some kind of a breakdown. Everything built up, and I just couldn't handle the disappointment. It was just too much! But, I am going to be honest with you. Every morning when I open my eyes, and it hits me all over again that I have to live another day without my husband and children, I can't help it. I wish I'd been with them. But you don't have to worry. I'm not going to hurt myself." Then she told her parents about the promise she and Alex had made to each other.

Barney took hold of Annie's chin and gently forced her to look at him. "I'm not going to tell you that I know how you feel, because I don't. But, I know how I feel. I've never in my life experienced so much pain. I've lived through a depression and a war. I've lost both my parents, and your mother and I have had to grieve for the loss of two unborn children, but nothing has compared to this. I know your faith in God has been shattered right now, but that is OK, because your mother's and my faith are strong, and even if you can't feel his love for you, I know that God loves you, and he'll get you through this. And sweetheart, I promise you that one day, it's going to get better!"

Chapter 5

The days following the breakdown seemed to be a little better, but it wasn't long after that Annie realized there was nothing more she could add to her to-do list. There was nothing left to clean or organize in the house, and the garage was so clean that she could have assisted Dr. Ray while he performed surgery in it. She had even found the courage to complete the last pages of her family's scrapbooks after she had found four slips in her mailbox informing her that she had four packages to pickup. It was a very tough moment when she realized the four packages contained the last photos of her husband's and children's lives, and it took her months before she could find the courage to open them.

The first package contained photos of their summer vacation in Yellowstone. As she looked through the photos, Annie thought about the night that Alex had come up with the idea of taking a vacation. She didn't think that they should spend the extra money, but Alex had been prepared to argue any excuse she made not to go.

After wrapping his arms around her, he'd said, "I knew you'd worry about how we'd pay for it, so I've already got that covered. I am going to get some summer project money, so we won't be cutting into our budget. Come on, babe, life is too short! You and I work too hard. Besides, it will be good for us to get away and spend time together as a family."

When Annie looked back, there were so many things that Alex had said that had seemed ordinary at the time, but now, she was convinced that he had known that he wouldn't live to be an old man.

There were photos of Molly riding on the hospital float at the Fourth of July parade. She was smiling from ear to ear as she pretended to be Lady Liberty. There were photos of Kara as she'd marched down the road with her dancing group. Looking at the photos, Annie thought back to how nervous Kara had been about dancing in the parade. After she had passed by, both she and Alex couldn't figure out why she had even stressed, because she had definitely been the best dancer in the group. There were photos of Jack and his baseball team. All of them had decided to dress up in their uniforms and ride their bicycles in the parade. Annie had to smile as she remembered how much fun he'd had drenching the crowd with his super water blaster.

There were pictures of the kids swimming at the city pool and jumping on the trampoline in the backyard. Their big smiles tugged at her heart, and even though she had to cry, she found that she could smile too, just by looking at their smiles. The very last photo was of Alex and Molly taking a nap together, all cuddled up in the big rocking chair.

The day came back so clearly in Annie's mind. Molly had spent the morning and early afternoon helping Alex in the yard. Around two, she'd marched in and announced that Daddy said that they needed twelve winks before they could go and get an Icee. Molly had ordered her father into the recliner, and as soon as she woke up, she had proudly counted to twelve and squealed, "Come on Daddy, we slept for twelve. Now it's time for one Icee."

Annie sorted the photos and wrote the dates on the back of each one before she put them in a shoebox. At first, she was just going to put them in a box in the closet, but she couldn't do it. When she lifted the box to the shelf, her hands couldn't let go.

"This isn't right and you know it!" She said, scolding herself.

Annie knew she had to finish the scrapbooks. How could she have even thought otherwise? She took her time and carefully decorated the pages with the different mementos that she had saved from the different events and the embellishments that she'd bought at the craft store to go along with each photo. She made pages until she ran out of photos, but she knew the books wouldn't be complete until she recorded the story of her family's untimely deaths. Annie used the photos that Karen had taken on the day of the funeral, the newspaper articles about the accident, the obituaries, and programs from the funeral service to make the pages in the last chapter of her family's lives. When she was finished, she added the finished scrapbooks to the pile of scrapbooks that had been sitting on the kitchen table since the day of the funeral.

Each night before she made her way to the couch, she would sit at the table and look through the scrapbooks. Then, with Buddy by her side, she'd take a few moments to walk through the house, and every night, she would find herself in the children's bedrooms, holding each of their pillows one at a time before wishing them goodnight. In her mind, she could hear their little voices answer back, "'Night, Momma." After the children's rooms, she would go to her own bedroom. She had tried to sleep in the bed a few times, but lying in the bed alone was only one more reminder of just how much she missed Alex. And as much as she hated to depend on the sleeping pills, each night after her walk through the house, Annie would take her pill, sleep for a couple of hours, and then wait for the long night to be over.

When Annie got to the point that she couldn't think of anything to do at her house, she would head to her parents' house, and they would find something for her to do. She knew they really didn't need her help, because that they were all quite healthy for their ages. It was just good for all of them to be together, and Annie knew they needed her just as much as she needed them.

As soon as Buddy was big enough, Annie started walking again. She started with the same old route as she had always walked, but with all the extra time she had on her hands, she made it a habit to walk around two more hayfields. Buddy grew quickly, and it wasn't long before he figured out that he could run ahead. He would scout out the area, chase a rabbit or tumbleweed, and then he'd circle back around to check on Annie. Then he would take off and do it all again. She liked walking out around the fields because she knew she wasn't likely to run into anyone. Most of all, she didn't have to worry about Buddy chasing cars, because that was the one bad habit he'd taken up. With only one main road to cross in her route, she figured that she could keep Buddy safe.

Before the accident, Annie had always loved to walk. She had used the quiet time to regroup and pray, and at least once a week, she and Alex would walk together. It had been a good time for them to catch up on their lives without interruptions from the kids. Now when she went for a walk, Annie spent the time remembering the past. It didn't matter which memory of her life she started with; she would always end up working her way to the accident, and then she would cry.

Annie couldn't believe that so many of her friends continued to check on her, months after the accident. Some of the visits were very uncomfortable, especially when she could sense that some of her oldest and dearest female friends spent their entire visits worrying that they were going to say something wrong. They would start off the conversations by asking Annie how she was doing, and then before she could even answer, they would start talking about the weather, fashion, or some other bizarre topic. Each time they did their best to avoid a conversation they felt might upset or remind Annie of what had happened, or heaven forbid, talk about Alex and the children, or the fact that they still had families. Annie didn't want her friends to feel guilty because they still had lives. Each time, she would do her best to reassure them that it was just fine for them to talk about their families. Then she would have to explain to them that she wanted to talk about her family. After all, their memories were all she had left!

Through it all, just as it had been since childhood, Annie knew that it was Karen, whom she could depend on to help get her through some of the darkest and heaviest days. Karen seemed to know just when she needed someone to talk to, or just when Annie thought she'd go insane from the loneliness. Matt and Karen would come by and take her out to dinner and a movie or an afternoon of bowling in Cedar. Annie enjoyed their trips to Cedar, because no one there knew or cared that she was the woman whose family had been killed. When she walked into a store, she didn't have to pretend that she didn't see the poorly camouflaged fingers that pointed her out or listen to the muffled whispers like she did at home.

She understood that for the most part, everything people said came from concern. Unfortunately, there had been a few times when she was standing in the middle of an aisle at the grocery store, and people had started talking, acting as if she were deaf. She'd had no choice but to listen to the conversation in the next aisle. A few times, she had felt as though someone had taken her heart from her chest, ground it in the meat grinder, and then shoved it back into her body with a force that compared to a 747 airliner as it took off from a runway.

As the months passed, Annie came to realize that she needed something to fill her time. There was nothing left to clean or fix. She knew that she and Buddy couldn't spend all their time walking, and she knew without a doubt that she was sick of watching movies. She had watched more movies in the past few months than she had in her entire lifetime. Something inside told her that it was time to go back to work. She had started working at the hospital as a nurse's aide when she was just sixteen years old and with the exceptions of when she and Alex had gone to school, and the six months maternity leave for each baby, working at the hospital had always been a part of her life. In fact, on the day that Annie finally decided to call and inquire about going back, her supervisor sounded as if she were going to cry. One of her full-time nurses had just informed her that she was pregnant and, because of complications, needed to be on complete bed rest, and another part-time nurse had just given her two weeks' notice because she was moving. At the end of the conversation, the decision was totally up to Annie. Did she want to work full-time or part time? She chose full time.

It wasn't difficult for Annie to get back into the working life. The only thing she had to worry about was what she was going to do with Buddy. She knew that on the days she worked, she would be gone at least thirteen hours, and there was no way she could leave him in the house alone for that long. Luckily, her worry was short lived because her father and Joe were more than happy to take care of Buddy. From the moment Buddy entered their world, he had captured everyone's heart. He was so easy to love, with his charming ways and good behavior, and even though no one said it out loud, they all felt that Buddy was their last connection to Alex and the children. Buddy gladly ate up all the attention everyone gave him, but no matter how much he enjoyed his popularity, his loyalty belonged to Annie.

The decision to go back to work turned out to be a good thing for Annie, for more than one reason. While she was at work, she could avoid all of the concern her family and friends had about her weight loss. She really couldn't understand what they wanted her to do about it. She had finally given in and talked to Dr. Ray, and he had given her a prescription. She had taken it exactly as it had been prescribed. The medicine had helped her stomach some, but eating really wasn't high on her list of priorities. When she was home alone, a cup of tea, a piece of toast, or a cup of soup took care of her need to eat.

The weight loss issue caused Lil to worry constantly about whether or not her daughter was eating enough. Annie swore that her mother had forgotten how to simply say hi. Instead of saying hello, the first thing she would say was,

"Have you eaten?" Annie couldn't figure out why her mother even bothered to ask because even when she told her that she had just eaten, Lil would still try and fix her something to eat. Each time Annie stopped by after work to pick up Buddy, it didn't matter if it was early in the morning or late at night, her parents would be waiting for her to join them for a meal. She really didn't mind the extra attention. She knew it was good for them to be together, but she did have to admit that she was glad that Buddy was there to help her eat the extra large portions of food that her mother served. After their meal, Annie and her father would wash the dishes together, just like they had done when she was a little girl, and then she and her Bud Dog would head for home.

It was after one of their meals that Annie decided it was time to tell her parents her plans for the upcoming holidays. "Mom, Dad, I've decided that I'm going to work as much as I can through the holidays. I think it will be for the best this year. I thought maybe you could come to the hospital on Christmas and we could have dinner with the geriatric patients."

Her father had nodded his head in agreement and replied, "That's a great idea, Annie, and I'll bet Buddy could stay with Joe and Gladys while we're gone."

Lil nodded her head in agreement.

One evening, Barney and Annie had finished with the dishes and were talking about an approaching storm. Lil was sitting quietly in her chair and thinking of all the things they would never get to do with Kara, Jack, and Molly. Silently, she prayed to the Lord, begging him to help her to fight off the evil bitterness that battled daily with her faith. She knew that if she gave in, it could destroy what was left of her family. She knew she had to be strong.

Annie was thrilled when she saw that the hospital had scheduled her six days a week from the middle of November through the end of January. The days were long, and she was exhausted by the time she was finished with her shifts, but that was the way she wanted it. Sometimes, it was hard to find the energy to stay and eat with her parents, but she knew she had to do it. The holidays were taking their toll on them as well. After dinner she would head for home, take a quick bath, and then she and Buddy would head to the couch and fall asleep listening to the TV. During that time, there were many days that Annie found herself wishing that she'd opted to run away to a deserted island, just so that she wouldn't have had to look at Christmas decorations. Every

Christmas light, tree, and ornament she saw made her feel as if she had been stabbed in the heart.

The holidays had always been such a big part of Alex and Annie's lives, starting each year off with celebrating the New Year and working their way to the granddaddy of all holidays—Christmas! Joe and Gladys had invited Annie and her parents over for Christmas Eve the first year that Alex and Annie had started dating, and they had shared the holidays together as a family ever since. They were disappointed when Annie told them about her plans for the holidays, but they understood completely. Joe and Gladys would have gladly joined them, but they knew they had to go on for their daughters and their families.

When Annie told them her plans, Joe had wrapped his arms around his daughter-in-law and with tears in his eyes and said, "You know, you're just like my own, and I know that you loved my son with all your heart. But one day, all this sadness is going to fade and life is going to be good again. I just know you're going to find another special person to share your life with." Annie had tried to stop the conversation because there was no way that she could or would think of replacing Alex with another man. But Joe insisted on finishing what he had to say. "Annie, I knew my son well, and nothing mattered more to him in this world than you. When you're ready, he would want you to go on and be happy. Gladys and I want that, too. We just want you to know that no matter what life brings your way, we will always think of you as our daughter, and that we will always want you to be a part of our lives. And I just wanted you to know how much we love you and how much we're going to miss you and your mom and dad this Christmas."

Joe's words comforted her. When he told her that he would always think of her as his daughter, Annie's love for Joe had grown even deeper, but as much as she had always valued Joe's advice, there was no way that she could see herself with anyone but Alex.

During the few days that Annie wasn't scheduled to work, she spent most of her time looking through the scrapbooks, reminiscing. She even found the courage to watch a few of the home videos. She, Alex, and the kids had always had so much fun as they worked together to decorate the house. Christmas time was a big deal to her family. They kept busy the entire month—shopping, decorating the house inside and out, wrapping presents, and baking. She had to smile when she thought of how she and Alex would lay awake every Christmas

Eve worrying that if they fell asleep, they would miss that first big moment when the kids would run to see what Santa had brought them.

At Christmas time, Alex reverted back to a child and became the biggest kid of all. She thought of how she had to hide his presents until Christmas Eve because he had such a bad habit of peeking. A time or two, she'd even caught him opening a few of her presents. Annie laughed when she remembered the time she had caught him peeking in one of her presents from her mother. When he looked up and saw that he had been caught, he just looked at her and with mischief in his eyes and replied, "I think that I'm really going to like this one." It turned out that Alex really did like the white negligee set more than Annie. A pair of flannel pajamas would have been more to her taste.

Every page of the scrapbooks held a special memory. There was a photo of Jack holding his first Valentine's Day box. Again, she had to laugh out loud when she thought of how competitive Alex had been when it came to making Valentine's Day boxes. Every year, he would come up with different ideas. His boxes were so famous that the entire grade school waited to see what the Davis kids' boxes would look like. Annie didn't know who felt the most pride when the kids walked into school the morning of the Valentine's Day party—Alex, the kids, or herself.

When she came to the book that contained pictures of Molly's first Easter, she thought of spring and how the kids were always the first to get the boxes of Easter decorations out so that they could practice hunting for plastic, Easter eggs. Annie smiled as she looked at a photo of the kids standing by the front window that Kara had decorated. She had spent hours decorating it with pastel-colored crape paper and Easter decorations. After she had finished, she had insisted that the family come and see her creation. As she led them into the front room, she had proudly announced that she had only used ten rolls of crepe paper and two rolls of scotch tape.

Annie remembered how she and Alex had fussed over Kara's creation and then later, quietly laughed together when they agreed that they wouldn't have to worry about closing the blinds at night for the next month.

Alex was just as crazy about Halloween as he was about Valentine's Day. He made sure the kids always had great costumes. Thinking back, Annie remembered how much they had all loved decorating the house and yard with scarecrows, fall leaves, and pumpkins, and then a couple of weeks before

Halloween, they would add an old stuffed dummy to the porch along with more decorations.

Now, the only thing Annie had to do to get ready for the holidays were to take flowers and decorations to the cemetery. Everyone hoped things would get better for her after the holidays were over, but January and February weren't much better, because Molly's birthday was in the middle of January, and Kara had been born on the last day of February. They'd always made a big deal over the fact she had been born a Leap Year Baby, but once again, the only thing she could do to mark the occasions was to take a decoration to the cemetery.

March came in like a lion, and like so many other years in the little town of Milford, the lion stayed around much longer than necessary to announce the coming of spring. After two weeks of opting not to go for walks because she didn't want to fight the thirty-mile-per hour gusts, Annie and Buddy were grateful when the wind decided to go elsewhere. As she walked along the dirt road, Annie noticed the small sprouts of green that were making their way through the desert floor. It was hard to believe that a new season had made its arrival, and it was even more unbelievable when she realized that it had been six months since the accident. As she walked, she reflected on the passing of time and how it had continued to march on, totally disrespectful of her feelings.

Annie looked across the field and watched Buddy as he hunted for gophers. Even though he was almost full grown now and a very fast runner, he wasn't fast enough to catch the young gophers, which seemed to enjoy teasing him with a good chase. They were into their walk about thirty minutes when Annie happened to look toward the West Mountains and see that the sun was just starting to go down. She also noticed a trail of dust but figured it was a herd of antelope running across the valley. Moments later, the dust caught her eye again, and she realized it came from a truck that was headed toward town. Annie had a bad feeling.

The truck was coming way too fast, and Buddy was headed to meet it head-on at a crossroad. She called for Buddy to come back, but he was too entranced with his hunt as he chased a gopher around a patch of tall sagebrush. When the gopher decided to run across the road, Buddy followed. Annie watched in horror as the truck and her beloved Buddy intersected. The driver slammed on his brakes which left an explosion of dust! A sick feeling of dread encircled

Annie's body as she raced to her pup. Pleading breathlessly out loud, over and over, "Please, God, please, God, let him be OK!"

As the dust began to clear, Annie could see that the driver of the truck was Jake Norton, and as she approached, she could see Buddy's lifeless little body. The impact had thrown him ten feet from the road. Jake had gotten out of the truck and was bending over him when she reached them.

This can't be happening! Annie thought as she fell to her knees. Her body started to tremble with fear as she reached for her pup. "Oh Buddy!" she cried.

At the same moment that Annie's fingers made contact with the soft black fur, Buddy opened his eyes and let out a small whimper, and then, as if nothing had happened, he jumped up and started wagging his tail at full speed. Annie was still shaking when she took Buddy in her arms and buried her face in his soft fur.

"Buddy, you're OK!" she cried. Then Annie took his little face in her hands and gave him a scolding as if he were a child but, that's exactly what he'd become to her: her child.

Jake was relieved when he saw the little dog move. He couldn't even bear to think what he would have done if the little dog had been hurt. After letting out a sigh of relief he said, "Annie, he came out of nowhere! I'm so sorry this happened!"

Suddenly, Annie jumped to her feet and began screaming and hurled herself at Jake, "You were driving too fast. What were you thinking? You idiot! Don't you know how to drive?"

Jake had known Annie forever, but, the person in front of him wasn't anyone he recognized. He'd been friends with Alex and Annie since the day they had gone to kindergarten. Alex had been his dearest friend. In all the years he had known Annie, he couldn't even remember her raising her voice. She was one of the sweetest, kindest people he had ever known. Jake knew how much this little dog meant to Annie, and he understood that her unusual behavior was brought on by more than just a near miss with Buddy. He was a big man, and she was a small woman, so he just stood there and let Annie pound her fists into his chest and scream words that didn't even make sense.

When Annie realized what she was doing, she was humiliated by her lack of self-control. She dropped her hands to her sides and lowered her head in shame as her weak body fell into Jake's strong embrace. "Oh, Jake, I'm so sorry.

I'm so sorry. I can't believe I acted like that. Oh, please tell me that I didn't hurt you," she cried.

Jake looked down at Annie and smiled when he answered. "You didn't hurt me. And just in case you've never noticed, I'm a pretty big guy. I think I can take a few hits from a gal your size. Right now, the most important thing is that Buddy and you are OK."

It was only a matter of seconds before Annie regained her strength and gently pushed away from Jake's embrace. "I'm OK. I'm just so embarrassed. I just can't believe that I acted like that," Annie confessed.

"Annie, you didn't act any way. You reacted. I know how much that little pup means to you," Jake replied. Then hoping he could help Annie to think about something other than what had just happened, he asked her how work was going. Annie was more than happy to talk about something other than making a fool of herself, and so for a few minutes, they visited by the side of the road. Jake was torn when he noticed the time. "I guess that I'd better get back to the shop before the guys start to worry about me. You know, it's getting kind of late. Why don't you let me give you and Buddy a ride home?"

"Jake, I appreciate your offer, but I'm OK, and it looks like Buddy's OK, too! We walk out here all the time. You don't have to worry about Buddy and me. Anyway, I've got my cell phone if we need anything," Annie answered. Trying to sound reassuring and still feeling sorry for the way she'd acted, she added, "Jake, this is going to sound kind of dumb, but I'm glad it was you. I just don't know what I would have done if…"

"I understand. If this had to happen, I'm glad it was me, too. There's no need to think of things that didn't happen!" Knowing he had to get back to work, Jake gave Annie another hug and then reluctantly walked around to the driver's side of his truck. Just before he slipped behind the wheel, he looked at Annie and added, "I miss Alex. There's just no one like him!"

Annie could only smile and nod in agreement, because she knew if she tried to speak, she'd start to cry again. After Jake pulled away, a cold chill ran down Annie's spine. As she headed down the field road, Annie tried to convince herself that it was the cool evening breeze, but she knew it was because she was still shaken by Buddy's near miss. Not wanting to interrupt her pace, she quickly untied Alex's old jacket from her waist and slipped her arms through the sleeves. The fleece lining warmed her a bit, but she continued to have cold chills. Annie slid her hands into the deep side pockets hoping to warm them, and that's when she felt the MP3 player. With her fingertips, she gently held on to it, and she thought about the last time Alex had worn the jacket.

He had come from school after a meeting with an irate mother who was upset because he had given her son an F in English. She had stormed into his room and informed him that he was terrible teacher. She said that it was Alex's fault that her baby wasn't going to be able to play football. Alex had confessed to Annie that after he had listened to that lady rant and rave for twenty minutes, he did something that was so far from his usual way of handling things. He had lost his temper and told the woman that it was far more important for her son to learn to write a complete sentence than it was to play a freaking high school football game. Needless to say, his afternoon had been wasted tending to one mother instead of teaching English to sixty students. Annie remembered how she'd tried to cheer him up, but the meeting had really gotten to him, and he had taken a walk to calm down.

It was still hard for Annie to believe that mother had behaved in such a way. Alex was born to be a teacher. If that woman had only known all the unpaid hours and care he put into his job, there would have been only one reason to stop by Alex's room, and that would have been to thank him. After several moments of running her fingers over the MP3 player, Annie took it out of her pocket and placed the earphones on her head. She really didn't think that the batteries would work, and she was surprised when she heard the music start to play. She was even more surprised when she realized she was listening to Alex's favorite song. She hadn't heard it since the funeral.

"Lord, I give you my life for you gave me yours."

The words to the song seemed to permeate every part of her body and soul. Just before the song ended, Annie thought of Alex and how much he had loved the Lord. Before the second song was over, Annie pushed stop and placed the MP3 player back in the pocket. She wanted to listen to the other songs, but the words and melody to Alex's favorite song were stuck in her mind, swirling together with memories and the horrible scene of Buddy and the white truck colliding and with her voice screaming, "Please, God, let him be OK!"

Annie's thoughts continued to race, and no matter how hard she tried, she couldn't clear her mind. It was strange, but it felt like her mind was fighting to take control of all of her body's energy. She tried to fight her way forward, but

Finally

with each step she took, her legs began to feel as though they were weighted with incredible amounts of steel until finally she found herself frozen, standing in the middle of the field road.

Sandwiched between two hayfields, she heard the person she used to be say, "If you don't want to talk to God, why did you call out to him? Some kind of faith you had, girl. As long as the tragedy belonged to someone else, you accepted his will. How many times did you look at people who'd fallen on tough times and tell them that it was God's will, and that you would pray for them? You hypocrite! Do you remember how many times you said that everything happens for a reason?"

Clutching her head with her hands, Annie's face grimaced with pain, and finally she screamed, "Everything is different now! I'm different now! I was who I was because of Alex and the children!"

Suddenly, images of her life flashed through her mind—moments that defined the woman she had been and who she had become.

The voice spoke again. "Your life has changed, but like it or not, you're still the same person. Was your faith in God based on Alex and the children? Maybe you never really believed!" Annie might have thought she was losing her mind, but she knew that wasn't. She understood completely.

Her body was still weak, but her voice was strong when she argued back. "Yes, I did. I believed. I still believe, and I will always believe!" And then with deep humility, Annie fell to her knees and cried, "Father, please forgive me. I've been so wrong! Lord, I can't do this without you. I've tried so hard to shut you out of my life, but I can't. I wanted to be angry at you for taking away my family. But how can I? They aren't mine; they never were! They are yours, and I should have been thanking you for each and every moment that you let me share my life with them. Oh God, I don't know why you have chosen this for me, but I can't go on without you. I've tried, and I can't do it. Forgive me for thinking that I could. I need you. Help me, God. Please help me!" With tears falling down her cheeks, Annie continued to pray. "I don't know why you took them home and left me here, but there has to be a reason. Please, God, please show me the reason and what it is you want me to do."

As she continued to pray, Annie was unaware that daylight had slipped away and that the sky had filled with twinkling stars. And it wasn't until Buddy wiggled his way into her lap that she noticed the gigantic spring moon beginning to peak over the Mineral Mountains. Ever mindful of his responsibility to protect Annie, Buddy had stayed by her side and waited patiently, but when the air cooled, and the sun sank into the west, he knew it was time to interrupt and let her know that it was time to get for home.

It was a perfect night. The air was still, and the light from the full moon made it easy for Annie and Buddy to see their way home. Annie walked in tune to the sound of crunching gravel and the hum of a locomotive's engine as it made its way into town. Just as she reached the golf course, she was surprised to hear what her grandmother always referred to as "the trumpets of spring." Her beloved grandma had always said, "Forget the groundhogs! Just listen for the anxious squeals of children playing outside. They will tell you when spring is here!"

At first, the echoes deepened the familiar longing, but then she remembered she wasn't alone. Before going home, Annie took one more look at the night sky and repeated one of her favorite verses from the Bible.

Psalm 139:16
All the days ordained for me were written in your book before one of them came to be.

Chapter 6

Once the house was finished, Annie and Alex had begun the process of creating a yard for their new home. After making a few preliminary plans, they spent countless hours clearing the lot, and in time they became semi-experts on building brick fences, forming and pouring cement, installing sprinkling systems, and landscaping. When it was all said and done, the flowerbeds belonged to Annie and the vegetable garden belonged to Alex.

Annie got an early start on working to clean up the yard after the long winter months. She did everything she and Alex always did, but, she didn't have the heart to touch Alex's garden. But as the days progressed, she couldn't stand to watch the weeds take over the soil that had once been her husband's cherished land. Step by step, she tried to do everything just like Alex. First, she pulled the weeds, then she raked and raked the soil until it was as clean and smooth as dirt could get. But after fighting with the rotor tiller for three hours, she gave up the notion that she had to plant the garden like Alex. And the first thing she decided not to do was to fertilize the soil with cow manure. She would have stuck with her decision, but she couldn't forget Alex saying, "You've got to feed the soil if you expect it to feed you!"

Always one to crack under guilt, Annie looked up toward the heavens and sighed. "OK, honey, you win! I'll call Sam!"

When Annie called Sam to ask if he had an extra truckload of manure that she could have, he laughed. Annie really didn't think she had said anything funny. Finally when Sam was able to stop chuckling, he replied, "Well yah, somewhere among my five hundred head of cattle, I'll bet I can find a truckload of manure. But ah, I think it would be a much better idea if, ah, I delivered it. And as long as I'm there, I can get that tilled into the soil for you."

As tempting as it was, Annie politely declined his offer and explained to him that she still needed to keep busy. She knew that if anyone could understand her feelings it would be Sam, because he'd been a widower himself for three years. Sam was sweet as could be about the whole thing, and he even apologized for laughing, but he insisted on loading her truck with his backhoe. On the day that they had agreed to meet, Annie and Buddy pulled into the farm right on time, but Sam was nowhere to be found. Annie didn't think too much about it. She just figured he would get there as soon as he could. To help pass the time, she straightened the inside of the truck and then tried to read an old newspaper that she had found under the seat. Her eyes grew heavy somewhere in the first paragraph, and she was quite surprised to wake up almost an hour later to the familiar sound of Buddy's dog tags jingling.

"I guess Sam's not coming," Annie said as she massaged the kinks out of her neck. "So I guess we'd better get started."

Buddy responded by jumping up from his comfortable napping position and then gave several excited yips to let Annie know that he totally agreed!

Sam's farm sat in the center of the Flats surrounded by acres of alfalfa and corn. The farm had supported four generations, starting with Sam's great-grandfather, who had turned the sandy sagebrush fields into lush carpets of green, and he'd even had the foresight to plant the entire south end of the property with Chinese elm trees. The giant trees alone made the property stand out among the other farms. There weren't many trees in the valley. Sam's farm was even more unique, because his family had been one of the first to irrigate their alfalfa with underground water pumped by electricity.

After opening the gate, Annie carefully backed the truck through the narrow opening and parked it next to the biggest pile of cow manure that she could find. As soon as she stepped from the truck, Buddy was right behind her, anxious to explore the new territory. Once she was standing in the corral with shovel in hand, Annie couldn't believe that she had spent so much time stewing about getting manure! Her body filled with confidence as she tightened her grip on the shovel's handle. Then with careful aim, Annie thrust the shovel deep into the mass of cow droppings. She scooped up as much as she could lift, and then, as if she had choreographed her movement, she turned and gave the oversized spoon a toss toward the bed of the truck.

"I can do this!" she shouted, realizing that the task at hand had a deeper meaning!

Unfortunately, her moment of self-discovery was interrupted when a very strong gust of wind burst through, causing the contents of the shovel to fly in the opposite direction. In seconds, Annie's eyes, nostrils, and mouth were filled with cow droppings! Totally sickened by the thought of what had just smacked her in the face, Annie dropped the shovel and tried desperately to wipe the goop from her eyes as she fought the urge to vomit! At the same moment, she became so preoccupied that she forgot to look where she was stepping, and that's when the bottom of her boots met with a fairly fresh pile of wet cow excrement, which in turn caused her body to soar though the air. When Annie landed, it felt as though she had been tossed for yards, though in reality it was a few inches. After landing face first, it took Annie a few seconds to figure out that the only thing injured was her pride. Quickly, she jumped to her feet and scanned the area to make sure that no one, especially Sam, had seen her moment of gracelessness. As she looked around, she noticed that Buddy was sitting at her feet, tilting his head side to side, and she realized how funny she must have looked to him, and she started to laugh hysterically.

"Oh, Buddy, I can't tell if you are amused or confused," Annie said still laughing.

Annie was totally surprised when Buddy jumped up and stood on his hind legs and begged for her to take hold of his paws, which, in his language, meant, "Will you dance with me?"

"Buddy, we can't dance here," Annie answered with a smile. "You know there's a reason why we dance in the front room with the blinds closed." But he wouldn't take no for an answer, and she couldn't resist his sweet little face. It must have been quite the picture. A little green woman, laughing and dancing with her pup on a dance floor made of manure. When the song playing on the radio came to an end, Annie curtsied to her partner and, with a big smile still upon her face, said, "Thank you so much! It was a pleasure dancing with you, sir." Then looking thoughtfully into Buddy's eyes, she added. "You know, Bud, after Alex and the kids died, I always thought that I got crapped on, but after today, I can honestly say that I did!" It could have been a moment that brought tears, but Annie decided it felt so much better to laugh, and so she chose to laugh.

A few days later, Annie was busy patting the soil around the last little tomato plant. After she stood up and admired her work, a smile came over her face, and she started to laugh again when she said, "Buddy, I hope you can acquire a taste for tomatoes, because I just planted thirty-six Super Fantastic Tomato Plants!"

Buddy looked up with his big brown eyes and wiggled his tail back and forth to convey to her that he would try. It was a lucky moment for Annie when she bent down to give Buddy a hug, because that's when she looked at her watch and realized she was going to be late for work. It was a close call, but she made it just in time for the end of shift report. The big news of the day was that the last flu bugs of winter had spread their germs throughout the small town of Milford and had caused the hospital to fill to capacity. Every nurse and nurse's aide who hadn't come down with the flu had been called in, and poor Dr. Ray was the only physician available, because both of his partners had come down with the bug, too!

The shift started at 6:00 p.m. and by 9:00, Annie had helped to admit three acute patients and administered IV fluids to four outpatients. Her hands were full of IV bags as she walked past the nurses' station. Dr. Ray saw her and asked her if he could buy her a soda on her break. He said he wanted to talk to her about something.

"That sounds good, Doc." Annie called back, knowing that she didn't have the time to stop. "I've got three more IV bags that need changing and a few other things that I need to take care of, and then I'll catch up with you."

Before she entered the patient's room Annie took one more look at the chart to make sure she had everything she needed. Mrs. Carter wasn't one of her patients, but Annie had insisted that the other RN (Marcia) who had come in early, take a break. As she looked over the doctor's order, her eyes kept going back to the name, Sherri Carter. The name seemed so familiar to her, but she couldn't remember why.

Mrs. Carter was sleeping, and Annie tried her best not to wake her up as she changed the IV bags, but as usual, even though she was trying to be quiet, the alarm on the IV pump decided to go off.

"I'm so sorry! I really wanted to get this done without disturbing you," Annie apologized.

"Oh, it's OK," Mrs. Carter replied with a sleepy voice.

"Do you mind if I check your vitals while you're awake, and then we won't have to bother you again for a while?" Annie asked.

"That would be fine," Mrs. Carter answered back sleepily.

After turning on the light above the bed, Annie took a moment and observed the patient to make sure that she was OK. As she did, they made small talk about the weather. Annie had always found that talking to her patients helped to ease some of their apprehensions, but she wasn't sure she'd accomplished that with Mrs. Carter, who seemed rather tense. After Annie had taken and recorded the vitals, she went to the supply room to get a warm blanket. As she did, she couldn't quit wondering why Mrs. Carter seemed so familiar to her. She knew it was nonsense to keep thinking about it, but she just couldn't shake the feeling.

Annie told Mrs. Carter goodnight and was just about to turn off the lights when she heard the soft and broken voice say, "I need you to know that it wasn't my husband's fault. He was a good man."

Annie was confused by what she heard and turned back around. She could see that Sherri was trembling. As she tried to compute the words, the inside of her brains felt like rusted gears slowly grinding, and then in a split second, it was if the gears started to turn at lightning speed, and the words began to make sense.

Sherri Carter, Ty Carter, God in heaven, Sherri's husband had been the driver of the semi truck. Annie's mind began to race with questions. *Why hadn't someone figured this out? Why was she or this patient, who was so very ill, put in this uncomfortable situation? How insensitive. How could this have happened?* Standing in the doorway with her hands grasping onto the doorframe for strength, Annie began to feel as if she were drowning. She wanted to run from the room, but she couldn't. Slowly she turned around and when their eyes met, Annie's anger and frustration melted away in an instant, because looking into Sherri's eyes made Annie feel as if she were looking at herself in the mirror.

It was Sherri who broke the awkward silence and said, "My little boys were supposed to go with their daddy that day, but they didn't go, because Wes had caught a bad cold. Wes, he's my oldest." She paused for a moment and looked down at her wedding ring. Then without looking up, she began to twirl the ring nervously with her right hand and said, "Ty decided that he'd better not take the boys with him. He didn't want to take Nick and leave Wes home to feel bad. He was worried that if he took Nick out on the road, it was more than likely he'd get sick, too. You know how it goes. If someone in the family gets sick, it seems like everybody gets sick. I'll never forget how Wes and Nick were both crying when their daddy left that afternoon. Ty was crushed, too! He told them that he would be back in two days. He promised that he would take them on his next trip, no matter what, even if they both had colds."

Annie released her grip from the doorframe and walked slowly back to Sherri. "How old are your boys?" She asked through the lump in her throat.

A smile came over Sherri's face before she replied, "Wes is eight. He's in the second grade, and Nick is six. He started kindergarten this year. Wes looks a lot like Ty, and everyone says that Nick looks like me. They're such good boys. I don't know how I could have made it through this without them." When Sherri realized what she'd said, she turned a crimson red and cried, "Oh, Annie, I'm so sorry! That must have sounded so awful."

"No, please don't apologize. Of course, they've been a comfort to you. God knows I would have felt the same if my children had lived," Annie admitted and then asked, "Do you live in Milford?"

Sherri was quick to answer back, but Annie noticed that the tone of her voice carried a bit of humiliation. "I moved here in January. We've been staying with my sister, but it's only temporary. As soon as I get feeling better, I'm going to see about finding some work. After the accident, I needed a little help. My sis was just so worried about me and the boys." She paused for a moment and then with a strong and proud voice added, "She's been my angel!"

Annie didn't know what to say, and even though it was only a few seconds, it felt like an eternity before Sherri spoke again. When she did, the tone of her voice became stronger. "The trucking company has tried to blame this all on my husband. I can't tell you how many times that Ty came home from work complaining about the overloaded trucks. I'm so sorry for all the pain you've had to suffer, but I needed you to know that Ty was a cautious driver. He loved trucking, and he was an excellent truck driver. I know this is going to sound crazy, but if he hadn't died, I know that he would have never been able to live

Finally

with himself. He loved children so much." The strong voice slipped away. "I'm just so sorry," she said in a quivering voice.

Standing next to the bed, Annie's heart filled with compassion and broke all over again as she thought of all the pain that Sherri and her family had been through. Annie's voice was trembling when she whispered, "Sherri, I understand, and I know it wasn't your husband's fault." When their hands connected, the two women were filled with an indescribable energy, and as their conversation continued, both realized that it was the first time since the accident that either one had talked to someone and felt that the other person had really understood what she was feeling. Annie didn't want to leave, but she knew that Sherri needed her rest and she needed to get back to work.

"I wish that I could stay, but I really need to get back to the desk. We could always talk later if you want to?" Annie asked, hoping that Sherri would agree.

"Oh, that would be wonderful, Annie. I feel so much better. I've wanted to talk to you for so long. More than once, I tried to dial your number, but something always stopped me!" Sherri confessed and then smiled when she added, "I guess we weren't supposed to have this conversation on the phone. Our meeting had to have been arranged by fate."

Annie smiled as she gently let go of Sherri's hand. "Sherri you really do need to get some rest, and I was just noticing that it's time for your night meds. Your orders say that you can have something to help you sleep. If you would like, I can get you a sleeping pill."

"That might be good idea," Sherri answered.

As soon as Annie was spotted back at the nurse's station, Marcia and the aides rushed to her side. Each of them apologized, and then Marcia confessed that it had been their intention to keep Annie and Sherri from meeting, but with all the confusion of the busy night, their plan had gone astray.

Dr. Ray, who had now joined the circle of concern, placed his arm around Annie's shoulders and added, "I'm sorry, too. I should have been more considerate. I hope that you will accept our apologies."

As she made her way around her circle of friends, giving hugs to each of them, it was hard for Annie not to fall apart. She couldn't believe that they had tried so hard to protect her. With a reassuring smile she said, "Guys, everything is OK! Really, Sherri and I are fine. It was the best thing that could have happened to the both of us, and please believe me, there's no need to apologize."

Once Dr. Ray was satisfied that Annie was OK, he tried to lighten the mood. "You know, if you need to go home, we understand. Heck, I can help Marcia. I might just be a doctor, but I'll bet that I could change a few IV bags if I had to."

With a big grin, Annie answered back, "No! No! Really, I'm fine! Just let me finish up, and if you're not too tired, I would love to get that soda that we talked about earlier. Besides, if I went home now, I'd only end up worrying myself silly thinking about a doctor trying to do the work of a nurse!"

Dr. Ray let out a little chuckle and said, "That was a low blow but probably so true!" And then in his soft and gentle way, he reminded everyone to get back to work.

As soon as Annie had given Sherri her meds, she hurried to find Dr. Ray, who was patiently waiting for her in the staff dining room.

"I know you said that it was OK, but I'm still sorry. I should have been looking out for you," Dr. Ray apologized as he poured Annie's soda over a glass of ice. "I know you like your soda from the fountain, but this is the best I can do at this hour. After what you've been through tonight, I should have called and begged Jessie to go in an hour early to the gas station, so I could have gone and gotten you one."

"No, really Doc, this is great!" Annie replied with a smile before lifting her glass to take a taste. "Besides, you know your life would have been on the line. I can just hear the choice adjectives Jessie would have shared with you had you told him that you woke him up early because you needed to get me a soda! Besides, I've already told you that I'm really glad that everything turned out as it did. But I've got to make a confession," Annie said and then lowered her head and looked away. This time there was no smile. "You know, I just can't believe how self-absorbed I've been. I haven't even wanted to think about the fact that another man was killed and that his family was hurting! I feel so ashamed."

"Young lady, you have had enough to deal with. You weren't being selfish," Dr. Ray argued back as he reached across the table and gently lifted Annie's chin, causing her to look him in the eyes.

"Doc, do you know anything about Sherri?" Annie asked.

"I know that she has two little boys and that she's living with her sister. She's a sweet lady, but I think she's also a very proud lady. I met her shortly after the accident. Sherri and the boys came in the office. All three of them had that bad stomach flu that went through the town last December. The boys rebounded quickly after twenty-four hours of IV therapy, but Sherri's health has struggled ever since. I think it's the stress," Doctor Ray answered. As a doctor, he had always been very careful about his doctor/patient confidentiality, but he knew he could trust Annie, and deep down, he was thinking the two women, who were both his patients, could help each other. Unbeknownst to him, they already had.

Suddenly, Annie felt overwhelmed with a different type of concern for Sherri and her boys. "Doc, do you know if she is OK financially?" Annie asked.

"Honestly, I don't think so," he answered and then added, "The trucking company placed all the blame on Sherri's husband. But I think someone at the top must have felt some guilt, because a couple of months ago, the company decided that Sherrie was entitled to Ty's health benefits and a small monthly income." His fists were clenched together, and he had to fight his urge to hit the table when he looked at Annie and said, "Just to hear the name of that company makes me so angry. I see one of their trucks, and I swear my blood starts to boil. It was just too damn easy for that big company to put all the blame on that young man. When I think of what they have done to all of you!"

Annie had to fight back the tears as she reached across the table and gently placed her hands over Dr. Ray's fists. "There have been so many things that I've had to work through or let go of. Tonight, I figured out that I needed to let go of the bitterness. There isn't anyone to blame. Sherri helped me to see that. I've got to believe in fate, and I want my friends and family to do the same."

Dr. Ray nodded and replied, "I don't mean to change the subject, but there's something that I have wanted to ask you." Dr. Ray nervously fidgeted in his chair and took several sips of his soda before continuing. "Annie, have you ever thought about doing something different? You know, maybe going somewhere else, meeting some new people? Now, I know this probably isn't any of my business, but it just seems to me that it might be good for you. Sweetie, I know it really hasn't been that long since the accident, but your parents and I, well, we're all concerned about you, and we think that it would be good for you to try something different. Annie, it seems to us that you're stuck in time."

It was a given that if anyone else had said that to Annie, she would have lost it, but Dr. Ray had a place in her heart like no other. He was her mentor, and she had always respected his knowledge and his advice, but this time she wasn't so sure. After giving the idea a few seconds of thought, she stared out into the dimly lit hospital garden knowing that she didn't want to look directly into Dr. Ray's eyes. "I know it doesn't look like it, but I, I think I have been working real hard to go on. I've been making great strides. You know, it's just not that easy, but I think that right now, I think I'm doing pretty darn good!" When she finally turned to face him, his gaze trapped her and forced her to speak the truth. "Oh, crap, who am I kidding? I know I'm not fooling anyone, or we wouldn't be having this conversation. You're right. I'm doing the same things that I did when Alex and the kids were alive. The only difference is that I just do it alone. You know, Doc, I have thought about trying something different, but I don't know where to go or what I would do when I got there. Besides, I've lived in Milford my entire life. Well, except for the four years that Alex and I went to college, but that probably doesn't count because we didn't even leave the state. But to be honest, I like living in a small town. I'm comfortable here. I just don't think that I could leave. Besides, everyone that I love and care about lives here."

Dr. Ray gave her a smile and then answered back, "Annie, you are my hero. You are an amazing woman. After all you've been through, you could have made the choice to give up, but you didn't. Just look at what happened tonight. We were all so worried about you, and then you came and gave us comfort." He patted her hand gently and then decided that he'd better get on with it before he lost his nerve. "Do you remember hearing me talk about my nephew, my sister's boy, the one who played professional football?"

"I knew you had a sister. But Doc, I don't remember anything about a nephew who played football. Man! I always knew that I wasn't in tune with what was going on. You're such a good friend and we've always been so close—how could I have missed that one? I can't believe that I didn't know that you had a nephew who played professional football. That makes me feel so stupid!" Annie answered.

"Annie, you are too hard on yourself. It's not like you haven't been busy having a life of your own. Besides, you and I both know you've never been much for sports. Well, at least not until little Jack came along," Dr. Ray said with a chuckle, thinking of how cute Annie had been when she watched Jack at his games. She was so excited when he scored his first touchdown that she had stood up in the stands and screamed, "Way to go, son! That was awesome defense!"

Dr. Ray's chuckle turned to a sigh and then he said, "Anyway, I got word about a week after the accident that my nephew, Bridger, had been in a terrible accident of his own."

"Gosh Doc, I am so sorry!" Annie said shaking her head in disbelief. "Why didn't someone tell me?"

"Well now, don't you think you had enough going on?" he answered.

Their conversation forced Annie's thoughts back to the time of the accident and it made her shudder. "There was a lot going on. Who knows, maybe someone told me after all," she admitted. "To be honest, there are days that are absolutely blank. But I am sorry. I wish I could have been there for you. Please, tell me what happened?"

Dr. Ray's face grimaced with pain. "The team had been out on a three-week road trip and had just got back to Seattle. In fact, Bridger called me from the airport while he was waiting for his bags. He always kept me up to date on how things were going. We talked for a few minutes, and then he said that he was going to head out to his mother's place. He told me that he was going to take a few days off and rest for a big game that was coming up." He paused for a moment, took several deep breaths, and then, shaking his head, he said, "He was having such an incredible year! Everyone in the world of football predicted that Bridger would be one of the starting quarterbacks at the Super Bowl. Anyway, a couple of hours later, his coach called me and told me that Bridger never made it to his mother's. Two stoplights past the airport, he was hit head on by a drunk driver. He suffered head trauma, and both of his knees were crushed like cracker crumbs. He was in the hospital for almost three months, and I lost count of how many surgeries he went through. After that, he spent several more months in a rehabilitation center, and since then, he's been living with his mom." Then Dr. Ray took a small detour from his conversation to ask Annie if she'd ever met his sister.

"Yes, I have," Annie answered. "She is a sweetheart! Alex and I spent quite a bit of time talking to her at your son's wedding reception. But now that I think about it, it just seems strange that I don't remember her mentioning anything about having a son. Does she still have the bed-and-breakfast that overlooks the ocean? She sent us some brochures, and we even talked about going there for our twentieth wedding anniversary."

"Yes, she still lives there, but she had to close the bed-and-breakfast. It was just too much for her. Right from the start, I thought she was taking on too much, but she insisted that she needed something to keep her busy after her husband died. Annie, between you and me, I never could understand why she just didn't find a hobby like crocheting!"

Annie smiled but didn't say anything.

Dr. Ray smiled back at Annie and then picked up where he'd left off. "Anyway, once Mary made up her mind to turn her home into a bed-and-breakfast, there was no stopping her, and it sure didn't take long for people to discover what a great place my sister had. The place got so popular that you had to make reservations a year in advance. That, I understood. Mary's home and property—it's like a little piece of heaven right here on earth, complete with two angels, Mary and Flora. As I said, I wasn't too excited about my sis taking on so much, but in the end, I had to admit that I was wrong. It turned out to be a real good thing until Bridger's accident.

"Anyway, Bridger is the one I really wanted to talk to you about. He's had a tough time, and he's had to have a lot of help since the accident. It takes his mother and Flora, the housekeeper, and a full-time nurse who lives at the house five days a week, and a weekend relief nurse to see to his needs. Whoa, I've got to back up here and apologize. I shouldn't have called Flora a housekeeper. Flora is family and has been since that first day that she joined our family. She's been a second mom to Bridger, and I thank God every day she's there, because it takes all of them to take care of Bridger. In fact, the last few times I've called, they have had me worried because they sounded so exhausted. I am very worried about Bridge. He has it in his head that because he can't play football anymore, his life is over. Between the physical pain and the pain of losing what he thought was his life; he's decided to just give up. It's been frustrating for those of us who love Bridger. The orthopedic specialists told us the outlook is good for him. They really believe that with intensive physical therapy he will be able to walk again. They said it was more than likely that he'd have to use a cane, but that all seems so minor compared to adjusting to a lifetime in a wheelchair or no life at all. Bridger doesn't see it that way. He has no desire to even try, and he refuses outright to do his physical therapy.

"After the accident, he was diagnosed with depression. He suffers from very intense mood swings, and his short-term memory was affected. Though my hope was renewed when I went to visit them a couple of weeks ago, and Bridge and I decided to play a few games of chess. I had planned to go easy on him, but I'll be damned, he beat the pants off me three times in a row, and it was some of the best chess I've ever played! He may have won, but I got something better! I got a glimpse of someone that I hadn't seen in a long time. I saw the old Bridger, and it gave me hope. I just know he's in there, and I believe with all my heart that he wants to get better. I didn't say anything about this to Mary and Flora, because I didn't want to get their hopes up. Oh Annie, my nephew has so much to give this world if he could just get through this." Dr. Ray paused for a moment and took a drink. After taking a long, deep breath he said, "I know I've been long-winded, and by now you're probably wondering what in the heck it was that I wanted to talk to you about. Annie, you are one of the most easygoing human beings that I've ever met. You are a loving person; you are caring; and the added bonus is that you are a highly skilled nurse. What I'm saying is I think you are the best there is! Now, I know you're used to working with more than one patient at a time, but I think you would adjust. You need a change, and Bridger needs a nurse like you."

Totally taken by surprise, Annie could only mumble, "Me?"

"Now, before you say anything else, just let me finish." Dr. Ray said, knowing he had to take control of the conversation.

Annie was so overwhelmed with what she'd just heard that she decided she would just take a long sip of her drink, sit back, and listen.

"I'm going to be upfront with you. He's been through quite a few nurses, and it's not because they left for better pay. His mother seems to think that the agency keeps sending her nurses who just haven't had enough experience or that aren't qualified to take care of him. She told me many times that he needs someone with a lot of patience and understanding, and that's how I thought of you."

"Me?" Annie questioned again. Throughout the entire conversation, she had been thinking that Dr. Ray had just needed someone to talk to. Her heart ached terribly for Mary and her son, and she knew that she would do most anything for her dear friend, but not this. Then without giving any consideration to what she was going to say, she just started rumbling and said, "Oh, no, I don't think so. I just can't leave my home, and what about Buddy? I'm quite sure Mary doesn't want my dog, and you know that I can't leave Mom and Dad. I've got to take care of them!"

The moment Annie's last word left her mouth, Dr. Ray was ready with his reply: "I've already talked to Mary about Buddy. She said she'd love to have a dog in the house again. Matter of fact, she used to have a white Schnauzer. Her name was Fluff. She was such a cute little thing. I don't think that I've ever known two more faithful dogs than Fluff and Buddy. She was as crazy about her little Fluff as you are about Buddy. There's one more thing, and I really hope that you're not going to be upset with me, but I've already talked to your parents. You know they have been so worried about you, and I needed their parental advice. When I thought up this plan and asked them what they thought, they said that it sounded like the perfect job for you."

Annie sighed before she replied, "I know you're all concerned for me, but honestly, I really don't think I'm the one you want. In fact, I'm absolutely sure. I'm absolutely sure that I'm not the one that Bridger needs. I don't have the patience that I used to have. Truthfully, I get very anxious over the littlest things. So if you're looking for a patient person, it definitely isn't me!"

Dr. Ray smiled and replied, "Annie, I know this is a big step. All I'm asking is that you don't make a decision concerning something of this proportion in five minutes. I know that you've been an adult for a long time, but why don't you talk this over with your parents—and Karen, too! See what they say." Dr. Ray felt bad that he'd been so blunt, but he'd do anything if he could help his sweet Annie find happiness again.

"Doc, you know that I'd do anything for you. So I'll think about it, but now it's my turn to be honest, and I just can't imagine changing my mind," Annie said as she stood up from her chair. When she pushed her chair in, she noticed the time and added, "Wow, I guess I'd better get back to the floor. Marcia is probably wondering what happened to me." Even though she was anxious to get back to work and away from the conversation, she had to stop and give Dr. Ray a hug, because, even though she didn't think much of his idea, she knew that he loved her and that he was just looking out for her. Before leaving, she gave him one last squeeze and said, "I really am sorry about all that has happened to your sister and her son, and I'll be sure to keep them in my prayers."

Finally

After report, Annie stopped by Sherri's room to check on her and tell her good-bye. The moment she walked in the room, her exhausted body was recharged when she caught sight of Sherri's warm and welcoming smile.

As soon as Sherri looked up and saw Annie standing in the doorway, she smiled and said, "Oh, I didn't think you'd really come. I thought you'd be so tired! Especially, after you worked so hard on your garden and then all night. You'd better get yourself home and into bed!"

Annie couldn't argue she was tired, and so she gave Sherri a quick hug and said, "I'm so glad that we met, and I'm really looking forward to meeting Wes and Nick. I'll be back in a few hours, and if you'd like, I could stop by on my break to visit for a little while."

"That sounds wonderful!" Sherri answered. "I'm just sorry that you have to work another night shift, but on the other hand, I'm very happy that I'll get to see you again. My sister told me that she was going to bring the boys by after work this evening, so maybe you will be able to meet them!"

"I'll make sure of that, and I'll see you later!" Annie answered back and then headed out the door.

Chapter 7

Annie was always one to keep a promise and for days it felt as though Dr. Ray's idea had consumed her. The more she mulled things over, the more she understood that it would be good for her to go somewhere else and meet new people, but she always came up with more reasons to stay than to go. To top off her dilemma, it didn't take her long to figure out that she wasn't the only one thinking about Dr. Ray's idea. During Annie's days off, many of her family and friends stopped by to offer their advice. Her father and Joe were first. She was working in the yard when the two of them stopped by to say hi before a round of golf. Immediately, she knew something was up because she'd never seen the two set foot on the golf course unless, they had an ice chest filled with water, soda, and beer.

Annie didn't even have time to pass the glasses of water out before Joe said, "Sis, I think it's a great opportunity. There's no one better than you when it comes to nursing, and if anyone can help this guy, it's you!"

Since talking with Dr. Ray, Annie had been thinking nonstop about what she should do, so she was rather quick to defend her reasons for not wanting to go. "Well, I just can't up and leave my home during the summer months and let the yard go to wreck and ruin. Alex and I worked too hard on it!"

"Annie, your dad and I kind of thought you'd say something like that, but we got it all figured out," Joe quickly replied with a smile. "We hope you don't mind, but we even talked it over with Kenny, because we knew leaving your yard would be such a big worry for you. It would be good for him, and it would be good for you. You know Kenny's going to be fourteen this fall. Your dad and I say it's high time that young man take on some responsibility. Now this is just between you and me, but my daughter babies him way too much. Heck, Alex was twelve years old when he got his first job bagging groceries at the market." Overcome by the memory of his son as a young man, Joe fell silent, lowered his head, and reached to wipe the tears from his eyes.

It broke Annie's heart to see her father-in-law hurt. His life had changed so much with the death of his only son. From the day of his birth, Alex had been his dad's "best bud." Knowing there was nothing she could say, she moved next to Joe and wrapped her arms around him.

With tears misting his eyes, Barney crowded in and said, "Ah let me in there!" Then moving closer, he wrapped his arms around his little girl and friend.

Even though it was a beautiful summer day, to the three of them, it felt like the dead of winter had descended as they huddled together. Of the three, Barney was the one who was able to find the strength to push them all forward. He gave Joe a couple of manly pats on the back and added, "Well, then, it's a given. He needs us!"

Surprised and a bit confused by her father's choice of words, Annie questioned, "Dad, who needs us?"

"Annie it's not you. Kenny needs us." Barney replied and then he looked directly at Joe and said, "Joe, just think what might become of that young man with us as his supervisors."

Barney's diversion worked. Joe's mind changed gears, and the two men started talking and became totally captivated with their plans to supervise Kenny. As they made their way to the golf course, Annie should have been irritated that they seemed to have forgotten that it was her yard and that she hadn't even said if she was going anywhere yet, but she couldn't, because she loved them both so much. She was just glad that her dad had been able to get Joe's mind on something else.

Even though she wasn't about to tell anyone, Annie knew that she had to agree with her father and Joe about one thing. If and when she decided to go anywhere, her nephew, Kenny, would be the right person for the job, but leaving him with the two old railroad conductors, who together had over sixty years of experience telling people what to do, seemed like a cruel thing to do to such a good kid!

"See, Buddy, there's one more reason we can't go," Annie said to Buddy on their afternoon walk. "I couldn't possibly do that to Kenny. Besides, Dad doesn't really want me living that far away, and I know he doesn't want me to move in with three strangers. He just said all that stuff for Joe's sake."

But the very next afternoon, Annie discovered she didn't know her father quite as well as she thought she did. She was out pulling a few weeds in the garden when he stopped by for another unexpected visit, and before she even had the chance to say hello or ask where her mother was, he said, "I just want you to know, I think that you should do it! Now, I know with your experience as a nurse, you could get a job anywhere that you want to, but heck, this place sounds so wonderful! I was remembering when you were a little girl. Do you remember how you used to play with that little basket of seashells your grandma gave you and how you used to tell me that when you grew up, you were going to live by the ocean? Well now, here's your chance. And just in case you're worried about leaving your mother and me, there is no need to, because we won't be here. We've decided that while you're gone, we're going to do the traveling we've always talked about. We were even thinking that we could head up that way to check on you. You know, I've always wanted to travel up the coastline and into Canada. Maybe we'll even go as far as Alaska!"

Annie was speechless, but it didn't seem to matter, because her father did all the talking. When he finished his little speech, he told his daughter that he loved her and that he'd be back to check on her later. Her father hadn't even driven halfway down the block when Annie heard the phone ring. It was Karen. She wanted to know if they could go for a walk. She said she really needed to talk to Annie about something.

Annie was frantic with worry by the time Karen got out to the house. She'd thought of just about everything that could or might have happened, but it turned out that the only thing Karen wanted to talk about was the same thing as everyone else.

They hadn't walked ten feet down the road when she blurted out, "I really think Dr. Ray's come up with a great idea. I think you should do it!" And then, just like Barney and Joe, Karen did all the talking, plus she felt compelled to give Annie an update on all the available bachelors who were living in Milford and the surrounding area. She had details about every man she named. She knew how many children they had, where they worked, and who their friends were. Karen had so much to say that it wasn't long before she had to stop and catch her breath.

"I was wondering when you were going to come up for air. You've probably worn yourself out sharing all of this information with me." Annie said. Then with a bit of an attitude she asked, "Are you going to be able to make it back, or do you need me to use my cell phone to call Matt and ask him if he can come out and get you?"

Karen completely ignored Annie's comments, and as soon as she caught her breath continued on with her lineup of available bachelors. "Well, let's see whose left. Oh yeah, how could I have forgotten Hank Thompson? I have to say that of all the guys that I've named, he is the hottest! But because he's got three ex-wives and five kids, just a date with Hank could be a scary experience! But don't fret, because there's always Stew Cash. Let's think about this. Stew thinks that he's working when he goes to the mail to pickup his unemployment check. And last but not least, there's my boss, Mr. Carrington. Just the other day, the girls at work said that he was wondering if you'd started dating again. You know, he's got his friend's retirement party coming up. Now that just might turn out to be one of the best time you'll ever have!" Karen let out a giggle and then with complete sincerity said, "Sweetheart, I know you're probably not very happy with me right now, but I'm trying to prove a point."

"And that point would be?" Annie asked with a smart sting.

"That there aren't a lot of men around here to choose from," Karen replied back sharply.

"Oh," Annie shot back.

"OK then. If you decide not to take the awesome offer, there is one guy who I think might be OK," Karen quickly added.

"And who would that be?" Annie had to ask when her curiosity got the best of her.

The sound of Karen's voice was back to normal when she said, "Well, I've never said anything to you, but every time that Jake sees me, he asks me how you're doing."

With a softer tone, Annie shook her head and said, "Just because Jake asks about me doesn't mean anything more than he's concerned."

"Not necessarily! A couple of days ago, he asked me what I thought you'd say if he asked you to dinner. Poor Jake, he's always been so shy, and that awful ex-wife of his didn't help him any. Sweetie, I know you're not ready to date yet, but you might be by the time that Jake gets up enough courage to talk to you!"

"I know what you're trying to do here, but it's not going to work," Annie said, trying her best not to get angry. "You are right! I'm not ready to date. I don't know if I'll ever be ready to date. But it's OK. Alex was the love of my life. He was my soul mate. You know what? Some people live a whole lifetime and never get to have what I had with Alex. I'm not worried about dating right now, and to be honest, I don't know if I ever will be. And besides, you and I both know that Jake and I could never be anything but friends, because Alex is the only thing that Jake and I ever had in common!"

Karen and Annie were still facing each other with their arms folded. As hard as they tried to hold their tough girl poses, it was only seconds before they both gave in and giggled at each other.

"I still love you, old friend" Annie said, smiling as she turned and continued on with their walk and conversation. Without breaking her stride and speaking very loud, Annie said, "Could we please talk about something else? You haven't even mentioned how or what Matt and the kids are doing. Oh and before we talk about another thing, how did your mother's tests at the doctor's come out? Oh come on, don't just stand there acting all mad because you couldn't really get mad at me any more than I could get mad at you! So let go of your pride and catch up! Besides, if you're going to help me eat that chocolate pie my mom left in the fridge today, we've got to start burning some calories!"

Karen was a little out of breath by the time she caught up with Annie, but she didn't let that stop her from speaking her mind. "OK, I won't say another word about bachelors, but I have one more thing to say, and I think you should listen. I really think this could be good for you, and just remember opportunities like this don't come along every day! So all I ask is that you think about it very carefully before you make your mind up."

Over the next few days, Annie didn't talk to one family member or friend, who saw it her way. Everyone thought it was a great idea, and she heard so many of them say, "I think you should do it," that she finally gave in, called Mary, and accepted the position. Mary was thrilled, but her enthusiasm caused Annie more stress. She could not imagine why Mary was so sure that she was going to be any different from the other nurses that Bridger had already gone through. Annie was absolutely certain there had to be someone far more qualified or capable of doing the job than she was.

As soon as Annie told Karen that she'd called Mary, Karen revealed her plans for a shopping trip. "You know, I think you're the most beautiful girl in the world, but honestly, you need to update your wardrobe, especially if you're going out into the big world. Matt and I were talking, and I told him that if you decided to go, I would have to take you shopping for some new clothes. He thought it was a great idea. In fact, I thought about going to Salt Lake City, but Matt said that we should go to Vegas. Girlfriend, we're going to have so much fun! Maybe we could even catch a show. Oh, and we could even go to a spa and have a massage and a facial! Oh, hurry up and say yes, or I'll start to whine, and I know how you hate it when I whine!"

As much as Annie hated to admit it, she knew Karen was right. When it came to fashion, she was out of date, and she really did need some new clothes. It wasn't until she started to plan what clothes she would take that she noticed that half of her closet consisted of nursing uniforms. If she were to be honest, she really wasn't excited about the idea of shopping. Shopping for clothes had never been one of Annie's favorite things to do, but spending time with Karen was, and how could she say no to her best friend, especially when she wasn't going to see her for months?

As soon as they got to Las Vegas, they checked into the hotel, got a quick bite to eat, and then hurried off to the mall. Annie wanted to hurry, pick up a few things, and be done with the shopping, but Karen was set on getting her a whole new wardrobe with matching accessories to boot. Annie had a plan of her own, and as soon as they walked through the front doors of the mall, she said, "Since both of your kids have birthdays in July, and since we don't get to shop in a mall every day, why don't we separate. You go and see if you can find them something, and I'll go and get started. Then we can meet back up, and, of course, you can give me the final approval!"

Karen agreed to the idea, but she was surprised when Annie called her an hour later asking where she could find her. As soon as they met up, Karen snatched up the sacks, gave them a quick scan, and said, "You wild and crazy girl. I leave you alone for one hour and by the looks of things, you went crazy! Let's see here, we've got two pairs of bibbed overalls, one pair of out-of-style khaki pants, two pairs of out-of-style jeans, two pairs of sweats, a sweat jacket, three new tank tops, and three T-shirts. Woo wee. You know the only difference between these clothes and your clothes in your closet, is that these clothes haven't been washed. Friend, did you forget that you were going to update your wardrobe?"

"I did update!" Annie answered with a whine. "Did you know that most of my jeans have holes in them?"

"Look, sweetie, it's time to quit hiding that cute little body of yours behind overalls, sweats, and high-wasted pants. If you're going to start dating again, we've got to spiff you up! Come on, we're not finished yet!" Karen announced as she grabbed hold of Annie's hand and led her down the mall. Annie didn't want to argue, so she followed and did as she was told. Annie tried on outfit after outfit and much to her surprise; she even liked the way she looked in some of the ensembles that Karen had picked out.

"OK, you were right!" Annie admitted as they made their way from the last dressing room to the register. "But, I'm not going to take even one shirt home unless you agree to turn around and get yourself a new wardrobe, too! Why should I be the only one who has to be updated? You know, old married women need to look good, too! Besides, I've wanted to do something special for you for a long time. I just didn't know what to do."

With a forced, stern look, Karen quickly replied, "I don't want you to spend your money on me. This trip is for you!"

"Oh, please, you would do the same thing for me. Besides, my accountant was wondering if he was ever going to have to work for his paycheck. He said that he hadn't even had to balance the checkbook. So please help me let him earn his keep," Annie argued.

"No, you should spend your money on you and your family, or the needy, but not me," Karen argued back.

"You know darn well that I can do that, too. Now, since you were the one who made such a big fuss about my wardrobe, you'd better pick out one of your own, or I'm going to head out into the big world looking like a geek, and it will be all your fault," Annie said, trying her best not to smile.

Karen pretended to think about it for a moment and then replied, "Oh man! I could never let you do that! OK, you win! But it's getting late, so I'll have to shop tomorrow. Besides, if we don't get back to the hotel, we'll miss the show."

This time it was Annie's turn to take hold of Karen's arm. "No! I know what you're doing. You won't go shopping tomorrow. You are as stubborn as a mule and as sly as a fox, but so am I. You don't need to worry about missing the show, because while you're trying on clothes, I'll call the hotel and get tickets for the late show. Remember, we're staying on the VIP floors! Now, get shopping!" Annie playfully demanded as she pulled Karen in the direction of a store.

While Karen was busy trying on different clothes, Annie thought to herself how glad she was that Karen had talked her into getting a new wardrobe. Still, as much as she didn't want to disappoint her best friend or the rest of her friends and family, Annie knew that she wasn't going to start dating again, not in the northwest or anywhere else. She was going there to work, and that was the end of story, no matter what everyone else had planned for her.

"Hey, let's go in here," Annie said, nodding in the direction of a hair salon as they made their way out of the mall.

"What in the world for?" Karen asked as she raced to catch up with Annie.

"I want to see if they can get me in for a haircut," Annie replied.

"What? Do you mean a trim?" Karen asked as she took in all the different kinds of people coming and going at the mall, not really giving much thought to what Annie had said.

"No, I don't want a trim. I want to cut it off! I've had hair down my back for as long as I can remember, and you know what else? I want some of those color strips or whatever you call them."

Karen was totally surprised by Annie's decision. "No way, you're not serious, are you? This isn't like you at all." she commented.

"Look, everyone including you, thinks I need to make some changes in my life, and it was just a few minutes ago that you told me that you couldn't let me head out into the big world, looking like a geek! So when I was trying on all those clothes, I took a good look at myself in the mirror, and I decided that I need a new hairdo to go with my new wardrobe. Do you want to get a new hairdo too?" Annie asked as she followed the receptionist to the waiting lounge.

Totally into the moment, Karen replied, "Let's do it, and, by the way, I really don't think you're a geek!"

Annie giggled, "Oh I know! Though when you call me a geek, I just think of all the times people told me that I look just like you!"

As soon as they stylist was finished, he turned the chair toward the mirror so that Annie could see the result. He'd done exactly as she'd asked and had cut her hair to her shoulders. When she first saw it, she wanted to cry, but the more she looked in the mirror, the more she decided that she liked it!

"You look ten years younger! I love it!" Karen exclaimed as she walked toward Annie.

As soon as she stood up from the chair, Annie hurried to give her friend a hug and squealed. "I love yours, too!"

Then with their arms still around each other, the two friends took one more look in the mirror.

"I don't know about you but I feel like a new woman!" Karen exclaimed.

"Me too," Annie agreed. "Yep, I think we look pretty good!"

"Yes, we do!" Karen replied. Then, with a big smile across her face, she said, "Now, let's go have some fun!"

The three days in Vegas seemed to fly by, but as much as Karen had enjoyed herself, she was relieved to get home, and it wasn't because she had wanted the trip to end. It was because it had been so hard for her to not confess her true feelings to Annie. Throughout the entire trip, Karen had to fight the urge not to tell Annie just how much she was going to miss her, but she didn't dare because she had been warned by everyone, including her own husband, not to say anything that might cause Annie to change her mind about leaving.

Annie, on the other hand, wasn't relieved to get home, because she knew that she would have to scratch another line off of her to-do list, which meant that her day of departure was getting closer and closer. She had a lot to do to get ready, and she liked to keep busy so that she wouldn't think too much but this time, her keep busy plan backfired, because how could she not think about going when everything on her list had something to do with the move?

She had a hard time trying to decide what to take, because she had never gone anywhere for longer than a week. But after days of deliberating, packing, and unpacking, she decided that she would only take, in addition to the essentials, her favorite framed photos and scrapbooks. It wasn't long before there was only one thing left on her to-do list, and that was the good-bye party. Not many days after she had made the decision to go, she had decided to throw a barbeque the night before she left town, and that day just happened to fall on Alex and Jack's birthdays. Even though she knew it would be hard for everyone, she knew it would be a great day to give tribute to her family.

Annie was grateful when her parents, along with Joe and Gladys, insisted on helping her with the party, but there was one detail that she took care of all by herself. Annie knew that she had wanted to do something special to thank everyone for all they had done for her, and that's when she came up with the idea to surprise everyone with a large fireworks show after dinner. It took some careful planning and a lot of help from the fireworks company, the county Fire Marshal, and the city crew for Annie to keep her surprise a secret. On the day before the barbeque, they had all worked together on the golf course, making it look as if they were doing repair work on the automated watering system.

Annie had seen the crews while she mowed the lawn, and just when she was about to relax and let herself think that her plan was actually going to work, she looked up and spied her father and Joe making their way down the fairway. Annie's heart started to pound as she watched Joe pull the golf cart alongside the city crew. She knew both her father and Joe would hound the workers with a gazillion questions. Annie kept an eye on them as she made her way up and down the yard with the lawnmower. It seemed to take forever for the two, old, lovable farts to get back to their game. When they pulled up in front of the gate, she knew they'd figured out her plans by the way they were both smiling.

"Annie, did you know the city's going to add some new kind of fancy pressurized pumps to the sprinkler system up on number one?" Joe hollered from the golf cart.

"Yeah, and they said if everything goes well, they're going to add them to the rest of the course," Barney added before they both started talking at once to tell her everything they had just learned. Annie took a deep breath of relief. She knew it wasn't that big of a deal if they found out, but it tickled her to think that they'd get to enjoy her surprise along with the rest of the crowd.

After a little visit, Joe and Barney continued on with their game, but it wasn't until they had stopped on the number four putting green that Barney felt it was safe to ask, "Do you think she believed us, Joe?"

"I think so. Annie must have worked awfully hard to pull off such a thing in a town this size. You know, we might have turned into two old busybodies, but there's no way that we'd do anything to ruin something like this." Joe replied as he picked up his putter. "I'm really looking forward to tomorrow night. It will be the first time we've all been together, since…" Overcome with reality, Joe's voice trailed off as his tears took over.

"I know, Joe. I know. It's tough," Barney agreed solemnly as he walked over to give his friend a pat on the back. "It's not going to be easy!"

The next twenty-four hours flew by, and before Annie knew it, her guests were arriving. The food was the center of the party. Annie, Lil, and Gladys had filled a table with all kinds of wonderful appetizers, salads, and desserts, while Joe and Barney served up incredible barbeque ribs, chicken, and burgers. The kids enjoyed playing in the sandbox, jumping on the trampoline, and playing on the swing set while the men and younger women played horseshoes. The older women had opted to gather under the shade trees and catch up on all the latest town news. Of course, there was still that familiar longing for those who weren't with them, but as this group of family and friends gathered together, they knew they had learned to have a greater appreciation for each other and for the time they spent together.

It was just about sundown when Annie's Aunt Emma stood in the middle of the yard and announced that she had something to say. In her dramatic way, she thanked Annie, her brother and sister-in-law, Barney and Lil, and Joe and Gladys for the great party. She wished Annie good luck and, in her usual bold style, told everyone it was time to pitch in and cleanup before they left! And to top off her speech, she made it plain and clear that she didn't want any lollygaggers visiting with Annie late into the night because she needed to get to bed and get a good night's rest.

Annie could only smile and laugh inwardly as she listened to her Aunt Emma. She had never been one to hold back what she was thinking, but you couldn't help but love the old gal. Everyone did as they were told, and the yard was cleaned up in less than fifteen minutes. Unfortunately, it was still a few minutes until the first salute. Annie tried not to panic when she looked at her watch, but she didn't want everyone to be in the front yard getting into their cars when it went off. Thinking quickly, she hurried to the gate and announced that she needed to make sure that she gave everyone a kiss good-bye. Facing the crowd, Annie stood in the middle of the gate with her feet spread apart and her hands holding onto both sides to block the opening. Uncle George and Aunt Emma were at the first in line, and she stalled them as long as she could, but she couldn't help letting out a great big sigh of relief when the first salute went off.

As soon as the first boom went off, everyone's heads turned in the direction of the golf course wondering what was going on. When Annie made the announcement that there was going to be a fireworks show, everyone reacted just as she had hoped. Before running for blankets, she explained that there was going to be a ten-minute delay in between the first five displays so that the town folks would have time to get out to the golf course to see the show. Annie knew that everyone from the town would come because there was no way, they could listen to huge booms going off in the night sky, and not come out of their houses to investigate and see what was going on.

Even though it was late when the fireworks ended, Annie had one more thing to share with her friends and family before they left. She gathered everyone in a circle and once again thanked them for all they had done for her. And then for the first time, she shared that she'd been given a very large settlement. She told them how at first she hadn't wanted anything to do with the money but now had come to realize that she could use the money to honor the lives of her family and, at the same time, give something back to the community that she and her family loved so much. Then she announced her plans to build a new library with a state-of-the-art media center and a second gymnasium at the high school. She told them that she was also going donate money for a new city park. It was hard for her to hold back her emotions when she looked at her father and Joe and asked them if they would do her the honor of overseeing the projects. Overcome with emotions of their own, both Barney and Joe nodded their heads in acceptance. The silence continued as everyone continued to take in what Annie had just shared. They all knew that the gifts would be wonderful additions to their little community, but they couldn't help but think of the real cost of the projects—Alex, Jack, Kara, Molly, and Ty Carter.

Looking out over the crowd, Annie was immediately sensitive to her friends and family's reactions, and she wanted to comfort them. She hurried and took hold of those who were standing next to her. "Guys, I understand how you're feeling. I felt that way for a long time after I talked to the lawyers. In fact, at first, I wasn't going to take the settlement. It felt dirty. But then, I realized that I could do good things for the people and the community that my family loved. It's important for me that you all understand that I've given this a lot of thought. I know with all my heart that this is what, Alex, Ty, and the kids would want me to do."

As soon as the word "do" left her lips, Annie felt sick, and her heart started to pound with apprehension. Maybe she'd been wrong. Maybe she shouldn't have taken the money. The sound of two hands coming together brought her back to reality. When Annie realized that it was her father and that he was clapping to show his support for her decision, she couldn't even begin to describe the love she felt for him. Her thoughts of apprehension quickly left when she heard another pair of hands coming together. It was Joe, and it was only seconds before the rest of crowd joined in.

After saying good-bye to her guests, Annie went to find Sherri, who was still helping with the last bit of clean-up. "Sherri, there's something that I've wanted to talk to you about," Annie said as they walked arm in arm toward the front yard. "Now, I know the minute that I tell you this, you're going to say no. So, before I begin, all I ask is that you please listen to me." Sherri tried to interrupt Annie, but Annie totally ignored her and hurried to add, "There is something that I need to do. This is purely selfish on my part, but I need to know that you and the boys will be ok financially."

Sherri tried speaking again, but Annie insisted she listen. "Please, Sherri, it's the least that I can do for you and the boys. I've already made the arrangements, so please just hear me out. When Wes and Nick turn eighteen, there will be a trust fund waiting for them at the bank. They can use the money for college or a good start in life. It's completely their decision, though I have to say that I'm hoping they will choose college. Also, I've arranged for a monthly deposit to be placed in an account for you. Now, when you're ready, you and the boys can get a place of your own. And maybe when things settle down, you'll be able to finish getting your teaching degree. You and I both know that there is no way money can ever replace what we've lost, but you shouldn't have to worry about providing for the boys when I can help you."

"I-I don't know what to say. Thank you is not enough," Sherri cried as she gave Annie a hug.

"Of course it is! But then again, I feel the same way about your friendship. Thank you doesn't seem to be enough. Sherri, you were the only one that I could talk to that truly understood just how much I missed my husband and children. I don't know what I'd have done without you, so please let me help you," Annie pleaded.

Gently, Sherri drew back from Annie's embrace and smiled. She said, "I guess all I can say is thank you, and then hopefully one day, I can become half the teacher that Alex was."

Once more, the two friends embraced and then Annie insisted that it was time for Sherri to get home and get to bed. Even though Sherri's health had improved a great deal over the past few months, Annie was still concerned about her and didn't want to take any unnecessary risks.

Annie said good-bye to Sherri and the boys and then it was Gladys and Joe's turn to say good-bye.

"Sweetheart, I just can't tell you how much we love you. All we want is for you to be happy." Gladys declared as she hugged Annie tightly.

"Hey, let me in there. I gotta get one last hug, too!" Joe added as he wrapped his arms around Annie and his wife. "You take good care of yourself, sweetie, and don't you worry too much about your folks, because you know we will look after them."

Annie was barely able to whisper that she loved them, because the lump in her throat was so tight. Her mother and father joined her just as Joe and Gladys drove away. The reality of Annie's departure hit Barney hard. It took everything he could muster to not break down and tell her that he was wrong and that he really thought that she should just stay home, where he would be able to look after her and know that she was safe. The pain in his heart was piercing. Oh, God in heaven, he was going to miss her so much, but deep down he knew that he had to let her go. Lil, on the other hand, couldn't seem to find any inner strength and totally fell apart when she reached for her daughter. Annie couldn't blame her; she knew her mother had to be scared to death of letting go of her only child.

"I'll be OK, Momma. I promise. I'll be real careful, and you know, I've got the Bud Dog to look after me," Annie said, trying to comfort her mother.

"Are you sure you won't come and spend the night with us or at least stop by in the morning and have some breakfast before you leave?" Lil pleaded.

"No, Mom. It would be too hard to go through this again. Besides, you know that I've got a schedule to follow, right Dad?" Annie replied with a teasing look directed at her father. Then she reached to give them one last hug and added, "Oh, I love you guys so much."

Annie made herself be strong, but as soon as her parents' car turned the corner, she broke down in a wrenching sob.

"You don't have to go," Karen confessed tearfully as she wrapped her arms around Annie from behind. "There, I said it, and I don't care if everyone gets mad at me! And I have one more thing to say. There are plenty of single men here for you if and when you are ready to date. Oh Lord in Heaven, what am I'm going to do without you?"

"I knew all along that you weren't being honest with me and that you didn't want me to go." Annie answered as she wiped their tears with the sleeve of her jacket. "But we both know that I have to go. It's going to be OK. I promise." She gave Karen a big squeeze and then reached in her pocket and pulled out a new cell phone. "Call me anytime, day or night. I just don't want you and Matt to have any financial trouble because of our need to talk to each other. And there's one more thing that I need you to do. Don't you dare open this envelope until after I've gone! I've written you a little note, and it's so sappy that once you read it, you won't be able to let me go!" Reaching to give her friend one last hug, Annie cried, "Oh, I miss you already!"

Annie and Karen were so in tune to each other that they had forgotten all about Matt and the kids, who had been patiently waiting in the car. "We all love you, Annie, but I've got to hit the road at 7:00 a. m. and it is now 12:30. So will you two dolls please have mercy on an old man who has to get up early! Besides, honey, did you forget about Aunt Emma's orders? If she comes back to check on Annie, oh man, is she going to get after you!" Both women tried to put on a brave front as they smiled and gave each other one last hug.

The party was over, all the good-byes had been said, and now there were just a few final things left to do on Annie's to-do list. Annie returned to the backyard and found Buddy, who had spent most of the night searching for leftovers in the grass, and then turned out the lights. Once inside, Annie and Buddy took their usual walk through the house. After straightening a few things in her bedroom, Annie knelt at the side of the bed and said her prayers. She was so tired when she finished that she didn't even notice that she had reached over and turned down the covers to her bed. She was just about to crawl in when she realized what she was doing. For just a moment, Annie thought she'd be able to sleep in her bed, but in the end, she still didn't have the heart or the courage to be there without Alex.

Chapter 8

Annie was surprised when she opened her eyes and realized that she had slept through the alarm. She had wanted to have that extra thirty minutes to have a cup of tea and wake up, but now she would have to skip that part of the plan if she was going to keep to her dad's schedule. She let Buddy outside and then hurried upstairs to get a quick shower. A little bit of makeup and a ponytail, and she was ready to go. Before heading to the garage, she and Buddy took one last walk through the house to make sure all the windows and doors were locked, and then because she had promised her father that she would, she double-checked all the appliances to make sure that they were unplugged.

With Buddy at her side, Annie pulled out of the garage, closed the door, took a deep breath, and put the car in drive. The smell of new SUV permeated her nostrils. She thought of Alex and how he had always loved the smell of new cars. She was glad that she had taken Karen's advice to get something bigger for the trip.

All along, Annie had wanted to share some of the settlement money with her parents and in-laws, but she had known that she would have to do it in a way that wouldn't make them feel uncomfortable. After much thought, she decided that on her way out of town, she would leave notes in their front doors that explained why there had been money deposited into their bank accounts. She was able to deliver all of her notes without anyone seeing her, until her last stop. Just as she was stepping off the front porch of her sister-in-law's house to run back to her car, she heard a familiar gruff voice say, "Whatcha doing there, Missy?"

Annie was startled by the noise but wasn't surprised when she turned around to see her sister-in-law's neighbor, Mr. Nichols sauntering across the yard toward her.

Annie hurried to him, hoping that he wouldn't talk too loud if she was standing next to him.

Mr. Nichols tipped his hat toward her and said, "They went to a big party last night!" It was their sister-in-law's going away party. You know the one whose husband and children were killed in that horrible car accident last year!" After pausing, he added, "That was one of the most tragic things ever. This family is good people and it just shouldn't have happened." He paused for a moment, shook his head and then added, "And, young lady, I've seen and heard a lot of stuff in my day. Why, I'm going to be ninety-four on my birthday next month."

Annie wanted to cry, but she realized that Mr. Nichols didn't have a clue who she was, and knowing there was no time for explanations, she quickly replied, "Oh, so that's why they didn't answer. Well, I guess they must have been up pretty late and they're still sleeping. So I'll just stop by a little later." Then speaking as loud as she dared, Annie said, "Hey would do me a favor? Would you tell them that I stopped by?"

Always the gentleman, Mr. Nichols tipped his hat again and replied, "OK, I'll do that for you, young lady." And then without thinking to ask who she was, he turned and walked back to his yard, grumbling to himself about the price of water. "I gotta get over there and change the water. It costs so damn much to water your lawn these days. Why, when I was young…"

Annie smiled as she watched Mr. Nichols walk back to his yard, and then she hurried back to the security of her vehicle. Now, all she had to do was grab a soda before she made her last stop. As she made her way across the dewy grass, she was glad that she'd decided to wear flip-flops, because her feet were soaking wet by the time she got to the graves. Annie couldn't believe how quiet the town was that morning. Even the birds seemed to be quieter than usual. As she gazed at photos of Alex and the children upon the headstones, she knew she had made the right decision. She wanted the world to know just how beautiful they were.

With a quiet voice, she said, "I know you're not here. If you were, I wouldn't leave."

Finally

Her thoughts and words jumbled as Annie wrapped her arms around herself to rub away the cold chills that had taken over her body on that warm July morning. "Oh, I know this is going to sound crazy, but I feel like I'm the one who left you. If only it hadn't been my birthday. If only you hadn't gone to get me a present, and I know you've heard me say that a million times, but I'll probably say it ten million more before I see you again. Oh, I'm trying, God. I'm trying!" Annie's voice quivered when she looked up at the heavens and said, "Alex, take care of our babies till we're all together again. Don't let them forget me." Then after kissing her hand and transferring the kiss to each picture, she called for Buddy and left.

The beauty of the morning helped Annie to feel a little better about things. The morning sun highlighted every detail of the Frisco Mountain Range. The big, blue western sky was packed with billowy clouds that were waltzing north, and just as she dropped into the Wah Wah Valley, she spied a zigzagged trail of dust left behind by a herd of antelope running across the desert. It didn't matter how many times she'd watched antelope run, Annie was always amazed at their awesome speed.

"Bud, don't you think the desert looks amazing this morning? That last rainstorm really did it a lot of good. Would you just look at all of those wild flowers?" As always, Annie talked to Buddy as though he were a person. She even felt a bit neglected when she happened to glance down and notice that he was lying across the seat with his eyes half closed. "Some copilot you are, Buddy! We haven't even hit twenty miles on the odometer, and you're taking your first nap! I'm telling you, you had just better sit up and take in all of this wide-open space, because it's going to be a while before we see it again." Buddy opened his eyes wide, lifted his ear, and as soon as Annie said the word "again," he stood up, wagged his tail, and pressed his nose to the window.

"The person who came up with the analysis that dogs only comprehend the tone of the human voice sure never met a pup like you, Buddy Boy!" Annie said as she reached across the console to scratch Buddy on the neck.

Then looking at the map on the dash, she thought of her father and all the time he had put into planning her trip. He had spent days studying maps and surfing the Internet before he decided that the drive across Nevada and up the California coastline would be the best route for her to take. He had made a very detailed map along with an attached itinerary for her and Buddy to follow. There wasn't a spot on the map that wasn't marked with some kind of a reminder. Using colored markers, he traced each highway, freeway, city, and town that she was going to drive on or through. After each major stop, he had written her estimated arrival time until the next major stop. He carefully marked where she needed to stop to get gas, where she might want to stop for a bite to eat, where she would stay, and even estimated spots where she might need to get a drink and go to the bathroom. The day he brought his carefully planned itinerary over to her house, Annie had made a big fuss over all his work and hoped that no one had told him that he could have done the same thing in about two minutes on the Internet or that she could use the GPS system in her new car.

When her mother first found out that Annie planned to drive, she had a complete come apart and argued the benefits of flying for days, but when she figured out that there was nothing she could say or do to make her daughter change her mind, she reminded Annie daily that she was praying for her safety.

Annie and Buddy were almost five hours into the drive. She had kept busy by singing and talking to herself nonstop as she drove across the western deserts of Utah and Nevada. Looking over at Buddy, she said, "Well, Dad will be happy to know that we're right on schedule!" Then she stretched and yawned several times before she looked back toward Buddy and whined, "Crap, I'm so flippin tired! I stayed up way too late and got up too early. I should have made sure that I had more sleep last night. I should have listened to Aunt Emma! But you know what, Bud? I never had to worry about being the only driver before. Whenever we took long, road trips, Alex and I always took turns driving. Oh, how could I have been so stupid?"

From his seat on the passenger's side, Buddy tilted his head from side to side, wagged his tail back and forth, made cute little doggie whimpers, and gave Annie one his best sympathetic puppy looks.

"Crap!" Annie yelled. "I swear we haven't passed a single car in the last two hours. OK, well, maybe I'm exaggerating a bit, but it's been at least fifteen minutes." As she was shaking her head, she caught a glimpse of Buddy and then added, "Oh, don't look at me with your cute little face! You know, if you wanted to be fair about this whole situation, it really should be your turn to drive! You've been sitting there all day, totally relaxed, having little catnaps and eating doggy bones while I have to drive. OK, I know I'm cracking! You aren't even old enough to drive yet, are you?" Annie added and then started to giggle. "Buddy, I'm so sorry. I'm just tired. I didn't mean to offend you. And I know that wasn't politically correct to say that you were catnapping. Man, now I think that I'm getting slaphappy. OK, I got to think of something and quick. Oh yeah, I know what we'll do, Bubba Doo. We're going to have a fire drill!"

Buddy stood up on the seat, stretched for a quick second, and then gave a soft bark in answer.

"Trust me! I promise. It will be fun! Karen and I did it all the time when we were teenagers, and besides, if I don't do something real quick to wake up, we're going to be in big, big trouble. Now, listen up, because here's the plan. We stop here in the middle of nowhere, and by the way, that is exactly where we are. Then, I open the door; we jump out, and then we start running around the car screaming, fire!" And because you can't yell, I'm expecting you to bark like crazy! And because you don't have arms, I'll squirt the water on us. Just trust me because this is going to be great!"

Annie brought the car to a stop right in the middle of the highway, picked up her bottle of water, jumped out, and then hurried to open the other door. Buddy welcomed the chance to stretch, but it was quite obvious that he was a bit bewildered as he watched his beloved owner put her plan into action, though it didn't take him long before he decided to join in. Every time Annie screamed, "Fire!" he'd echo with a long howl as if he were the siren.

After several minutes of chasing each other around the car screaming, laughing, and barking, Annie was forced to stop and catch her breath. Instantly, her carefree laughter faded and was replaced with an uneasy feeling that only deepened as she looked to the road in front of her. As her breathing returned to normal, she made a half-turn and looked back in the opposite direction. Then she repeated herself several more times, looking to home then looking to the future. Sensing that something was wrong, Buddy whimpered for Annie's attention. Her eyes never left the road as she lowered herself and reached for him. Even as she held him close and whispered words of comfort, Annie repeated herself several more times. Looking at the road home made her heart long for the safe and the familiar. Each glance forward into the future became more frightening and lonely. Finally, overcome with exhaustion, Annie made her way back into the SUV, and Buddy followed.

She hadn't found the feeling of refreshment that she had been looking for; instead, she found herself staring at the long road ahead. Tears started to fill her eyes, and then with an explosion of frustration, she screamed, "What the hell am I doing? I don't know what to do! Alex, why did you leave me? This isn't fair! Why did you take my babies away from me? Why? Why did you leave me? Didn't you love me as much as I loved you? I wouldn't have done this to you. This isn't fair." She was so lost in her own desperation and sorrow that she didn't even notice that a man and woman were standing next to the car. As soon as Annie heard a voice say, "Excuse me, miss, is everything OK?" Annie was completely brought back to life and very overwhelmed. Annie closed her eyes for just a second and hoped that when she opened them again, the two people standing by her car would be gone, but when she opened them again, she saw that they were still there, and she knew she was in deep trouble! When she turned her head to face the police officers, Annie caught a glimpse of herself in the rearview mirror, and she almost didn't recognize herself. Her hair and shirt were soaking wet, and her eyes and cheeks were blazing red, smeared with smudges and streaks of black mascara. It even took several attempts for her to clear the frog from her throat before she could answer with a weak, "Yes. I'm fine, officer. Really, I'm fine. Umm, yeah, I'm fine."

The large man standing next to the window, tipped his mirrored sunglasses, stared into Annie's eyes and asked, "Miss, have you consumed any alcohol today?"

Annie felt totally dumfounded, and then without even thinking, she answered, "No, sir, I didn't drink. Well, that's not true. I had a soda. No! No! I'll bet you want to know if I drank any alcohol. No, I didn't! But that was just today because sometimes, I like a glass of wine when I eat Italian food. And sometimes, I like a margarita with Mexican dishes. And once in a while, when I'm at a barbecue, I like a wine cooler or a really, really cold beer, and I always have a few glasses of wine at Christmas time, sometimes at Thanksgiving, too. And maybe just a little champagne on New Year's, but I promise, I didn't even have any this last year. I swear and I swear with all my heart that I didn't have anything to drink that had alcohol in it today!"

It was at that moment that Annie realized that she must have sounded even crazier than she looked. Then the man said that he would need to have a look at her driver's license and that he wanted her to step out of the car. How could this be happening? Annie started to shake. The trembling started in her hands and then like a colossal Dominoes display, the trembling rippled through her entire body. When Annie looked over again at the giant man, she tried hard not to cry, but she couldn't stop herself. "I swear to you. I'm not drinking. I'm not on drugs. I'm a nurse. I'm a good nurse. I live in Milford, Utah. My name is Annie Davis. Everybody said, 'Oh you need to go. You need to do something different.' But what I want to know is how come everyone but me seems to know what it is that I need. To be perfectly honest with you, Buddy and I were doing just fine. Well, that's not completely honest, but I've already had that discussion with Dr. Ray. It's just that after my husband and my children were killed in a car accident in the Minersville Pass, it has been a living nightmare. It was really hard! It's still hard. I don't know what I'm supposed to do. But, I don't think going to live with three strangers is really going to make everything all better. How could it? I don't think anything is going to be better again." When she finished, Annie continued to sob as she unsuccessfully tried to wipe her face with the bottom of her shirt.

 The sheriff and his deputy had been totally unprepared for the poor woman's admission. Throughout their careers, they'd had to listen to some pretty wild stories after asking someone to step out of their car, but nothing had compared to Annie's. Both of the officers' instincts told them that there was nothing threatening about the situation, but after Annie had told them that her husband and children were killed in the Minersville Pass, the deputy recalled a news report that she had seen on several national TV channels. She remembered the story had gotten to her because she was a police officer, even more so because she was a mother.

 To get the sheriff's attention, the deputy tugged on his pants and then covering her mouth with her hand whispered, "Claude, I believe she's telling the truth. I remember the story on the news. In fact, it was on every national news channel. Let's go easy on her. I think life's already done a number on her."

 After taking a quick moment to think things over, Claude shook his head in agreement. "Miss, why don't you take a deep breath and get yourself settled down a bit, and then maybe Faye and I can help you out." Looking at Annie, he reached into his pocket, gave her a kind smile, and gave her his clean white hankie.

Annie sniffed as she reached for the hankie. "Thank you. I know that this is going to sound completely stupid, but I was tired, and I'd been driving for hours. I've never had to drive this far by myself. I've always had someone with me. And that probably sounds really stupid coming from a person my age." Before she could continue, she had to stop and blow her nose several times. "I was just so tired, and I needed to wake up. The only thing I could think to do was have a fire drill like I did when I was a teenager. And then Buddy and I, well we were actually having fun, and then I guess that I got a bit overwhelmed and that's when I kind of lost it. I really didn't mean to cause any trouble, officers. I'm so sorry." After she'd stuttered her way through an apology, Annie looked down at the soiled hankie and wasn't quite sure if she should give it back.

Again with a gentle smile stretched across his face, the sheriff reached over, gave Annie a gentle pat on her shoulder, and said, "Oh, that's OK dear. You can keep it. Ah, I've got plenty more at home."

"So how far are you going today, Annie?" The deputy asked in a friendly tone.

"I need to get to Reno. Buddy and I have reservations for tonight," Annie answered.

Offering his hand, Claude said, "You know, we haven't even introduced ourselves. My name is Claude Hayward. I'm the sheriff of this fine county, and this is my deputy, Faye Evans."

Graciously, Annie accepted their hands as she formally introduced herself and Buddy.

After a few moments of small talk, Claude said, "Hey, I've got an idea. Why don't you let Faye drive you as far as Fallen? It would give you a chance to rest up a bit. We'll get you some lunch at our favorite diner, and then you can decide whether you want to keep going or if you want to turn around and head for home."

And then without the slightest bit of hesitation or even giving a thought to the fact she was with two complete strangers, Annie agreed. As strange as the whole situation seemed, she felt completely safe, and it didn't hurt that she trusted Buddy's instinct and judgment far more than her own. Had he barked or fussed, she would have been scared to death, but it had been the complete opposite, and he'd instantly taken to Claude and Faye.

Finally

After getting Buddy settled in the back seat, Annie gratefully slid herself into the passenger side of the SUV, and as soon as Faye steered the car back onto the highway, the two women started gabbing as if they were old friends. Unfortunately, it was only ten minutes into the conversation that Annie's weary body forced her to rest, and she fell asleep in the middle of a sentence. She didn't move again until after Faye pulled the car into the diner's parking lot and turned off the engine.

"Whoa, I guess I really was tired!" Annie mumbled as she tried to wake up.

"I think the word exhausted would be more fitting! It's a good thing Claude and I came along," Faye replied with a smile. "It's OK if you let Buddy out for a run while we get something to eat." Then she chuckled and added, "You don't have to worry about the dogcatcher getting him because Claude and I know the Animal Control Officers well."

Annie laughed and replied, "Sounds like home! I should have him on a leash but he is really good about staying close to me. By the way before we get something to eat, is there somewhere that I could freshen up?"

"Yep, come on and I'll show you," Faye answered, motioning with her hand as she gave the front door to the diner a push.

"This is the best place in the world to get a cheeseburger!" Claude called out as he caught up to them. "That is, if you like cheeseburgers. Sometimes, I forget that there are people who just like to eat the green stuff."

"Not me. I love a good cheeseburger with a big red tomato and onion," Annie commented. The diner was small and reminded her of the little diner at home. The dining area consisted of six tables, and there was a small bar that ran in front of the open grill.

When Annie looked at her reflection in a mirror, she felt extremely lucky that Claude and Faye hadn't arrested her. After muffling through her bag for a brush, she gave her hair a quick once-over and freshened up her ponytail. The cold water that she splashed on her face felt good and after freshening up her makeup, she almost felt like a new woman.

After taking the chair next to Faye, Annie was able to get a good look at Claude. Now he actually reminded her of a big, old, loveable, teddy bear. She had barely sat down when another big, teddy bear of a guy came out carrying a tray covered with cheeseburgers, fries, and shakes.

"I went ahead and ordered. I hope that's OK. I got your cheeseburger just how you said you like it," Claude said, smiling.

It was amazing how much Annie, Claude, and Faye, all had in common. They talked about living in small towns, going to small schools, family, and Annie even talked about the accident. Claude shared with her that he'd been married for forty years and was looking forward to retiring after the holidays. He told her that he had four children and was the proud grandpa of eight grandchildren. Faye told Annie that she was a single mother raising a boy and a girl, who were the same ages as Kara and Molly. It wasn't hard to tell that they were the light of her life when she opened her wallet to show Annie their photos.

Claude had to excuse himself from the table to take a phone call, and since he was going outside, he told Annie that he'd check on Buddy, which made her feel better. She was just starting to worry about him and wondered whether she should be getting back on the road.

As the two women sat and drank their shakes, Faye looked over at Annie and said, "Annie, I know we've just barely met and you can tell me to shut up if you want, 'cause I know that it's none of my business, but I think you ought to give it a try. I think you need to keep your car going in the same direction. It was five years ago that my husband up and left me. And every year since then, I tell myself that this is the year that I'm going to take my kids and move up to Tahoe. I would make twice the money, have more benefits, and there's got to be a heck of a lot bigger selection of single men up there for me to choose from. And then for some reason or another, another year comes and goes, and well, I'm still here." Faye paused and then reached over and took hold of Annie's hand and smiled reassuringly. "Annie, do it for all us older gals who are just too set in our ways, or maybe just too scared. You've gotten this far. Don't give up now. You can do it. You've been through far more than this. I know you can do it!"

After listening to Faye, Annie knew she was right. "You're absolutely right, Faye. I can't go back, at least not yet!" Annie answered back with a smile.

Shortly after making this decision, Annie decided she had better check on Buddy and get back on the road. Claude was just coming back in the door as Annie and Faye were heading out, and he was sorry that he had missed out on their conversation. They walked Annie to her car. As soon as she opened the door, Buddy jumped in and gave a bark to let everyone know that he was ready, too.

"I can't forget this little guy." Claude said as he leaned into the car to give Buddy a small cheeseburger that had been made especially for him.

Before getting in the car, it felt so natural for Annie to reach over and give Claude and Faye a hug. "I just want you both to know that when I look at you, I don't see officers of the law. I see two angels! Thank you for everything. You have both been so wonderful. I'll never forget what you've done for me," Annie said as she wiped a few happy tears from her cheeks.

Faye patted Anne on the shoulder and said, "I'm so glad that we got to meet you, Annie. Oh, before I forget, here are our cards. If you ever need anything, you be sure to give us a call."

"Hey, when you head back home to visit, don't forget to stop by and see us," Claude added.

"I would love to!" Annie called out as she steered the car back on the road. Standing side by side, Claude and Faye watched their new friend drive off in the same direction she'd started.

Claude turned toward Faye and said, "I'm glad she kept going."

Faye smiled and said, "Me too!"

Chapter 9

As she neared Seattle, Annie reminisced about the time that she and Alex had visited the city for a teaching convention. Because of limited time and funds, they had only had a chance to see the downtown area and take a short tour of Puget Sound. On the first night, they decided they'd skip the get-to-know-you party. They had a wonderful seafood dinner down at the pier and then took a leisurely stroll along the waterfront. Before she and Alex even made it back to the hotel, they'd both fallen in love with the city.

Annie's mind was full of thoughts of the past and worries about the future, but it turned out to be a good thing, because it helped the last part of the drive to pass quickly. Before she knew it, she was steering the SUV up a private tree-lined road and around a circular driveway. After placing the car in park, she took several breaths, very thankful that the trip was over but equally as anxious about having to get out of the car and introduce herself to her new employers. She decided the best thing to do was to stay put a little bit longer and take in her new surroundings from the comfort and safety of the car.

As she looked around, she was surprised to discover that she had driven right passed the front of the house. Its privacy was maintained with several rows of staggered trees and flowering shrubs. Annie was impressed with the green lawn. It was massive compared to the lawns back home. As she surveyed the area, her eyes zeroed in on each of the flower gardens in the yard, each owning a canopy of perfectly placed shade trees. The most inviting garden had a huge hammock attached to the tree limbs.

"Wow, Buddy, would you just look at those gardens! I hope Mary will let me do some weeding!" Annie admitted and then added, "And I know where I'm going to do my reading."

Buddy expressed his excitement with a few woofs.

"Oh, I know what you're thinking, and I was going to talk to you about that. Now, I know it's instinct, and I know you have to mark your territory, but mister when you do, could you please try and remember your manners?"

Again he answered, but this time there was more volume to his bark, and his little body wiggled with excitement as he tried to communicate that he was ready to get out of the car. Still not ready to open the doors, Annie avoided making eye contact with Buddy and took a better look at the house. In just seconds, she decided that the brochures Mary had sent didn't begin to do the house justice. She was intrigued that such an extremely large home could have the allure of a small, country cottage.

The color of the house was a striking, tulip yellow, trimmed with white, and the windows were accented with hunter green shutters. The entire exterior was adorned with a large, wooden wraparound porch. Both the second and third levels had decks, and, like the main porch, they were filled with wicker furniture and decorated with unique whatnots along with buckets and baskets of greenery and flowering plants.

When Annie finally stepped from the car, she intentionally took her time getting to the front door, pausing in between steps to take in more of the enchanting yard. As she did, she couldn't help but feel a bit envious on behalf of her beloved desert. As she reached for the doorbell, Annie's nerves started to get the best of her. Her body started to shake; her arm felt like it was filled with lead. She moved her hand in slow motion toward the bell, but before her fingers ever touched the button the door had burst open.

Standing in the doorway was a little Hispanic woman with a beautiful smile that warmed Annie's heart from the very second she looked at her.

"You take forever to get out of the car. I've been waiting for you! I am so happy to meet you. I'm Flora, Flora Garcia Medrano. And of course, you are Annie! Oh my, Mary and I are so, so, so excited to have you here," Flora giggled and then reached over and gave Annie a quick hug before she gently scooted her through the front doors. "Oh, I hope you don't mind me squeezing you so soon after we just met, but I am a squeezer. You'll get used to my squeezing. There now, let's go inside! You know, you are the answer to our prayers. Oh my, but you are so beautiful!"

One of Annie's worries was quickly put to rest. There had been no need to worry about her first words making a good first impression, because she didn't get much of a chance to speak. Though, she had to smile as she listened and watched Flora. It seemed as if her arms and hands were somehow connected to her tongue, because every time she spoke, they moved excitedly through the air. Almost instantly, Annie fell in love with the sweet, little woman who radiated enthusiasm for life with every move she made, but Annie decided that it would take her a little bit of time to understand Flora, and it wasn't because of her Spanish accent or even because she changed the subject and giggled frequently. It was because she talked so fast!

"Mary wanted me to tell you that she is so sorry that she isn't here to greet you, but she had to go to the dentist. She wanted to cancel her appointment and wait for another, but I said no way! She's had a toothache for a long time. I told her not to worry and that I would be here to welcome you. You know, it's a good thing I'm here to look after Mary, because she is very good at looking out for others but not for herself. So I look after her. So where is Buddy? I am so excited to see him!"

Annie was glad when Flora asked about Buddy because she was getting a bit worried about him herself. She hadn't seen him since she'd let him out of the car. Both women turned back toward the door when Buddy came running up the steps and through the door to make his grand entrance.

The moment Flora laid eyes on him, she let out a squeal. Then she got down on her knees and showered him with affection. "Oh, my goodness; oh, he is so cute! Come here to me, sweet little puppy!"

Buddy ate up the attention, and while he and Flora took a moment to get acquainted, Annie took advantage of the time to look over the house. The foyer was bigger than her entire living room. To her right there was a beautiful great room that connected to a dining room. The décor of the house was a charming country seashore style mixed with a potpourri of family photos and displays of treasured mementoes. Annie would have never believed that a home of this proportion could feel so warm and inviting, but now she knew she'd been wrong. The house was definitely a home!

"Come, Come!" Flora gently commanded as she took hold of Annie's arm and led her into the great room. After a quick tour of the great room and dining room, Flora hurried over to a serving table and poured two glasses of iced tea.

"First, I will show you the lower level, and then I will show you to your room. You need to know where you are. Am I right? Mary and I just want you to be very comfortable. If you need anything, all you have to do is ask. Here dear, I make sweet tea for you. You will love it!" Flora handed Annie the glass of tea and then called for Buddy. "Now, for you, Mr. Buddy, come with Flora, and she will get you a fresh drink of water. You know, Mary ordered this special for you. This is the same kind of water that she used to get for her little Fluff."

Annie really didn't like her tea sweetened, but she didn't want to offend Flora, so to be polite, she thanked her and drank the tea. To her surprise, it was delicious. She had to smile when she saw the type of water that Flora was serving Buddy, it was some type of imported bottled water and she was pouring it into a crystal bowl. It took every muscle Annie had not to giggle, as she thought of how Buddy drank his water at home. Even though she always made sure he had a full bowl of tap water upstairs, downstairs, and in the garage, Buddy's first choice to get a drink of water was from the toilets. Then, as if he had read her mind, Buddy looked up and gave Annie a look that said, "But mom, you never filled my bowls with imported water!"

"Here you are, dear," Flora said as she refilled Annie's glass. "I see you were very thirsty. Did I not tell you that you would like my tea? It was my Poppy's recipe."

"It's delicious! And it really hit the spot!" Annie said.

"So you come from the little town where Dr. Ray lives?" Flora asked, but before Annie could answer, Flora continued. "Never been there myself, but maybe someday." Flora continued to talk as she busied herself straightening up the serving table. "Oh, that Dr. Ray, he is such a good, good man! He is the one who helped me to find work with his sister. I have been very happy here, and I know that you are going to be happy here, too! Come now, and I will show you the kitchen. Mary is such a good woman to work for. I cannot say enough good about her as well as her late husband. We were all so sad when he passed on, but Mary is such a strong woman. She had to be, you know, for Bridger. It was soon after her husband passed, that she turned the house into the bed-and-breakfast. I know that Dr. Ray has already told you all of this, though he doesn't know all the good times that Mary and I had then. We will have to share them with you. Oh, you will never know how happy Mary was when you called to say that you were coming. It was the first time that I saw her smile like that since Bridger's accident."

Flora led Annie and Buddy on a tour of the kitchen, laundry room, sunroom, and study. They had just made their way through the hall that circled back to the great room when Flora turned to Annie and with deep sincerity said, "Bridger, he is like a son to me. The first day that I come to this house that little boy melted my heart. He was a good boy." The constant smile that had been on Flora's face dimmed when she spoke her next words. "I will never forget the day the hospital called. It was a living nightmare! Mary and I thought we were going to lose him, so we prayed and we prayed. Thank the Lord, he answered our prayers, and he gave us a miracle. But our boy changed. He needs lot of love now. No, he is not the same." Flora paused for a moment before she moved her face closer to Annie's and whispered, "So again, we pray and pray, and now you are here, praise God. We have been given a second miracle! Now things are going to get better, and once again this family will be happy!"

As she listened, Annie's heart filled with compassion for Flora, but when she heard Flora refer to her as a miracle, Annie felt a rush of panic go through her body, first Dr. Ray, then Mary, and now Flora. What in the world did they think she could do for this man that other healthcare professionals hadn't already tried? Her face felt as if it was turning ten shades of red but Flora didn't seem to notice. Annie could hear Flora chattering away, but she was feeling so overwhelmed that she couldn't understand a word that she said until she felt Flora pinch her stomach and say, "Oh my dear, you are such a skinny girl. I think that Flora is going to have to do some extra cooking for you. I cannot even find anything to pinch on your belly! You like dessert, yes? I think you are a chocolate girl. Oh, I am so excited to cook for you! Come, come and follow me, and I'll show you to your room."

Annie and Buddy did as they were told and followed Flora upstairs. When they got to the door of Annie's room, Flora opened the door and said, "Ah, here you go, little sweeties! Oh, and before I forget to tell you, the cleaning service comes every Tuesday and Saturday, and laundry service comes every Monday and Thursday but, if you need something washed in between, there is another laundry room on this floor, and I would be happy to wash for you. We have also checked with our friends who have puppies, and they recommend Patty's Pet Grooming. This girl comes right to the door in a traveling van. They said that she is wonderful!" Flora looked at Annie with a very serious face and added, "We hope that is OK?"

"Oh yes. It was sweet of you to do that for us," Annie answered as she followed Flora into the room.

Annie was surprised that the room was so large. There was a sitting area, which she especially liked. The couch faced a beautiful brick fireplace, and on each side of it there were two large picture windows that displayed unbelievable views of the ocean. There were two TVs—one in the sitting area, and the other was hidden in a console at the foot of the bed.

"See, you push this button and the TV comes up, then you push this button and the TV goes down. It's so crazy, don't you think?" Flora announced proudly as she pushed the button four times.

"Yes! Technology is crazy!" Annie agreed with a smile.

"So do you like your room?" Flora asked.

"Yes! It's beautiful. I'm sure that I'll be very comfortable here," Annie answered.

"OK now, you get yourself refreshed, and I will go and have Tom get your things. Oh, I forgot to tell you about Tom. He comes daily to help with things around the house and yard. He is such a sweetheart! I do not know what Mary and I would do without our Tom. Now, I go. I will be down in the kitchen. I have made my decision for your dessert." Flora announced as she walked toward the door.

"Excuse me Flora but before you go, I was wondering when I would get to meet the patient. Is he at home?" Annie asked, already feeling guilty that she hadn't met Bridger yet.

"Oh yes, yes, he is home. Bridger is in the room next to you, but you need to rest and refresh yourself. Do not worry about Bridger. You can meet him when his mother gets back. Maybe, you should wait till tomorrow. He is with one of the temp nurses. He is OK. I will check on him." Flora paused in the doorway and turned to look back at Annie. With a very serious voice, she said,

"Sweetheart, sometimes Bridger is not very nice, but it's like I told you before, he is not the same. But now, I do not have to worry because you are here. Oh yes, before I go, did you know that you can get on the Internet to order your groceries, and they deliver it to your house within an hour! That is good! But yes, technology is crazy! OK sweetie; I go now. I have lots to do!"

As soon as Flora left the room, Annie looked over to the bed. It had to be the most inviting bed she had ever laid eyes on. It was an oversized, pillow top queen, and its fluffy comforter seemed to be calling her name! And the more she looked at it, the more she thought how nice it would be to have a fifteen-minute nap. Unfortunately, she knew that she wouldn't be able to sleep because she had worked herself up about whether she should wait for Mary, or just go and introduce herself to Bridger.

Annie had to smile when she noticed how prepared the room was for Buddy, who was already stretched out across his new doggie pillow. There was a cookie jar full of doggie treats and another bottle of high-priced water dripping into a continuous doggie water bowl. With a bit of sarcasm in her voice, she said, "Well, mister, I guess you're not too worried about when you're going to meet Bridger. Now that you've got your new water bowl, does this mean that you're going to give up your bad habit of drinking toilet water?" Annie asked Buddy with a chuckle. "This place is so incredible. I'm beginning to wonder if this is for real! It's hard to believe that we are here to work. Heck, sometimes when I was on call at the hospital and had to sleep there, I thought they were treating me pretty good when they let me sleep on a bunk bed that was in an old closet they'd fixed up and called the nurse's lounge!"

With heavy eyelids, Buddy wiggled his tail several times and then drifted off to sleep.

Annie was enjoying the view of the ocean when she heard Tom knock on the door. After a brief introduction, he asked if he could get the keys to the SUV. He was a good-looking young man in his early twenties, and he was as sweet as he was handsome. Annie wanted to go back downstairs so that she could help him carry her things, but he was very insistent when he said, "Oh, no thank you, Miss. I appreciate your offer, but Mary and Flora wouldn't be very happy with me, if I let you carry in your belongings. Anyway, you're probably tired from your trip. You should use this time to rest up from your long drive."

"That's funny; Flora said the same thing. I must look pretty bad!" Annie joked.

"Oh no, I didn't mean that! You look real nice. It's just that I thought that you might be tired after driving so far," Tom replied with a smile and then turned bright red with embarrassment.

Annie felt bad that she'd embarrassed Tom and quickly apologized. "I was just teasing. A little nap sounds very tempting, but I think the first thing I need to do is meet my patient."

Before he turned to leave, Tom gave Annie a garage door opener and told her that he would park the SUV in the garage just as soon as he unloaded it. After taking a couple of steps toward the door, he turned back, nervously cleared his throat, and said, "I'll hang your keys on the key hook by the back door, and then you can get them when you're ready. And, I, ah, I hope that you won't think I'm being too forward, but I just wanted to say that I hope you won't let Bridger get to you! I know he's going to try! He puts on the tough guy act, but the more I've gotten to know him, the more I've figured out that he's a pretty good man. He just likes to keep it hidden. And I've just got to say that I agree with Mary and Flora. I think you're the one!"

Annie didn't know what to say, and so she just stood there in the middle of the room with her mouth open, thinking how stupid she must have looked. Then she was mad at herself that she had forgotten to ask Tom, why Flora had wanted her to wait for Mary before meeting Bridger. She started to feel frustrated. Why did everyone keep saying that she was the one? For crying out loud! She was a nurse, not a miracle worker!

Annie calmed herself back down, checked to make sure Buddy was still sleeping, and then quietly slipped out the door and walked slowly toward Bridger's room. Making her way down the hall, Annie couldn't help thinking how it might have been if the house were still a bed-and-breakfast and she and Alex had come here to celebrate twenty years of marriage. She knew it didn't do any good to have what-ifs, but sometimes she just couldn't help herself.

Annie only had to wait seconds after she had tapped on the door before facing a very angry woman who instantly declared, "I thought you would never get here!"

Annie was so completely caught off guard that all she could think to do was offer a handshake and say, "Hi, I'm Annie Davis."

Finally

The woman totally ignored Annie's gesture. She just glared at Annie and replied, "I was told that you would be here yesterday!" Then she turned and angrily stomped in the direction of a coffee table. Once she reached it, she picked up several books and began shoving them in the bag. The woman frowned at the closed door on the opposite side of the room, and her voice sounded possessed when she barked, "The patient is in there!" Then she turned and stomped toward the door. "Now that you're here, I see no reason that Mr. Jones should need my services. Besides, I've got better things to do with my time than to waste another second of my life with that mean, spoiled rotten, no good, unappreciative, super jock, has-been, son- of- a -bitch!" Then she stomped out the door, and once again, Annie was standing in the middle of the room, wondering what she should do.

Seconds later, the door opened and Annie was very surprised to see the woman had returned. She didn't come in. She just stood in the doorway with a sorrowful expression on her face and said, "Look, I'm sorry! I shouldn't have taken that out on you. It's just that Mr. Jones and I have had a couple of really bad days! I hope things will work out for you. I know that you came a long way and that Mary and Flora are very excited that you are here. I really haven't been here that long, but I can tell you that you'll love working for those two cuties. I came back because I wanted to tell you that his records and daily chart are in the top drawer of the chest of drawers. If you have any questions, you can call the agency. Their number is on the front of his chart. Anyway, I really do have to go because my friends are outside waiting for me. And by the way, from one nurse to another, if you should decide to stay, don't let him know that he gets to you! He thrives on it like a wild animal that enjoys tormenting its prey before killing it." Then without giving Annie a chance to reply, she quickly turned and shut the door.

Looking at the closed door, Annie replied. "Uh, thank you! I think."

After her encounter with the nurse, it took a few minutes for Annie to regroup. Once she approached the next door, she was still a bit hesitant about knocking. The woman's words were so fresh in her mind. She wished that she had stayed in her room and waited for Mary as Flora had suggested. But there was no turning back now; she knew that Bridger had to know she was there. There was no way that he had not heard them talking, and what would he think of her if she didn't go in and introduce herself. With her hand stuck midair between herself and the door, she gave herself a pep talk. "OK Annie, you can do this. Just knock on the door. He can't be that bad!" She let go of her fears and tapped softly on the door.

Surprisingly, there was no reply. *Oh, maybe he's sleeping. Maybe he didn't hear anything,* Annie thought.

But that wasn't the case. A man's voice thundered, "If you are expecting me to open the door, you might just as well stand there and wait until hell freezes over!"

Annie felt like she had jumped a hundred feet straight in the air. After taking a couple of deep breaths, she reluctantly let herself in. The room was dark, and it took a moment for her eyes to adjust to the darkness. Standing in the doorway, she quickly scanned the room and spotted Bridger sitting in a lounge chair with his back toward her. The only thing she could see of him, was the top of his head and his right hand which was on the arm of the chair, and his hand that was holding the TV remote control.

"Do you mind if I turn on a light?" Annie asked as she quickly eyed the room for a lamp.

"Whatever floats your boat," he answered, holding onto his sharp tone.

After she turned on the lamp, she thought it was odd that Bridger hadn't even attempted to turn around to get a look at her. "Thank you. I can see better now," she replied as she made her way to the chair. Now that she could see, the first thing that caught her eye was his wheelchair. It was sitting against the wall to his back. There were big heavy draperies drawn over the windows, and the room was in total chaos. The bed was unmade, and there were piles of dirty towels and clothes scattered about the room. Annie couldn't believe all the stacks of papers, magazines, and books scattered about the floor, dressers, and tabletops. The more she took in, the harder it was for her to believe that she was in the same house. Her nerves started to get the best of her, and even when she could have made eye contact with Bridger, Annie delayed the moment by pretending to be interested in what he was watching on TV. That's how she noticed he was pretending to watch the TV intently, while he channel surfed.

Only minutes had passed since she'd entered Bridger's bedroom, but it felt more like agonizing hours. To add to the unbelievably awkward moment, Annie could feel an absurd amount of heat rising from her neck up to her cheeks!

When she finally forced herself to look at Bridger, she discovered that he was staring at her and by then, she just knew that her cheeks must have turned a crimson red.

Even though he probably hadn't shaved in three or four days and his hair was tumbled, Bridger looked like a male model sitting there in his white V-necked T-shirt. Every characteristic on his face was perfect. He had a defined chin, high cheekbones, and an olive complexion. His facial qualities complimented his dark, sandy blond hair, and his eyes were a riveting hazel color. For a moment, Annie was totally mesmerized until she heard a scornful voice in her head say, *"What is wrong with you, girl? Say something! Quit acting like a star struck teenage girl. So he's handsome. Big deal; you've had good-looking patients before. Act professional! Introduce yourself"*. The situation only worsened when she tried to speak. She couldn't get her tongue to cooperate with her brain.

But Bridger didn't seem to notice that she was having a problem, because he was too busy spouting off. "So you're the wonder nurse who's come all the way from Uncle Ray's wonderful little town, huh? The way my mother and Flora have gone on about you, are you sure you're not an angel sent from the holy heavens above? How does someone like yourself get to be so specialized in saving has-beens in the big city of Milford, Utah?" His stare deepened to a glare, and the tone of his voice was nothing less than offensive when he added. "Oh but then again, I'll just bet little old Milford has got a whole bunch of has-beens! You know, I used to go there when I was a kid. That place was such a hole in the wall. What was there—something like three flippin' trees in the whole freakin' town?"

Annie wasn't offended by Bridger's comments toward her, but she was offended when he went off about her hometown. But she knew that she couldn't let him know that because that was exactly what he wanted. Forcing herself to smile, she replied, "You just might be surprised to know that Milford has come a long way; in fact, I think we've got close to six or seven trees now!" Then trying to be as gracious as she could be, she offered her hand and added, "That was a real bad start. Why don't just start over. I'm Annie Davis."

He wouldn't respond with his hand—just his mouth. "Oh, I know. I know all about you!"

A knot tightened in the middle of Annie's stomach. *Does he know everything?* She asked herself.

"Oh yeah, I've heard over and over how much Uncle Ray thinks of you and how he thinks that you're the one who will know what I need! Just answer one question. How in the hell do you know what I need?"

Bridger wasn't the only one questioning Annie's ability. In just the few minutes that she'd been with him, she had begun to question it herself. Still trying, she looked at Bridger with another very fake smile and said, "Your nurse told me that I would find your records and orders in the nightstand. If you don't mind, I would like to take a look at them." As she walked toward the dresser, she was grateful that she didn't have to look at him, even if it was for just a few seconds.

Bridger's voice was full of distain when he replied, "Yeah, you do that! But I can save you the time and the trouble. I know them by heart. My history will tell you that I'm just not the same as I used to be, and you're going to read the reason is I've got some problems with my head. You know, it took half of the medical profession to make that diagnosis, the dumb bastards. Oh, I'd better not forget to tell you about the daily orders, because they are even better. You won't have to worry about distributing too many meds. It's not like I have cancer or aids. About the only thing you will need to give me is something for the pain and the brain. I'm supposed to do physical therapy several times a day, because if I do, there's a good chance that someday, I'll be able to walk with the help of a cane. To that I say, big freaking deal!"

With her back still turned away, Annie tried to read through the records, but Bridger's comments made it very hard to concentrate on anything other than what he had to say, and he made it clear he wanted her attention, because his voice got louder with each sentence. "I haven't seen too many successful quarterbacks carrying canes lately! How about it, Toots, have you? Have you got to the patient's daily evaluations? I love how all of my lovely nurses and the therapist wrote that I don't cooperate. And I so enjoy reading the part where they emphasize that I still can't get to the bathroom by myself. You have to agree that it makes for good reading."

"I guess that I would have to say that I would rather read a good novel, Bridger." Annie answered sarcastically, and then, just to make small talk, she asked if it would be all right if she sat on his bed while she read.

"And just so you know, I don't care what you do as long as when I need something to eat, you get it! And when I'm not comfortable, you make me comfortable! And when I need a bath, you bathe me! And when I need to take a shit, you make sure you help me get to the bathroom, or I'll just sit right here and shit in my pants, and then you can clean it up!" Bridger replied and then after a forced chuckle, he added, "I guess if you can do all that, then I'd have to agree that you are the one."

Bridger's comments and stares were unnerving, and Annie was grateful that she had the records to look at, because it gave her a reason not to look at him. As she thumbed through the pages, she saw an order highlighted in red. "All controlled substances are to be locked in the safe and only administered to the patient by the nurse." In parentheses were the words "mother worries son may try to harm himself." The rest was pretty much standard except for the area of physical therapy: "patient will not apply himself."

"Are you comfortable? Do you need anything?" Annie asked, trying to bond with The Beast.

His face was still scowling when he bellowed, "Did I ask for anything?"

"It says that you are due for your meds in an hour. Would you mind if I were to go back to my room and check on my dog? Then I'll come back and give them to you." Annie was trying her best to hang on until she could get out of the room.

"Oh, yeah, the wonderful nurse from Milford was even going to bring a wonderful dog! Whatever, I like to be alone. Here is your pager. You are to wear it at all times and if I need you, I'll let you know." Annie was a bit surprised when she noticed that he'd lost a bit of the growl.

"OK then, I'll be back," she replied as she hurried to the door.

"Most don't come back!" he added with a snort.

Turning around to face Bridger, Annie remained calm and with a matter-of-fact attitude replied, "Oh, I'll be back, Bridger. I feel like I just drove a gazillion miles to get here, and I'm not ready to turn around and do that again. Besides, I haven't got anything else to do."

As soon as she closed the door, it took Annie a few seconds to calm down. She was so thankful for the space. She knew she needed to think and clear her mind. Most of all, she was thankful she didn't have to hear his voice for a moment. After she had cleared her head, Annie hurried back to her room to take Buddy outside. Once they were outside, Buddy and Annie both enjoyed their walk through the beautiful yard. After living her whole life in a desert,

Annie was amazed that she could hear the ocean surf from a backyard. She discovered a paved pathway across the way, and she decided that it might lead to the shoreline. Just thinking about walking the trail made her want to go and put on her walking shoes, but she knew she couldn't do that yet, because first she needed to figure out what to do with Bridger. While it was quiet, she thought she had better give her parents a call and let them know she'd made it.

She'd barely even said hello when her father wanted to know what was wrong. Knowing that her father could always sense when something was wrong with her, caused her to think quickly and reply with a voice that she hoped would be convincing. "I'm fine, Dad, maybe a bit tired. It was a long drive. Man, it sure is beautiful up here. I'll e-mail you some photos as soon as I get a chance." She knew her father was worried enough about her, so she tried her best to sound cheerful and excited. Annie asked how her mother was and decided to make the call short, knowing the longer they talked, the more time he would have to figure out that she was absolutely miserable.

After hanging up the phone, Annie bent down and cuddled Buddy. With her head next to his, she whispered in his ear, "Oh, maybe this wasn't such a good idea, Bud. Maybe we should have turned around when we had the chance."

While she was still on her knees holding Buddy, Annie heard a door close and a sweet welcoming voice call out, "There you are! It's been such a long time. I hope you remember me." Annie stood up as Mary made her way across the lawn. As soon as she reached Annie, Mary opened her arms with a welcoming hug and said, "I'm so glad you're here. How was your trip? Do you like your room? If you don't, we can see if you like another one better. Flora and I thought you'd like that one because of the view. Did you want to be that close to Bridger? If not, we can move you."

Mary, like Flora, seemed to ask a hundred questions without waiting for answers. As they continued to talk, Annie had to laugh inside; she couldn't help but wonder if Mary and Flora were ever able to have a conversation with each other, because neither seemed to pause once they started talking.

Thinking it was time for some attention, Buddy let out a little bark, and, as usual, his strategy worked. Mary stopped talking midsentence, got down on her knees, and made a big fuss over him. "Oh, he's so cute! It's too bad he and my little Fluff never got together. They would have made beautiful puppies."

Standing back up, Mary confessed that she was worried about Annie's first encounter with Bridger. "You know, dear, he's been through so much, and he's lost so much." Looking directly at Annie, her constant smile faded, and her voice changed from pleasant to apologetic. "I had no right to say that to you. Nothing in Bridger's life could compare to what you have been through. I'm so sorry to have said that, and I want you to know that Flora and I are so very sorry."

"Thank you, Mary, I appreciate that." Annie replied and then added, "But when I made the decision to come up here, I was hoping not too many people would know what happened to me. I just thought maybe something different, maybe, oh, I don't know." Her voice quivered as she fought the tears. Mary reached to take hold of Annie's hand. "Oh, I understand completely, dear. Don't worry; Flora and I are the only ones who know, and you have our promises that we will completely respect your wishes. But if you ever need to talk or need someone, please let us help you!"

Unable to speak, Annie smiled, wiped away her tears, and nodded her head to show Mary that she accepted her offer. Then hoping to change the conversation, she said, "Right now, I think it would be best for everyone if we just concentrated on Bridger and his recovery." As she spoke, Annie hoped that she hadn't given away any of her negative feelings about the man she had named The Beast.

The welcoming smile returned when Mary replied, "I just know you're the answer to our prayers!"

"I hope so, Mary, but right now, I'd better get back up and see if Bridger needs anything," Annie answered, while at the same time thinking that Flora and Mary were just far too hopeful about her.

Annie turned to leave and was just about to call for Buddy, who had wandered across the lawn when Mary asked, "Dear, do you mind if Buddy stays in the yard with me? I'll watch him close. I really want to be his friend."

Annie nodded her head and said, "That would be great, Mary. He's ready for some space; he was so tired of being cooped up in the car!"

"Oh thank you, and dear, if it's OK, we'll have dinner at seven. But if you're hungry sooner, all you have to do is ask, and Flora or I can get you something, or if you'd rather get it yourself, you'll find we have plenty of snack foods. Annie, please feel free to do whatever you need to do. We want you and

Buddy to feel welcome, but more important; we want you to feel at home! Before you go, I wanted to ask something of you. I know you just got here, and I know you're tired, but I was thinking maybe, just maybe you could ask Bridger if he would have dinner with us."

As much as Annie wished she could convince Bridger to come to dinner and make his mother happy, she knew that the odds were against her. As she started to leave, Annie smiled and said, "Mary, thank you so much for making me feel so welcome. About Bridger coming to dinner—I can't make any promises, but I'll see what I can do."

Chapter 10

Annie felt weary and after her talks with Mary and Flora. It was hard for her to decide what thought was weighing heaviest on her heart—Bridger's ill-mannered ways, or knowing how much faith the two ladies had in her ability to help him. She stopped by her room to freshen up, hoping that she could freshen up her spirits as well as her body.

After splashing a cold continuous stream of water on her face for several minutes, Annie looked at her reflection and wondered to herself why she had told Bridger that she had nowhere else to go. She gripped the edge of the sink, leaned forward, shook her head in disapproval, and began talking to herself. "Home, you can always go home, and at this moment, I'm thinking you should have stayed there!"

After throwing herself a few more disgusted looks at the mirror, Annie turned and hurried to her suitcases. She rummaged through the bags until she found a white tank, floral skirt, and blue sweater. By the time she was half dressed, Annie had managed to get herself into a better frame of mind. Then after slipping on a pair of flip-flops, she hurried back to the bathroom, pulled her hair up into a ponytail, added a fresh touch of makeup, brushed her teeth, and decided she had stalled long enough. Annie knew Bridger wasn't going to be too receptive about her decision to open the draperies, and just as she had predicted, the moment his eyes caught the sunlight, he let out an outburst of profanities. This time his words didn't bother her because she had prepared herself.

"Bridger, I just wanted to make sure that I had enough light. I have to read the doctor's orders when I give you your meds." Annie called out with a loud but sweet voice of victory. "And I just thought you would enjoy looking at the beautiful sunset!"

Without bothering to look out the window, Bridger snarled and said, "I don't give a damn about the sunset, and the next time you need to read, turn on a damn light!"

The sunset may not have done much for Bridger, but its beauty did wonders for Annie. With her eyes fixed on the sky and ocean, she smiled and said, "You know, Bridger, if I'm going to take care of you, I've got to be able to see, and to be honest, I can see much better with natural light. So you'll just have to get used to the sunlight again." Annie didn't bother to move away from the window until a loud grunt of impatience from Bridger brought her back to the real world. He didn't say he wanted anything and with nothing else to do, Annie decided to pick up the dirty laundry. She was on her way to the pile of dirty laundry with her second armful of clothes when she decided it was time to ask Bridger about dinner. "Hey, Bridger, before I forget, your mom was wondering if you would like to eat dinner downstairs tonight."

Looking up from the TV, Bridger answered, "No, I wouldn't. I eat in my room, and why don't you just leave my stuff alone. I like things just the way they are!"

Annie totally ignored him and continued to work her way through the room. As she waded through the mess, it was still so hard for her to believe that she was in the same house. When she realized that she'd already filled up two cans of trash, Annie decided it was time to let Bridger know how she felt. Without stopping, she glared directly at Bridger and said, "Well, I don't like the way things are, so you had better get this through your head right now. I came here to work as a healthcare professional. I take pride in what I do, and I cannot and will not allow any patient of mine to live in a pigsty!"

Annie continued to work, but it wasn't long before guilt started to get the best of her. She had never been one to like confrontations. She decided she had better try and smooth things over. As she continued to tidy up the room, Annie began telling Bridger about her and Buddy's drive up the coast, and how beautiful she thought his mother's home and yard were, and how excited she was about walking by the ocean. He didn't join her in conversation, but he wasn't totally ignoring her, because several times when she had looked up, Annie saw that Bridger was looking at her. Had she been in any other place or situation, his staring would have made her nervous. Annie didn't blame him for watching her; after all, she was going through his things. In a weird sort of way, Annie started to think things were going pretty good.

But things changed quickly when Bridger growled, "I gotta take a leak, now!"

At that moment, Annie was thankful her arms were full of dirty laundry because she knew that she would have smacked Bridger if they hadn't been. It would have been so easy to act as if she hadn't heard him, but she couldn't, so she dropped the bundle of clothing and went to help him. As she helped Bridger transfer from the lounge chair to the wheelchair, her feelings of anger changed to empathy when she realized the degree of pain he had to endure.

Annie rested her back against the wall while she waited outside of the bathroom. She shook her head in frustration. "He just can't stay cooped up in this room, staring at a TV," she whispered softly to herself. "He just can't!"

After Bridger had washed up, Annie asked him if he wanted to change into a fresh shirt. Again, his reply wasn't anything that she hadn't expected. "You just haven't got it yet, have you? So listen up: I really don't give a rat's ass if my shirt is clean or dirty."

Annie's and Bridger's eyes locked together in the reflection of the mirror. She forced a smile and said, "Well then, would you like me to get you a comb so that you can comb your hair?"

Bridger shook his head in disbelieve and barked, "Lady, are you flippin' nuts or what? Don't worry about my hair! Just get me back to my damn chair!"

Annie didn't say anything. She just nodded to let him know that she understood and then turned the wheelchair around and pushed Bridger back into the bedroom. Instead of turning the chair toward the TV, she spun it around in the opposite direction and took off at a run, pushing Bridger out of the bedroom, through the sitting room, down the hall and toward the elevator.

"What the hell are you doing, woman?" Bridger shouted as he watched his bedroom and sitting room fly by in a blur. He was about to say more but stopped when he caught sight of his mother, who luckily for Annie's sake, just happened to be standing next to the elevator door.

The elevator had been one of Mary's top priorities when she had decided to turn her home into a bed-and-breakfast. Even when her contractor had suggested using less expensive items that were within the building code, Mary insisted that she would only have the best products for her guests. She had no idea that her own son would be the sole recipient of her extra efforts.

Mary's eyes grew large with excitement, and a big smile formed on her lips as soon as she saw Bridger and Annie coming toward her. "Bridge, I can't tell you how happy I am that Annie was able to talk you into having dinner with us."

Before looking at his mother, Bridger quickly looked back at Annie and mouthed the word, "forced!" When he turned back around, he gave his mother a half smile and stuttered, "Ah, I, ah, me too, Mom."

Mary and Buddy took the stairs and met Bridger and Annie in the hall. Flora had been patiently waiting for Annie and Mary in the dining room and squealed with excitement when she saw that Bridger had come with them. "Oh this is wonderful! Praise the good Lord! Finally, our boy has come back to the dinner table!"

Once everyone had settled at the table, Flora and Mary started talking up a storm. They wanted to know how things were going in Milford, and even though they asked Annie a million questions, they were both very careful not to tread near anything too personal. Buddy, who was still worn out from the trip, got comfortable on the floor between Annie and Bridger's chairs, but it wasn't until dinner was almost over that Annie was able to figure out why he kept staring at Bridger. At first, she thought that Buddy was checking him out. But then she happened to glance down and saw that Bridger was slipping him food. As she watched them interact, something in her heart told her that Bridger might not be the Beast he tried so hard to be.

There wasn't much conversation throughout dessert, which was perfectly understandable, considering they were all enjoying a delicious cake that Flora had baked. Hopeful the night wouldn't have to end with dinner, Mary looked over at her son and said, "Bridger, before you head back upstairs, would you like to sit on the porch and get some fresh air?"

"Thanks for asking, Mom, but I don't think tonight is a good night. I'm real tired," Bridger answered, but as soon as he looked across the table and saw the disappointed look on his mother's face, he added, "Maybe we could do it another time, real soon."

Annie's heart felt like it dropped to her stomach when she saw the looks on Mary's and Flora's faces, but when she looked back at Bridger, he really did look exhausted. Hoping to ease the mood, Annie told Flora how delicious the meal was and thanked the ladies for everything before she said, "I'll help Bridger get back to his room, and then after he's settled for the night, I'll come back and do the dishes." Seconds later, she knew she had said the wrong thing. Before she even had the chance to stand up, the two little ladies scolded her and made it very clear that they would do the dishes. Then they gently took her by the arm and escorted her, Buddy, and Bridger to the elevator.

As soon as the door shut, Annie looked down to check on Buddy and realized that he was scared. He'd never been in an elevator. The elevator was quite small, so when Annie quickly grabbed on to the arm of the wheelchair, and dropped to her knees to reassure him, she was very close to the wheelchair. With her head cuddling his, she cooed, "It's OK, baby. Don't be afraid! Momma is with you!" Annie totally forgot about Bridger, and it wasn't until the sound of the elevator doors opening that she glanced up and noticed that he was staring at her with a strange look on his face. *What? Does he think I'm crazy?* Annie thought as she looked away. Just thinking of what he might say made her angry. It had been a long day, and she wasn't in the mood to hear anymore of his smart-aleck comments. He didn't have any right to judge her, especially when he had no idea just how much the little dog meant to her. Annie decided that if Bridger said even one thing that she considered offensive, she was going to let him have it! With her hands still clasped on the chair for support, she gave herself a push to stand back up, but found herself unable to go any farther than mid-point. She was frozen, face to face with The Beast.

Bridger was at the mercy of his emotions as he stared deep into her eyes. "You have the most beautiful color of blue eyes."

The sound of his voice was so sweet and so unexpected that for some strange reason, Annie didn't hear what he'd said. Unconscious of her actions, she moved closer and said, "I, ah, what did you say?"

As soon as Bridger realized she really hadn't heard, he backpedaled. "I, ah, said that I, I've never met anyone who cares about their dog like you do! Ah, well, except my mom. She really loved her dog, Fluff."

The sound of Bridger's sweet-sounding voice seemed to cast a spell on Annie, because had she let her guard down like this at any other time in her life, she would have turned crimson with embarrassment and slithered away. Before Annie stepped behind the wheelchair, she returned Bridger's smile with an even bigger one and nodded her head to agree with what he had said.

For the first time, Bridger and Annie actually had a pleasant conversation as they made their way back to Bridger's room, but as soon as she asked him if she could help him get a bath, things went back to the way they had begun.

Without looking up, Bridger steered the wheelchair in the direction of the television, grabbed the remote, turned on the TV, and turned up the volume. Then he roared out the answer to Annie's question, "No, I don't need a bath. I'm a grown man, and I know when to have a bath!"

Bridger's mood wasn't the only one that changed, and he was very surprised when he saw Annie's reflection on the TV marching toward him. The sweet smile that had been on her face just moments before was long gone, and as she zeroed in on her target, she gave the clothes that she had just searched for a toss, and then lowered herself until they were eye-to-eye.

"Bridger, I know how old you are because I have read all about you! Excuse me once again for thinking that it is my job to do things for you that would help you feel more comfortable. Whether you know it or not, a hot bath and a massage would help you relax and ease some of your pain, so that, just maybe, you could have a good night's rest! But if you would rather, I can just throw you on the bed and leave you for the night, and I want you to know that I can do that without the slightest bit of hesitation!"

The stare down lasted several long moments before Bridger shrugged his shoulders and said, "OK, I'll have a bath."

Annie wasn't too thrilled with Bridger's tone of voice and choice of words, but she decided that she would keep her thoughts to herself this time. After forcing a small smile, she nodded her head and went to get things ready. It took her a while to find what she was looking for, because she was too stubborn to ask Bridger for any help. In her search, she found a basket that hooked to the tub and a hand mirror, thinking it would be easier for Bridger if he could shave while he was in the tub, and she was able to fasten the mirror to the basket with some bandage tape that she had discovered in the back of a drawer. During her search, she spotted a bottle of bubble bath and decided to pour some of the fruity solution into the tub. Even though she was quite sure that Bridger wasn't a bubble bath kind of guy, she was hoping it might make him feel more comfortable and that he would stay in the tub and soak.

Annie's assumption about Bridger was accurate, because as soon as he spotted the bubbles, he said, "Gee, thanks! I love bubbles! Did you find some toys, too?"

"No, I didn't, but I think we've finally found something that we have in common, because I love bubble baths, too."

The automatic lift helped with transferring him from the chair to the tub, but Annie could see it was very painful for Bridger. She was thankful the lift also had a safety device to keep Bridger from slipping. As soon as he was settled, Annie said that she would wait outside the door, and he could call for her as soon as he was finished. Annie stepped out of the bathroom, took a deep breath and leaned her body on the wall. Buddy, who had been patiently waiting close by walked over to her, snuggled a moment, and then headed into the bathroom. Annie had to smile when she realized that Buddy must have thought it was his turn to look after Bridger. After watching his cute little stubbed tail disappear into the bathroom, Annie decided it would be a good time for her to change the bed sheets, and to her surprise, several times she heard Bridger talk to Buddy.

Just as she finished smoothing out the bedspread, Bridger yelled, "I'm done."

"OK, I'm coming," Annie answered as she walked to the bathroom. "I was wondering if you wanted me to wash your hair."

"No, I am quite capable of washing my own hair. My arms work just fine!"

"OK, let's just get you out."

As Annie helped Bridger make the transition back to the chair, she thanked God that his arms were still strong, because, even with the lift, it took all of her strength, the strength of his arms, and the little bit of strength his legs had, to get him out, dried, dressed, and into bed. By the time they had finished, Annie could see he was exhausted and in a lot of pain, and she was glad that she had thought ahead and got the night meds ready.

Annie covered Bridger with a comforter and was very sincere when she said, "Bridger, I'm so sorry that you have to live in such terrible pain."

Bridger nodded his head in appreciation for her understanding and then, much to Annie's surprise, said, "I wasn't always like this. It's just, I don't know." Bridger looked away and then added, "That son of a bitch never even said that he was sorry."

"You've been through a lot." Then hoping to lighten the moment, Annie said, "You know, a lot of my patients have told me that I give a pretty good backrub, and my offer still stands if you'd like one."

Bridger nodded his head, gave a half smile, and rolled over to his side. As Annie massaged the lotion into his back, she couldn't help notice that his upper body didn't have any muscle atrophy, and the more she moved her hands over and around the different parts of his back and arms, the less she could stop herself from admiring Bridger's athletic torso. She knew she wasn't acting professional, and to top it off, she was totally embarrassed by her thoughts and the surge of hot energy that had rushed up her chest, neck, and face, leaving her with bright red cheeks. She continued to massage Bridger's back and hoped and prayed that he wouldn't turn back around. After ten minutes of silence, Annie realized Bridger was sound asleep. Before carefully moving herself off the bed, Annie looked toward the heavens and mouthed the words, "Thank you." Then she quietly turned off the lamp and quickly tiptoed out of the room.

Once she was in the hall, Annie had to take several deep breaths before she could even decide whether to head straight back to her room or go to the kitchen to see if she could find a diet soda. After deciding on getting a soda, she walked into the kitchen and was very surprised to see Flora and Mary sitting at the table. It took Annie a second or two, to realize that they had been waiting and hoping she would come. Annie gave each of the sweet ladies a big smile and asked if she could get a soda as she let Buddy out the backdoor.

Mary and Flora both answered excitedly, "Of course you can!"

Flora gave Annie a big smile and added, "Ray told us that you liked to drink soda, so we picked some up at the store last week, when we were shopping!"

Then it was Mary's turn, "Dear, we just want you to feel at home. We know and understand that caring for Bridger can be very difficult, and we just want you to know that we will do anything to help you."

Mary and Flora both thought that they needed to get up and help Annie, but when Annie realized what they were up to, she decided it was time to give

Finally

them both a sweet scolding. "Now, you two just sit yourselves back down. You've done enough waiting on me today, and besides, if you really want me to feel at home here, I've got to know where things are, and I've got to be able to do things for myself!" With her feet planted firmly, Annie didn't make a move toward the refrigerator until both women sat back down in their chairs. When she finally made it to the refrigerator and opened the door, it took everything Annie had to keep from giggling after finding an entire shelf filled from top to bottom with her favorite kind of diet soda.

"There's more in the pantry, too!" Mary called out.

"Just in case," Flora added.

As she walked to the table, Annie knew that she had already fallen in love with Mary and Flora. "Well, that was very sweet of you. Thank you!"

Mary waited for Annie to sit down before she said, "You know, that's the first time that Bridger has eaten dinner at the table with us since the accident."

"Well, I think things went pretty well for the first day," Annie said, trying to sound hopeful.

Mary reached for Annie's hand and gave it a gentle squeeze. There were tears in her eyes and a loving smiling on her face when she answered, "Flora and I are just so grateful that you're here."

Hoping to avoid her own tears, Flora jumped up excitedly and hurried to the cupboard. "I think that I should get us all a piece of cake!"

Even though she was still full from dinner and exhausted, Annie didn't have the heart to do anything but stay right where she was, eat a piece of cake, and visit. Somewhere in the conversation, Annie confessed to Mary and Flora that she didn't know much about Bridger's football career, and then they proceeded to take turns filling her in. At first, Annie had listened with interest, but every time she heard the word, football, she thought of Jack, and after a while, instead of listening about Bridger, she found herself lost in her own memories.

She remembered the day that Jack had come home with his first official team jersey and the day her handsome little boy had made his first touchdown. She was so deep in her own thoughts that she didn't even notice that Mary and Flora had stopped talking. When she did, she tried to act as if she'd been listening. Without even thinking, she said, "Well, I really didn't have much time to watch television. I was so busy being a, and a, —well, anyway, I was just busy."

Mary and Flora felt terrible. They hadn't meant to go on about Bridger. Thinking they needed to apologize, Mary said, "We're so sorry, dear. We've just gone on and on, haven't we?"

"Oh no, I want to know about Bridger. It's just, well, I have to admit that I'm a bit tired," Annie replied still trying to sound as if nothing was wrong.

Flora hurried and wrapped her arms around Annie, gave her a big hug, and said. "Of course you are, dear. Now you go and get yourself off to bed. We've got plenty of time to talk ahead of us."

Annie let Buddy back in the door, said goodnight, and was just about to head back upstairs when Mary called out, "Annie, before I forget, I wanted to tell you that you don't have to worry about getting up early, because Bridge likes to sleep until around noon."

Mary's comment confused Annie because after reading Bridger's records, she had planned to wake up early, so that she had time to help him get ready for his physical therapy. "Excuse me, Mary, but Bridger's orders say that he's scheduled for physical therapy in the morning."

Annie waited for Mary to say something, but it was Flora who said, "Oh, sweetie, Bridger doesn't have physical therapy anymore. He said that it didn't do him any good and that it was just too painful. So we just let him sleep because rest is good. Isn't that right, Annie?"

Again, Annie was confused by what she'd just heard, but feeling like she needed to acknowledge Flora, Annie nodded. She agreed that Bridger needed his rest, but more importantly, she knew that Bridger, his mother, and Flora, understood very well that if he was ever going to walk again, he had to have physical therapy.

With Buddy at her heels, Annie walked back upstairs and straight into the bathroom, turned on the bath water, and poured an atrocious amount of bubble bath into the tub. Then she hurried back in the bedroom and opened the boxes that she had packed her favorite photos in. After setting them around the room, she hurried and grabbed one of Alex's old pairs of boxers and a tank top. Once she was back in the bathroom, she hopped in the tub, turned on the jets, and let her body sink deep into the hot, fragrant water; for just a few moments, she forced her brain to compute nothing but the sound of the pulsating water. Thinking she was in control again, Annie took a deep breath and spoke out loud, "Rest is good." The word, "good" had barely left her mouth when she torpedoed from her comfortable relaxed position to sitting upright. Her movement was so abrupt that it woke Buddy up from a sound sleep. He hurried across the tiled floor, stood up on his hind legs and placed his front paws on the tub.

"Oh sweetie, Bridger had to quit his physical therapy. He said that it didn't help him and that it was just too painful!" While Annie was busy quoting Flora, her brain insisted on flashing mental photos of Bridger's torso as well as analyzing everything she had seen and heard. "Bud, there is just no way that Bridger could have retained that much muscle. It's been too many months. Buddy, I think our new patient has been working out. So here's what I think. If he can work his upper body, then I think he can work his lower body."

Buddy let out a little bark to add his opinion to which Annie replied, "Oh, I know he's in a lot of pain, but if he doesn't start doing physical therapy, it's going to be too late! Besides, we didn't come here to be maids, did we, baby?"

With bubbles on his paws and nose, Buddy let out several yips to let Annie know he was in total agreement.

Chapter 11

Annie was sure that she sounded wide-awake when she answered the phone. Unfortunately, her acting didn't make much of an impression on Dr. Ray.

"Well, my dear, if it's going to make you feel better to act like you weren't asleep, go ahead with your acting, but, I think I'd be safe to bet my right arm and leg that you were sound asleep, and I'm just going to say this, "It's good to know that you are finally catching up on some much needed rest. Now, before my pager goes off, I had better hurry and tell you the reason for my call. Annie, I have decided that I'm just a meddling fart who should have just minded his own damn business!" Then without giving Annie a chance to respond, Dr. Ray asked, "Are you OK? Is my nephew behaving himself?" Because if he isn't, I just want you to know that I'll be on the next flight to Seattle."

Annie knew that Dr. Ray had always had the best of intentions for her, especially when he'd come up with the idea of this move. "Oh, Doc, I'm fine, and I can honestly tell you that my first day on the job wasn't too bad."

Dr. Ray chuckled. "Oh, I had a feeling you were going to say that," and then before he could finish up what he was going to say, his pager went off and he had to say good-bye.

As soon as Annie hung up, she decided she wasn't in any hurry to get out of bed, so she pulled the covers back over her shoulders and turned on her side to get comfortable. At the same moment, she started to drift off back to sleep; she thought of Buddy and realized he wasn't in the bed. In an instant, she was wide-awake. Annie jumped from the bed and hurried to find her beloved pup.

After making a quick but unsuccessful search of Bridger's room and the second level, she hurried downstairs to search the main floor.

The second that Mary heard Annie call Buddy's name, she hollered back to let her know he was in the kitchen. Annie was relieved when she spied Buddy sitting between Mary and Flora at the breakfast table.

"Annie, I'm so sorry if I caused you any worry. I went to get a load of laundry from Bridger's room, and Buddy must have heard me, because he started fussing at the door. I tapped on the door a couple of times, but when you didn't answer; I figured you were still sleeping. You were so tired last night, and I thought it would be good for you to get a little more rest. I only wanted to help. Oh, I hope I haven't done anything to make you upset with me. Buddy, tell your momma what a good boy you were, and tell her how much fun you have had with Flora and Mary this morning."

"Oh Mary, there is no way I could ever be upset with you. I just don't want Buddy to get in your way."

"There is just no way that he could! I meant it when I told you that we've missed having a pup around the house. After Fluff died, it took me a long time before I could even think about getting another dog, and by the time I did, well, I just didn't think it would be fair for a lively little puppy to have to live with two old gals, like Flora and myself."

"It looks to me like a dog couldn't find better company!"

"Annie, let me make you some breakfast," Flora said as she jumped up from the table and hurried to the refrigerator. "How about pancakes and sausage, or do you like waffles? I could make you eggs and bacon, hot cereal, or we have cold cereal. Whatever you like, I will fix it for you."

"Thank you, Flora, but I've never been much of a breakfast eater. I usually just have a cup of tea and something like a piece of toast," Annie answered.

With her hands flying though the air, Flora replied, "OK, I will fix you some toast and tea, but I tell you, it's no wonder that you are so skinny! I'm sure your mother has told you that you need to have a good breakfast!"

"You are right on that one. She has said it to me more times than I can count, and she is going to be thrilled when she hears how well you two are treating me."

Annie enjoyed a quick breakfast with Mary and Flora and then excused herself. When Annie walked back into her room; she happened to catch her reflection in the mirror and realized that she had run out of her bedroom in Alex's boxers and the old tank top that she had worn to bed. She was embarrassed, but at that point about the only thing she could do was be grateful that she was with two very understanding women and not Bridger.

Annie took a quick shower and once again searched for something to wear. As she looked through her suitcases, she wished she had time to unpack but decided she had better put in a call to Bridger's doctor and physical therapist before it got any later. Luckily, fate was working with her, and she was able to talk to both of them. After the calls, she told Buddy that it was time to go to work. As they walked to Bridger's room, Annie looked down at her little dog and said, "It is definitely different wearing sweatpants to work, but I love the fact that you get to go with me!" The first thing on Annie's agenda for the day was to open the curtains and let some sunshine into Bridger's dark and dreary world. "Good morning, Bridger," Annie called out loudly as she tied back the first drape.

Bridger opened his eyes, took one look at the clock, let out a growl and pulled the covers back over his head but as hard as he tried, he couldn't go back to sleep because every move that Annie made sounded as if it was amplified. As he listened to her move about the room, his nerves started building up like the timer on a bomb, and he was just about to blow when he realized that the room had turned silent. He hoped that Annie had given up and left. Unfortunately, when he pulled off his covers, there she was standing next to his bed with a smile on her face, holding a washcloth and wanting to know if he wanted to freshen up before Flora brought breakfast.

Before he even had a chance to answer, Flora danced into the room and with her usual jolly voice and said, "Good morning, my boy! I was so excited when Annie told me that you wanted to have an early breakfast. I made your favorite omelet and toasted you fresh English muffins. Oh, Bridger, you made your momma and me so happy last night when you came downstairs to have dinner with us. It has just been too long!"

Taking advantage of the moment, Annie stepped backward, placed herself behind Flora, and gently tossed the cloth to Bridger. With a bit of sarcasm and a sugary sweet voice, she said, "Don't forget to wash your hands before you eat!"

Bridger caught the cloth, wiped it across his face but instead of wiping his hands, he rolled the cloth in his hands several times until he had shaped it into a ball. Then he looked Annie straight in the eyes and gave the cloth a hard, angry toss to the middle of the room, but to his and Flora's surprise, Annie shot her arm out and made a great interception. Playing professional football may have made Bridger the better thrower, but the years of being a mother had made Annie an expert at catching unanticipated flying objects.

After watching all the action, Flora decided it was a good time for her to leave.

As soon as Bridger was sure that Flora had left, he glared at Annie and said, "Let's get another issue straight."

"And what is that issue, Bridger?" Annie asked calmly.

"I don't like to get up early, and I don't want you or anybody waking me up. I'll get up when I'm damn good and ready."

Acting as if she didn't hear a word he said, Annie just smiled and said, "Bridger, we have a lot to do today, and we have to get some things figured out, so just be a good boy and eat your breakfast. I am so sorry; I meant to say 'man."

At that point, Annie figured she had pushed Bridger's buttons far enough and decided it would be a good time for her to take care of a few things downstairs. As soon as she reached the door, Buddy got up to follow her, but she told him it was his turn to look after the Beast. Bridger rolled his eyes when he heard Annie's voice, but he was amazed when Buddy walked backed and sat down by the bed. When he was certain the coast was clear, Bridger looked down at the little dog and said, "Buddy, has she always been this bossy?"

A smile came across Annie's face when she got back to the room and saw Buddy sitting on the bed sharing breakfast with Bridger, but as soon as he saw that she was back, he graciously took one more bite and ran to her.

After giving Buddy a little love pat, Annie asked Bridger if he was ready to get dressed.

"Why do you even bother asking me? Even if I tell you that I'm not, you are going to throw some kind of clothes on me anyway."

Annie smiled as she listened to Bridger's reply and he did his best not to smile when he heard hers.

"You're wrong. I would never just throw clothes on you but I would make sure that you were properly dressed."

After helping Bridger dress, Annie was a little more understanding of how easy it was for Mary and Flora to give into him. She had only known the man less than twenty-four hours and it was horrible to see how much pain he had to endure just to put on a pair of sweat pants. She almost decided not to go through with her plans but deep down she knew she had to.

As soon as Bridger was in his wheelchair, Annie gave him a little bit of time for the pain to settle down before she said, "I thought this would be a good time for you to do your daily workout and I thought as long as you were working out, I would work out, too."

Looking at Annie from his wheelchair, Bridger shook his head with disbelief. "You know what? I like to work out in the afternoon so you just go right ahead and work out after you help me into the recliner."

Annie totally ignored Bridger and pushed the wheelchair toward the mat. After she had set the brakes, she moved to the front of the chair and tried to figure out how she was going to help him get to the floor.

Bridger watched Annie struggle with her thoughts for a few seconds before he told her to move to his side, then he maneuvered the wheelchair over to a lift bar and lowered himself down to the mat. Once he had settled, he looked at Annie with a half smile and said, "Getting to the mat is easy. Getting back in the chair is the hard part."

Annie smiled and nodded in agreement as she lowered herself alongside of him on the mat. "OK, what do we do first?" she asked but when Bridger didn't answer right away, she looked over at him and giggled. "You didn't think that I was serious when I told you that I was going to work out with you, did you?" Before he even had a chance to answer, she started asking him what weights she should use and she didn't quit asking questions until the workout was over. Bridger didn't seem to mind sharing his knowledge of weight lifting; in fact, he actually seemed to enjoy the workout. Just as they were finishing up, there was a knock on the door and Bridger was very surprised when he looked up to see his team's physical therapist enter the room.

After making his way to Bridger, Chris extended his hand and said, "Bridger, it's good to see you, man! I was so excited when Annie gave me a call and said that you wanted to start doing physical therapy again."

Instead of offering his hand, Bridger looked at Annie, shook his head and said, "This is crap!"

Thankfully, Mary had followed Chris into the room, and Bridger shut up as soon as he saw his mother.

Mary was beaming from ear to ear as she made her way across the room. "Christopher, it's so good to see you. Congratulations. Did you bring a picture of your new baby? I'll bet she's a beauty!" Mary continued to visit for a few moments and then she said that she and Annie needed to start cleaning Bridger's room.

After the accident, Chris had tried many times to get Bridger to do his physical therapy, but it didn't matter what he said or did, he couldn't get him to budge. When he got the call from Annie, he had been very hesitant to set up the appointment, but she had seemed so optimistic about everything that he just couldn't say no. As soon as he walked into the room and saw the look on Bridger's face, he was certain that his instincts had been right. Surprisingly, an hour later, he was glad he had come. Chris could not believe how cooperative and easygoing Bridger was, and he was stunned when Bridger started asking him how some of his old teammates were doing.

Throughout the physical therapy, Bridger did his best not to acknowledge that Annie was in the room, but as hard as he tried, it seemed he couldn't. To make matters worse, each time their eyes met, she was smiling at him. At first, he thought it was a gloating, "I won kind of smile, but then he realized she wasn't gloating. She was encouraging him.

After their physical therapy session, Chris helped Bridger to his lounge chair and then stayed and visited with Mary and Annie for a bit. Throughout their conversation, Bridger heard each of them say something about scheduling another appointment for Monday, and his nerves started to get the best of him. He was glad when he finally heard his mother tell Chris that she and Annie would walk with him to his car.

When Annie returned, she was carrying a couple of hot packs. "Chris thought this might help you with the pain. We were worried about you. It's been a while since you've used some of those muscles." Annie took care to elevate Bridger's legs before she put the hot packs on. Thinking that she had done something good, Annie smiled at Bridger and said, "Does that feel OK?"

"Really, do you ever stop?" Bridger asked with his growl at full strength and then added, "What do you want me to say? Do you really think that moving my legs a little and then putting a couple of hot packs on them is going to make my legs feel OK?"

Finally

Moving her face inches away from Bridger's, Annie retorted, "Bridger, it's like I told you, yesterday. I am here to help you recover! The sooner you figure that out, the better, and just in case you have had a brain fart and have forgotten, your doctor told me that he has informed you on several occasions that at this point, your recovery depends on what you do to help yourself. He told me that if you do the things you need to do, and if I do the things I need to do, you could be walking again. Your doctor told me that if you would put some effort into you physical therapy, he really thinks that you could be walking within six months, and that is when I will stop doing what it is that I do, and Buddy and I will be happy to pack up and be on our way back home." Throughout the conversation, Annie had moved her face so close to Bridger's face that at that moment they could feel each other's breath. Buddy, who had been enjoying a little nap in a patch of sunshine on the floor, woke up to the sound of their voices and quickly sensed he was needed. After making a mad dash from across the room, he placed himself between the two and placed his front paws on Bridger's lap. Then he barked several times as if to say, "That is enough!" Annie felt bad that she had upset her pup and quickly stepped back.

"So you've talked to my doctor, too?" Bridger asked calmly.

"Bridger, of course I've talked to your doctor," Annie snapped back. After realizing she wasn't acting professionally again, she took a deep breath and with a calmer voice, added, "I needed to know what his orders were."

Bridger leaned back in the chair, folded his arms, and then with another round of his own snippiness asked, "So who else are you going to call?"

At that moment, Annie knew she was running low on patience and figured it was a good time for a break. After standing up, she forced a smile and said, "You had an intense therapy session, and your body isn't used to that much of a workout. I'll bet you're exhausted! It's time for me to take Buddy outside. While we're gone, maybe you can get some rest."

Annie didn't stick around for Bridger's reply, but as she and Buddy stepped out of the room, she wasn't surprised when she heard Bridger say, "You're right; I need lots of rest!"

Annie learned quickly that she would use the excuse of taking Buddy outside many more times during the coming days. She also learned that Bridger was the most stubborn, spoiled man she had ever met. It didn't matter what she suggested or tried to do to help him, he would argue about it or refuse to do it.

By the end of the first two weeks, Annie had decided she was ready to throw in the towel and head for home. Then for some unexplainable reason, Bridger's attitude changed. Annie wasn't sure if his mother had said something to him or if he just decided that he wanted to try. She really didn't care how or why he changed; she was just thankful that he did.

At the end of her third week, Annie decided to take Mary and Flora's advice and take her first Sunday off, but unfortunately, when Annie introduced the new temp nurse to Bridger, she knew in an instant that Bridger was going to give him a hard time. Annie hurried and introduced Randy to Bridger and then asked Randy to follow her so that she could give him a quick tour of the house. Randy and Annie connected instantly, and from the moment they started talking, it was as if they had known each other for years. Annie learned that Randy had just graduated from nursing school and was happy to come and earn some extra money. He told her he needed the extra money to help pay for his student loans and the ring he had just given to his fiancée.

"There really isn't much for you to do," Annie said as she led him down the hall. "Bridger is in one of his moods today, so you might want to watch TV or read something out in the sitting room. He'll let you know if he needs anything; he is very good at that! Flora will bring your lunch trays when we get back from church, and here's my cell phone number, just in case you need me."

As soon as they walked back into Bridger's room, they heard him growl, "This is ridiculous! I'm not two years old and I don't need a babysitter!"

That was all it took for Annie. Her patience were gone. "Bridger, this isn't about you! This is about your mother. You know she would worry herself sick if she left you here by yourself. You know perfectly well that you are not strong enough to go to the bathroom by yourself. Why are you so flippin selfish?" Annie snapped as she moved toward him, bent down and looked him directly in the eyes. "You know today is my day off, and eventually you will need some help. Do you really want your mother to help you?"

Bridger knew she was right but he wasn't going to admit it.

Feeling frustrated and trying not to explode anymore in front of Randy, Annie quickly changed the subject. "Bridger, before I forget, would you mind if Buddy stayed here with you while I go to church? And one more question, does that walking trail across the street eventually end up by the shore?"

"Why?" he asked.

"Because I thought Buddy and I could go for a walk later," Annie replied.

"I really don't think you need to take off walking in a place you know nothing about," Bridger answered back almost shouting.

"Bridger, I bet that the trail is paved and marked! Can't you answer just one question and be nice?" Annie replied. "But I guess if you're that worried, you can come with me." The moment the words left her lips, Annie couldn't believe that she had just invited him to accompany her. She didn't want his company; she needed some time to herself. *Please Lord, don't let him want to go*, she prayed silently.

"Oh, I guess you think that I'm just going to get up and walk down the trail?" he answered.

"You have a motorized wheelchair downstairs. Don't you get sick of this room?" Annie asked with a scolding tone. *Why in the world did I just say that? Why can't I just shut up?* Annie shouted in her mind.

Randy had sat quietly throughout the conversation, not daring to move, watching the two of them go back and forth. Then, thinking he could soften the situation, he asked, "So how long have you two been married?"

Bridger and Annie both turned toward him in unison and eerily at the same moment answered, "We're not married!" Then without missing a beat, they went back to their squabbling.

Bridger could not believe that Annie had just given him a lecture about him worrying his mother, when she was planning to take off on a trail that she had never been on before. He figured he had better go with her so that she wouldn't end up lost. He just knew his mother and Flora would have a nervous breakdown, if something happened to their precious little Annie. Man, she was such a pain! He really didn't want to spend the day wheeling through the trees. He was as surprised with himself as she was when he said, "OK, I guess I'll go with you."

Annie almost fell over when Bridger announced he wanted to go, but all that she could think to say was, "Great."

After church, Mary and Flora hurried home to fix a picnic lunch for Bridger, Annie, and Buddy. By the time they left, Annie was glad Bridger had decided to go. She really didn't know the area and still wasn't used to doing things like walking alone in strange places. Now, she was just hoping that everything would go well. When they left, Annie and Buddy were strolling by the electric wheelchair, and Flora and Mary were standing on the porch. Both of them waved good-bye as if Bridger, Annie, and Buddy were going to walk the Oregon Trail back to the East Coast.

Annie and Bridger were silent as they followed Buddy, who ran ahead to check out the new territory.

Bridger was the first to break the silence. "Tell me something, Annie. Why did you really come here?"

With his voice pulling her back to reality, Annie said, "I'm sorry, what did you say?"

"Why did you come here?" he asked again.

Annie really didn't want Bridger to know what had happened. She had come to help him, and she wanted him to focus on his own healing. Most of all, she really wasn't ready to share anything too personal with him."

"OK, I'm going to be honest with you. I work for the FBI, and I needed to lay low for a while. When I saw your mother's ad for a personal nurse, I decided this would be the perfect place," Annie answered, trying to keep a straight face.

Bridger held back a smile when he asked, "So you're not even a nurse?"

"Don't worry too much about me not being a real nurse, because I've watched a lot of those hospital dramas on TV, and there's really not much to it. You just stick a needle here or there, write a few things down, and fluff a pillow. I've got it all under control," Annie added.

When they reached the end of the trail, there was a little park with another breathtaking view of the ocean. There were more beautiful green trees and gorgeous wild flowers indigenous to the Washington shoreline surrounding both sides of the park, and, to top it off, it was a gorgeous day. Annie couldn't believe that she and Bridger were the only ones there. They picked the table closest to the shore and after settling in, they enjoyed the lunch that Mary and Flora had packed. As usual, there was way too much food. Even Buddy couldn't eat it all.

Annie giggled and said, "We'd better not take any leftovers back, or we'll get in trouble."

Bridger laughed and added, "Big trouble."

Annie was still laughing when she said, "I can't believe it! We actually agreed about something."

Finally

Bridger nodded his head and said, "Hmm that is pretty amazing." Turning his gaze toward the ocean, he added, "Why don't you and Buddy go and put your feet in the water and look for some seashells? I know that's something you can't do in Milford."

Annie said that she could do it another day, but he insisted. Deep down she was glad that he had, because she'd been looking forward to doing just that since she'd arrived.

From his wheelchair, Bridger watched Annie and Buddy as they walked down to the shore. He missed not being able to walk. Maybe Annie was right; maybe he could be walking at the end of six months. His mind would not let go of how quickly she had avoided answering his question about why she had come. It was obvious she was an exceptional nurse and there was no question that she could have gotten a job anywhere. His mind continued to race with more questions. Something had to have happened in her life. Why was she there?

After a bit, Annie looked up to check on Bridger and noticed that he had fallen asleep. She felt a stab of guilt for keeping him out so long. "Come on, Buddy, we'd better get Bridger and head for home." As she and Buddy were walking back to the picnic area, her phone rang.

"Hey, I miss you," Karen said as soon as she heard Annie say hello.

A large lump had started to form in Annie's throat when she replied, "Oh, I miss you too! Just hearing your voice makes me want to cry."

After they had said their hellos and told each other how much they had missed each other, Annie and Karen caught up on how things were going. As the conversation continued, Karen sensed Bridger must have been nearby, since there were a few things that Annie would not share, but the two friends found plenty of other things to talk about.

Annie wanted to know how her parents and in-laws were doing. Karen did her best to reassure Annie and told her that she had checked on all of them, and they were all fine. Then she gave Annie a report on Kenny.

"I saw Kenny downtown. When I asked him how things were going, the poor kid told me that he has to have a lecture at least once a day about how he should take care of your yard. He said that he really likes the job, but he added that it was kind of tough having Stalin and Hitler for supervisors."

"Do you really think those two old guys are that bad?" Annie asked and then added, "Because if they are, they are in big trouble!"

"Oh, I think it's good for Kenny. Please don't worry. I'll watch out for him," Karen answered reassuringly and then she asked Annie if she had gotten a chance to see their old pal from childhood, Robert?

"Oh my gosh, I forgot all about him! I will have to ask Bridger if he still lives around here. He was such a cute little guy, but oh my, he was so shy, wasn't he?" Annie replied.

"I think you're being too nice. You've got to admit, he was a nerd!" Karen laughed.

"He was not. Robert was a good kid!" Annie quickly snapped back. "We always had fun hanging out with him at the old swimming pool."

"Was he fun, or was he a stalker in training? Didn't you ever think it strange that he always seemed to know where we were? It didn't matter if we were swimming at the park, playing night games, getting a soda at the diner, or sitting on the corner listening to the radio, he always seemed to find us." Karen said sarcastically.

"Karen, he wasn't a stalker!" Annie said.

"Oh, stop it," Karen said, trying not to giggle. "That kid had the biggest crush on you, and when I think back about how shy he was, I still can't believe that he followed us like he did. But then, I guess a boy will do anything to see the girl, he's in love with.

"Did you ever think that something bigger is going on here? Maybe it's fate and I'm supposed to see Robert again!" Annie replied, trying to sound dramatic. Just as she was about to try to explain that she had been kidding about the fate stuff, Annie noticed that Bridger looked uncomfortable and was waking up. She quickly told Karen that she would have to call her later and then hurried back to Bridger.

After gathering up their belongings, Annie and Bridger started back for home. While they were walking, Bridger said, "So you remember Robert the Nerd?"

"I didn't call him a nerd," Annie answered, a bit embarrassed that he had overheard their conversation. "What were you listening to my phone conversation?"

Finally

"Just the tail end, now don't lie; the kid was a skinny nerd, and I'm sure he wore out his welcome!" Bridger shot back as they headed back up the trail.

"By the tone of your voice, I will take it that you and your cousin don't get along, but if I can arrange it while I'm here, I would love to see Robert again. Does he still live nearby? Did he get married? Does he have children?" Annie couldn't believe she had just asked so many questions about Robert.

"Don't ask me!" Bridger answered sharply.

"Whatever, Bridger but, if I want to find Robert, and have a visit, I'll just ask your mother." Annie replied.

"No, don't do that!" Bridger shot back quickly.

"Easy there, I get it!" Annie answered. "I wouldn't want to do anything that might upset your mother."

For most of the journey home, Annie and Bridger didn't have much to say. Annie felt bad that she had brought up the subject of Robert. As she and Buddy walked up the trail beside Bridger, Annie decided that if she wanted to find out anything more, she'd just have to ask Dr. Ray.

Chapter 12

Once Bridger's strength started to improve, Chris suggested turning one of the guest bedrooms into a workout room so that he could get Bridger working on different exercise machines.

Mary looked at Bridger, who was sitting directly across from her and said, "I think that sounds like a wonderful idea. Besides, it's about time you started spending some of your money, Son. And you know what else? I think all that stuff would be good for your old mother and Flora, too!"

By the time Mary was finished with the remodeling; she had turned the bedroom into a state-of-the art gym. Workout time turned out to be the best part of everyone's day. Mary and Flora dressed in their exercise outfits from the eighties, leg warmers and all, and to top things off, they insisted on listening to disco music.

When Annie had first talked to Chris about getting physical therapy for Bridger, he thought he would be able to come by the house every day. Unfortunately, after a couple of weeks, he realized he just couldn't keep up with the team and stop by every day. Annie even had a chance to fret about the situation; Chris had pulled her aside and said, "Now, before you start looking for another physical therapist, I want you to hear my plan. I want you to take over when I am not here."

At first, Annie was hesitant. "I can't do that!"

"Why not, Chris asked?

"Because Chris, I'm not a physical therapist," Annie replied.

"OK then, if it will make you feel better, I'll give you some training. I will stop by two or three days a week, just like I am doing now, and then you can take over the other days. That should take care of Bridger's PT."

To Annie's amazement, by the time the conversation had ended, Chris had convinced her.

The other room in the house that Annie truly enjoyed was the library. In fact, she had decided it was her favorite room when Flora had given her the tour of the house that very first day. Annie was amazed at the fact that Mary's collection of books outnumbered the books at the Milford library, two to one. One particular afternoon when Annie was visiting the library, her eyes caught sight of a beautiful chess board that had mahogany carved figures. Her mind flooded with memories, and she took a step back in time, as she reverently ran her fingers across the smooth, checkered board and each carved figure. She thought of all the times she and Alex had played chess, and as she did, her heart filled with the familiar longing and heartache. She thought of Jack. He had only had the chance to play a few matches, but he played chess just like everything else he did. He had picked it up quickly and he was good at it! She smiled as she remembered the look on Alex's face when Jack had reached over and taken his king.

Annie was brought back to reality when she heard Bridger ask, "Do you play?"

The sound of Bridger's voice startled her so much that her body launched forward, and when she tried to catch herself on the chessboard, she learned that the board wasn't secured to the stand. Luckily she was able to catch herself, but the sound of the falling chess pieces slapping against the wood floor caused her to jump again.

After the last piece had fallen to the ground, she turned to Bridger and said, "Holy crap, you scared me! I didn't hear you come in."

Bridger found the situation comical, but he didn't dare laugh, because he wasn't sure how Annie would react. It took him a few seconds to clear his throat a couple of times and then stuttered, "Ah, well, you were pretty lost in your thoughts." Then because his curiosity got the best of him, he added, "Anything you want to share?"

"No, I…I was just thinking about my secret chess strategies," Annie stuttered. She didn't want to tell him what she had been thinking about. As she picked up the fallen pieces, she continued," It's been a while, but I've been told I can play a pretty good game of chess."

"Sounds like a challenge." Bridger replied as he placed the pieces back in their starting positions. It didn't take Bridger and Annie long to figure out that they were evenly matched. One game led to another. Eventually, they ended each day with a game of chess, after Annie helped Bridger into bed. And it didn't take many matches for Annie to discover that Bridger's competitiveness extended beyond football. She used her discovery to her own advantage. If she didn't want to go back to her room, Annie knew that win or lose, Bridger would challenge her to another game.

It was during their late-night chess games that Bridger began to let down his guard and share some of his past. Most of his stories were about football, the friends he had made, and the things he missed. There were even a few moments when Bridger thought that Annie was going to share a bit with him. She would start talking small talk about Milford or the old days, but then she would change the subject and make light of whatever she had said, just as she had the day she said she worked for the FBI.

After the late-night chess games, Annie returned to her room and in the darkness of night, she allowed herself to miss Alex and her babies. The longing to touch them and to hear their voices was just as strong as it had ever been, maybe even stronger, and she wondered if the pain would ever ease. Annie knew she needed to talk about her pain, and there had even been a couple times she thought she was ready to open up and tell Bridger everything. At home, she had been the one who had encouraged her friends and family to talk about Alex and the kids, so why were things different now? Even though Annie had found a way to avoid her pain during the day, the nights in Washington were the same as they had been in Utah. After the usual tossing and turning, the sleeping pill would take effect, and Annie would drift off to sleep. A sleep filled with nightmares.

Even though the nights were the same and the hurt felt just as deep, Annie was glad her days were full. When she wasn't busy with Bridger, she kept herself busy doing things around the house and yard for Mary and Flora, and taking Buddy for walks. Overall, she felt things were going well and even decided that she had made the right decision to take the job. Mary, Flora, Bridger, Annie, and Buddy had developed a routine. Friday night became movie night. Mary was glad to see the theater room put to use again, and Flora was thrilled because she was in charge of getting the snacks. As with everything she did, Flora put her all into it. When it was time to shop for movie night, Flora would stop by a specialty shop so that she could pick up gourmet beef jerky for Buddy. Most of all, Mary and Flora were happy about the fact that they were spending time together with Bridger, Annie, and Buddy. Bridger even liked the idea of movie night, but he still thought he was being outvoted when it came to picking out the movies. He complained that there were too many chick flicks and not enough action shows.

One particular afternoon, Annie had finished with her duties and was just about to head out the door and take Buddy for a walk. When she walked past the dining room, she caught sight of Mary and Flora sitting at the dining room table going through boxes of photos. As she approached the table, she could see that the photos and newspaper clippings were of Bridger and his football career. Mary and Flora noticed that Annie seemed more interested than she had before. Annie knew immediately her urge to work on scrapbooks took over. Excitement filled her voice as she hurried toward the table. "You know, I could help you put all of these pictures and things into a scrapbook. Well, it would actually take quite a few scrapbooks by the looks of all those boxes."

The color drained from Mary and Flora's faces when they heard Annie's idea.

"Oh, I don't think we'd better do that. Bridger doesn't even know we look at his things," Mary replied quickly.

"That is so sad! I don't understand. Why would you want to keep all those wonderful memories in old boxes? They need to be properly preserved so that they don't get ruined," Annie replied passionately, as she reached to pick up a pile of photos.

"Sweetheart, it's just too hard for Bridger" Flora said, as she placed the papers she'd been looking at back in a box and hurried to pick up other photos. "When he looks at these things, it reminds him of how much he lost. You know, Annie, there is more in these boxes than Bridger's football career; there is the memory of his father and all the things they did together. He had a real tough time when his father died. They were so very close. It's just too painful for him to look at these things."

Finally

"I guess that I just see it a different way," Annie replied softly. She ignored both Mary and Flora and continued to look through the stacks of photos while they tried to put them away. "To me, each memory is a blessing that should be treasured."

As the three women stood around the table, they were startled when they heard something hit the doorway, and they were very surprised when they realized that the sound had come from Bridger. When he saw what they were doing, he quickly steered the wheelchair toward the table and spun it around to face them.

As soon as Annie saw the look on Bridger's face, she knew The Beast had returned. In an instant, she was filled with the need to protect Mary and Flora. "This is my fault! I was looking for a sweater that your mom was going to let me borrow, and I discovered these boxes. Once I saw the labels, I just started going through them, and then your mom and Flora came and we started looking." At first, her voice had been strong. She was determined not to let Bridger intimidate her, but by the time she had finished, she was stuttering. "And I, I thought we could sort through everything and then I thought we could put all of it into scrapbooks! And I…I, umm…well, I thought it would be good for your recovery."

For a few seconds, the room was absolutely still but it wasn't still for long. Bridger's voice thundered throughout the room as he glared at Annie and shouted, "No, we won't do that!" The volume of his voice wasn't quite as loud the second time, but his stare was just as fierce when he added, "Would someone please explain to me why you've come here and taken control of our lives, and then tell me why in the hell we just stepped back and let you. I want you to understand something. The things in theses boxes are mine. These are my memories, and it is none of your damn business where or how I keep them. I don't want to sort through this shit with you, and I sure as hell do not want to make scrapbooks with you. You leave my stuff alone! Do you understand? And don't you dare talk to me about blessings because I don't believe in them! You know, you have some nerve, lady, suggesting that it would be good for my recovery to sort through my life, when you don't even admit to having one!"

Mary and Flora had been witness to many of Bridger's rants, and because of their deep love for him, they had always found a reason to excuse his bad behavior, but this time was different. This time, they were both so ashamed and shocked that neither knew what to say or do. Even more, they were ashamed at themselves for letting Annie take all the blame.

As she thought of what she would say, Annie felt she was becoming smaller and smaller with each word Bridger spoke. But then something inside, told her that she didn't need to be treated that way. After swallowing her tears and taking several deep breaths, she squared her shoulders and with a strong voice said, "Bridger, I do believe in blessings, and I believe with all of my heart and with every fiber of my soul that God doesn't waste anything, and no matter how bad it may seem, there are reasons that things happen. Bridger, I am very sorry for what happened to you. I had no business getting into your things without your permission. I am very sorry for that too. I guess that I just got carried away when I saw all your pictures and awards, and I thought of how wonderful they would look in scrapbooks."

Before he had even finished with his outburst, Bridger felt like the Scum of the Earth, and by the time Annie had finished speaking, he was sure there wasn't a word in the dictionary to describe how he felt about himself. He was ashamed and wished with all his heart that he could take back the awful words he had just said. Bridger turned away and looked out the window. He stared at the sea and tried desperately to think of how he should apologize. In reality, he had only looked away from Annie for a few seconds but to him, it felt like an eternity had passed. Quickly and still without knowing what to say, he turned back around only to discover that she was gone. Staring at the empty doorframe, Bridger realized that his life had reached a defining moment, and everything that he used to think was so important, suddenly seemed small and insignificant.

Mary and Flora remained silent as they finished putting away the rest of the photos. Unable to face them, Bridger could hear them slapping the items back into the boxed. When he finally managed to turn back around to face them, much to Bridger's surprise, neither his mother nor Flora spoke to him. They pretended like he wasn't even there and continued with what they were doing. As soon as they had placed the lids back on the boxes, they walked toward Bridger, stopped and gave him a looks that could kill before they left the room. Unbeknownst to Bridger, they were just as angry and disappointed with themselves for letting Annie take all the blame.

Finally

As soon as Annie's feet touched the path, her tears turned into sobs. With her heart located somewhere in her lower stomach and Buddy at her heels, she unconsciously headed down the trail that led to the ocean. She'd been dreading this particular day for weeks, because it was her birthday and the first anniversary of Alex's and the children's deaths. If it hadn't been a Tuesday, she would have come up with an excuse to stay in bed, but she couldn't because Tuesday was the day that she and Bridger went to town. At first, they had started going into town for Bridger's doctor appointments, and then as he started to feel better, he asked Annie if they could run a few errands, usually to the bank or a store.

On one of their trips to town, they were just about ready to head back home, and out of nowhere Bridger totally surprised Annie and asked her if she wanted to get something to eat. Before she even had a chance to reply, he asked if she wanted to go to a movie, too. After the shock wore off, Annie was thrilled. As much as she enjoyed herself at Mary's, she was happy to do something different. Everything went so well that they did the same thing the next week, and the next week, and then, somehow, Tuesday became their day for going to lunch and a movie. Annie looked forward to Tuesdays, and it didn't take her long to figure out that Bridger did, too. Several times a week, he'd get online and print out information about the movies that were playing and ask her several times what movie she wanted to watch.

For just a second, as she and Buddy made their way down the walking path, Annie wished she'd brought her cell phone, but she quickly changed her mind, knowing that if she had talked to Karen or her parents about what had just happened, they would only worry more about her than they already did. With a gazillion thoughts racing through her mind, she couldn't help but think of how ironic the events of the day had turned out. As she'd tried to prepare herself for her birthday, she had insisted to her parents and Karen that she didn't want anyone to fuss over her. Her reasoning was that if she just pretended that it was another day, the day would be easier for her to get through.

With Buddy by her side, Annie found herself at the picnic area where she and Bridger had gone for their first picnic. After making her way to the line of trees that separated the park from the shore, she found a tree with a big trunk and leaned her tired body next to it. She thought about all the different things that she and Bridger had made routine. Sunday had become their picnic day.

After they enjoyed Flora's picnic basket full of food, they would spend the afternoon playing with Buddy, reading, playing a game of chess or talking. As they became more comfortable with each other, they found that they enjoyed each other's company, so much that sometimes, they would just sit next to each other and watch the ocean. So many things had gone right, but now that she thought of it, maybe more things had gone wrong. After a few minutes of standing, Annie let her exhausted body slide downward along the side of the tree's trunk. As soon as her bottom made contact with the ground, she curled her body into the fetal position and let her weary head fall to her knees. Feeling the need to hold something, Annie pulled her hood over her head and then wrapped her arms tightly around her faithful pup.

By the time Bridger had made his way into his motorized wheelchair, his arms were shaking. Even though nothing felt right, he was glad to learn that he had regained more strength in his legs. Bridger knew that he had to give Annie the credit for his newfound independence. He knew the only reason that he had come this far was because Annie had pushed him with her kind words and encouragement. If she hadn't come, he knew that he would never have been able to be this independent. Angry at himself, he shook his head with despair. His voice thundered with regret as he shouted. "How could I have treated her that way?"

After Annie left the house, Bridger's instincts had told him where she was going. His mother and Flora must have had a pretty good idea about where Annie would go too because they were waiting for him at the bottom of the porch ramp to give him two jackets.

"Thank you," he said humbly. Unfortunately, they were still giving him the cold shoulder. Not knowing what else to say, he added, "I know I'm a jerk but I do love you two old bugs!"

They refused to speak, but, nodded their heads to let Bridger know that they agreed with his self-description.

Bridger knew there was no time to waste; he needed to get to Annie as fast as he could. He pushed the forward control of the wheelchair down and took off down the trail at full speed. He knew he was pushing the chair but he had to find her, and nothing was going to stop him! As he made his way around the last curve, he was glad the picnic area was just a bit further. He began to feel even more confident that he would find Annie. It was strange, but it was almost as if he could feel that she was near. Instead of watching the path and paying attention to his driving, his thoughts filled with all the things he was going to say to her. Unfortunately, he forgot the last turn was a switchback. He was going too fast and lost control. The wheelchair fishtailed on the trail before it spun out-of-control and headed for a small embankment. As soon as the chair and the embankment collided, a strong force sent Bridger flying. Thankfully, when he came back down, he landed on a much larger embankment of sand.

"Shit!" he yelled as his arms stretched forward, trying to help break the fall.

After a good cry, Annie felt she needed to talk to Bridger and decided to head back. Her mind raced with a million thoughts as she hurried back up the hill. She was so focused on her own thoughts that it took her a few seconds to realize that she heard a voice and the sound of bushes snapping and cracking. For a brief moment, she was frightened about what lay ahead, but when she saw that Buddy wasn't barking, she took it as a good sign and figured she wasn't in any danger. As she rounded the turn, she was totally surprised to see Bridger sitting in the bushes, with a bloody nose, his chair five feet away and leaning into an embankment.

"Bridger," Annie shouted as she and Buddy ran to him.

"I'm OK. I just can't get back in my chair," he said.

Annie saw one of the jackets and grabbed it. As soon as she reached Bridger, she began wiping the blood from his face.

"I'm OK. Really, it's just a little cut on my forehead and a bloody nose," Bridger said.

"Are you sure? Does anything feel like it might be broken? Are you bleeding anywhere else? Oh my gosh, Bridger, this is my fault," Annie said as she tried to figure out the extent of his injuries.

Bridger sat leaning back on his arms and watched Annie as she nursed him. Instead of thinking about his body and what he'd just put it through, he thought of how glad he was to have her close to him. He was thinking how good she smelled. As Annie looked closer to see if the thorns from bushes had penetrated his skin, Bridger became totally captivated by her kind and smiling blue eyes, but the closer he looked, he could see that her eyes were sad, and he was angry with himself that he had made her feel that way. She hadn't deserved to be treated the way that he had treated her. She had come here to do a job and had done so much more.

As she continued to wipe the blood from his cheek, Annie said, "Bridger, I know I'm pushy. When there is something to be done, there is something inside of me that takes over, and I guess, I just don't know when to stop. Again, I'm very sorry I got into your things," she said continuing to cover for Mary and Flora. "And I guess, well, what I'm trying to say is, I think I've done all I can do for you. You've come such a long way in such a short time and I really think you are going to be just fine. What I'm trying to say is that I think it's time for me to go home."

Her words brought him back to reality with a pain that was much deeper than any of his injuries.

"No, please don't go, Annie. I'm so sorry. I had no right to treat you that way. I'm sorry for the way that I've treated you. I know that I have been a jerk but I'll change. I have changed and I know I can change more. I would still be sitting in my room, watching television and not trying if you hadn't come," he said as he gently cupped her face between his hands and wiped away the tears that were falling down her cheeks.

Bridger put his arms around Annie and held her. He didn't want to let go out of fear that she really would leave. His wanted so badly to kiss her but his instinct told him the closeness was enough for now.

In the safeness of his arms, Annie let go and let him be her strength. It was then that she confided, "Bridger, I had a life. I just can't talk about it. I'm not ready. I'm just not ready."

Bridger was caught totally off guard. He didn't know what to say or do, so he continued to hold her. She seemed so small, like a little rag doll that he was holding together. He laid his head down against hers and held her tight. "It's OK, Annie. When you're ready to talk, I'm here," Bridger said as his own tears fell upon her head. It was then he knew that something bad had happened to her. Something very bad, and he meant what he said—he would be there for her whenever she was ready to talk. Bridger picked up the jacket and wrapped it around her. It was the first time, he had done something for her and it felt so good and so right.

Buddy took his place next to Bridger and Annie and s stood guard over the two people he loved most.

Finally

When Annie finally started to stir, her first instincts were to take care of Bridger, "Oh my gosh, Bridger, you must be in so much pain. Here, we've got to get you up."

"I'm fine but I have to confess that I think it would be a good time for me to move." If he hadn't been in so much pain he would have stayed there and held her, but his body told him he had to move. Between the two of them, they managed to get him back into the chair, which luckily hadn't been damaged. As they started back up the path, Bridger reached for Annie's hand and she accepted the offer. Before they reached the road that would lead them to the house, Bridger stopped, looked at Annie and said, "I was thinking since we missed our day to go to town, maybe we could go tomorrow. I'll bet we could find one of those girly stores, where they have lots of things to make scrapbooks."

"How does a guy like you know anything about girly stores with scrapbook supplies?" Annie asked with a small grin.

"Remember, I've been watching a lot of TV. I've learned all kinds of things. You told me yourself that's where you learned to be a nurse," Bridger answered back with a chuckle.

Annie laughed too. "I think that sounds like a great way to," then she paused for a moment and said, "To start again."

By the time they made it back to the house, it was nearly dark, and Mary and Flora were pacing the porch. When they looked up and saw Bridger's bumps and scrapes, their instincts told them to rush to him.

But just as they started to move, Mary stopped and gently took hold of Flora's arm, and whispered, "Look, they're holding hands."

"Praise Jesus, I tell you, Mary, the Lord's got a plan going here!" Flora whispered back.

Chapter 13

Bridger felt his life had truly changed for the better the day that Annie took hold of his hand. He knew he loved her, and he had from the moment he had first laid eyes on her. Annie liked the person that Bridger had become, and she liked being with him. She liked the way he made her feel, but the old feelings and the new feelings battled within her. She couldn't face either, so she just kept going. Late in the fall, as Halloween approached, Flora and Mary started planning a big Halloween celebration. Mary insisted that they were all to dress up in costumes, including Buddy, to greet the children for Trick- or- Treat. Annie's old holiday spirit seemed to take over. She helped with the decorating, and wherever Annie was and whatever she was doing, that's where Bridger wanted to be. The night of the party, Mary surprised Annie and Bridger with their costumes. Annie was Sleeping Beauty, Bridger was Prince Charming, and Buddy, Mary, and Flora were the good fairies.

One by one, they arrived at the front porch. They all laughed when they saw each other. They talked and joked with each other and then anxiously waited for the children. Bridger couldn't take his eyes away from Annie. She truly looked like a princess to him. If only he could walk and take his princess to the ball. *Someday, I will,* he thought to himself.

It was tradition for every kid in the neighborhood to make his or her way to Mary and Flora's. All the kids knew they would find the best treats there. The five of them had a very busy night, but most important, they had fun and they were all sad when the last little witch made her way down the path.

"Well, I guess that's it," Flora said as she stood up from one of the porch chairs, thinking she should start to clean up.

"Oh, but wasn't it fun!" Mary said as she got up to join her.

It was then that Bridger insisted his mother and Flora go in and get warm.

"I'll bet Annie will help me clean up out here, and then I was thinking in the morning, we could start getting ready for Thanksgiving," Bridger said teasingly.

All the ladies started laughing.

"What have we done to you, my Bridger?" Flora said with tears now rolling down her cheeks from laughing.

"Movie night taught me that I can't win. So I figured out that I might as well join in. Besides, Buddy is the only other male, and I know darn well that he is going to do whatever you girls want to do, but that is only because you all feed him more than I do."

After Mary and Flora gave Bridger and Annie a hug and kiss goodnight, they went inside, giggling.

After turning off the lighted decorations, Buddy, Bridger, and Annie followed them into the house with the empty candy dishes and made their way into the kitchen.

"Are you up for some hot cocoa and a game of chess?" Bridger asked, not wanting the night to end.

"I am! Let's change and get you into bed, and then I'll beat the pants off you!" Annie replied not thinking about what she had said.

"Wow, all I really wanted to do tonight was dance with the princess," Bridger teased.

Annie's face turned bright red.

"It's OK; I was only teasing. Wow, you are red. I didn't know ladies your age still blushed," Bridger said, trying to ease the moment.

"Oh, so now I'm old," Annie replied.

"Maybe we'd better get that chess game started," Bridger said.

Annie hurried and changed into a pair of sweats and a T–shirt. Walking into Bridger's room, she was about to say that she would go and get the cocoa when she noticed that Flora had already set a tray of hot cocoa and chocolate chip cookies by the bed, along with the chess set.

"I'll bet you're ready for your night meds," Annie said as she helped Bridger into bed.

In a more serious tone, Bridger asked, "Annie, do you think the pain will always be this bad?"

Taking hold of his hand, she replied, "I really don't know, Bridger. I know you don't like to talk about God, and I know you and I don't have the same thoughts about the subject. But I do believe, and I want you to know I pray for you every night."

"Thanks, Annie. It means a lot to me," he said.

Walking down the hall to get the meds, she thought about what she had read in Bridger's medical history. All the specialists had the same prognoses. Everything medically had been done that could be done. The doctors felt that with continued therapy, Bridger would eventually be able to walk with the help of a cane. But there had been so much nerve damage done to both legs that there was not much hope that he would ever live without pain. Fortunately, Mary, Flora, and Annie believed in something much stronger than medical predictions; they believed in the power of prayer.

After two sets of chess and a win for each, Annie laid her head back on the pillow on the opposite side of the bed and thought she would rest for just a minute before she headed off to her own bed. Looking over at Bridger, she yawned and said, "I'm really tired." Her eye lids were heavy and before she knew it, she fell asleep. Before she did, she mumbled, "It was such a good day. Wasn't it, Bridge?"

Bridger knew that when Annie woke up, she was going to have a fit and say things like, "I'm so sorry. I shouldn't have done that." But he wasn't about to wake her. She was sleeping too peacefully. After checking on Buddy, who was asleep at the bottom of the bed, Bridger turned off the light and watched her sleep by the light of the moon that shone through the opened curtain. He tried his best not to fall asleep. He didn't want to let go of the moment, but his own exhaustion overtook him, and soon he was asleep too.

Later in the night, Bridger woke when he felt Annie move.. As he became more awake, he heard Annie say, "Alex, I can't reach you. I can't. My babies, my babies, Alex," she cried over and over.

"Annie, honey, wake up," Bridger said, shaking her gently. Bridger tried and tried to wake her but her nightmares had too deep a hold. As she trembled, Bridger reached for her and took her in his arms and was very surprised when her body responded. She held tightly to him and in the safety of his arms, she let go of the nightmare. Even though Annie was safe in his arms, Bridger couldn't fall back to sleep. The question of what had happened to her and why she wouldn't talk continued to plague him. Before his body finally gave back into sleep, he knew he had to find out what had happened to her because he knew that until she let go of her past, he would have no future.

When Bridger woke up, Annie was gone. He was so worried. Would she regret that she had spent the night in his arms? He became anxious for her return and it felt like an eternity, but it was only moments before he looked up and saw Annie coming through the door.

"Morning," she said with her usual smile. She had already showered and was wearing a pair of blue jeans, a white V neck T-shirt tucked in with a belt, and her hair was pulled up in a ponytail. She didn't look like a grown woman of thirty-six; she looked more like a young girl he had once known. He liked the way she dressed. She looked just as beautiful in a pair of jeans and t-shirt as she had been the night before dressed as a princess.

"Good Morning. Did you sleep good last night?" he asked nervously.

"You know what? That's the best I've slept in a long time. I feel great today!"

Bridger was totally surprised. He hadn't been expecting such a wonderful reply.

"Bridge, today is my day off, and the temp can't come in. Do you think you would be OK if I left for a while?" Annie asked as she helped him to dress.

He knew he'd be fine, but the thought of not being with her seemed worse. "So are you going shopping?" he asked.

"Nope," she answered.

"Are you going walking?" he asked, feeling a bit stupid for prying.

"No. But would you like to come with me?" She asked without giving him any details. Since her birthday, except for the time she walked Buddy, Annie really had only taken a few hours a week to herself. The last few weeks, she had wanted to ask Bridger to come with her, but she hadn't had the courage to ask him to go, and this moment seemed like the perfect time.

Finally

"Sure," he answered, just happy knowing he was going to be with her. "So are you going to let me in on where we're going?" he asked.

"Not until we get there. I think you've forgotten who I work for. Everything is top secret with the FBI." Annie answered laughing. It was total instinct, but after she had handed him the sweater that she had picked out for him to wear, she leaned over and kissed him on the cheek.

It didn't take Bridger long to figure out that they were headed into Seattle, a place he hadn't even considered that she might be going on her time off. As he listened to the music, he thought of all the things they had in common. They liked the same music. He had even grown to like her Christian music. They liked being outdoors, working around the house, watching movies, reading, playing chess—the simple stuff of life as Annie had called it.

Bridger was the first to break their moment of silence. "It's strange when Buddy isn't with us."

"Yeah, it's kind of strange not to have him here, but today, I let him stay with your mom and Flora. I swear, I've never seen such a spoiled dog," Annie said laughing.

"Children's Hospital," Bridger questioned as Annie took the exit.

"Yep, I have met some very special friends there, and today you're going to meet them," Annie answered.

"I should have guessed that you were going to some place like this, but I just want you to know beforehand that I'm not very good with sick people, especially sick kids." After wiping away the nervous perspiration from his brow, Bridger added, "Heck, I haven't even dealt very well with my own illness!"

"Bridge, please don't get nervous. After watching you yesterday, I know you are going to enjoy this."

As soon as the elevator door opened, Bridger took in a breath. He hated the smell of hospitals. Truth be told, he had had enough of hospitals, and he hated everything about them. Reluctantly, Bridger followed Annie down the hall, into an elevator, through several more halls, and then into a recreation hall. The first thing he saw was about twenty kids, and they were all waiting for Annie. As soon as they spotted her walking through the door, they started clapping and cheering. "Annie, Annie," they chanted.

"Oh, stop it, you guys," Annie replied humbly as she made her way around the circle, hugging and kissing each one of the children. There were two new children, and when she came to them, she stopped, knelt down beside them, and took extra time to make them feel welcome. After she had greeted all of her friends, she walked over to Bridger and said, "Hey guys, I would like you to meet my friend, Bridger. He came to help me today!"

Curtis, who was eleven, clapped his hands together and with undeniable excitement shouted, "You're Bridger Jones, the Bridger Jones. Oh my gosh, my dad's never going to believe this!"

Bridger seemed to eat it up. It had been so long since he'd had any contact with fans. After the introduction, Bridger went over and talked to Curtis. As she watched from a distance, Annie could see that Bridger and Curtis had already become friends.

Annie opened one of the bags that she had brought and passed out little individual bags of arts and crafts that she had prepared for the kids. When they got out of the car, Bridger had been so nervous that he hadn't even noticed the bags she had hung on the back of his chair. Now, he wanted to notice everything. He jumped right in to help. He loved watching Annie work with the kids. She was a natural. But as he continued to watch her, a heavy feeling of sadness came over him when he thought of what she had said in her sleep.

After the kids had finished their crafts, it was story time. Annie and the nurses helped the kids that could lay down or sit to form a circle on a big, shaggy rug. The children and Bridger were totally captivated with her passion for each story. After she had read a couple of stories, Annie got up, walked over to Bridger, and whispered in his ear, "Bridge, I need to go to the restroom. Will you please take over?"

"Annie, I can't do that. It's just not my thing!" he tried to whisper back, but just like everything else, she got her way. She went to the restroom, and Bridger read to a room full of children.

When she returned, Annie didn't hurry back to her place on the rug. Instead, she stood behind the doorway and listened to Bridger read to the children.

Annie smiled and thought, *who would have ever thought The Beast, would be so good with kids?*

A nurse, who was standing next to Annie, leaned over and very quietly said, "So that's the famous Bridger Jones. Knowing his reputation, I would have never thought he would be so good with children!"

"Me either," Annie replied. "Me either!"

Finally

After Bridger finished reading the book, it was time for the children to get back to their beds. Annie cleaned up from the crafts, and Bridger volunteered his services to give kids rides back to their rooms. Before they could leave, Annie said that she needed to go and stop by the rooms of two more of her friends who weren't able to come. Knowing how Bridger felt about hospitals, Annie explained to him that the two children were very ill, and he needed to decide whether he wanted to go with her or wait for her. It was a hard decision for him, but as he followed her into the rooms, Bridger couldn't tell who was happiest to see each other, Annie, the children, or the parents. Annie had little gifts for each of them, and it was plain to see that they had been chosen with loving care.

The last little girl they visited with was Lauren. Annie gave her a book of Bible stories, and when she handed the gift to Lauren, she smiled and said, "I told you that I would find one that had the story of, *Joseph and His Amazing Coat*.

Lauren's mother stayed at her daughter's side twenty-four hours a day. Lauren was worried about her mother not getting fresh air. Annie wanted to help both of them, and after a little persuading and the promise that Bridger would stay and read to Lauren, she was able to talk Lauren's mom into going for a short walk.

When they returned, Annie had her arm around the distressed woman. Bridger didn't have a lot of medical knowledge, but it didn't take a medical degree to figure out that Lauren didn't have long.

Once Annie was back in the room, she walked over to Lauren to give her a hug and kiss. When she moved to stand up, Lauren pulled her back and looking up at her and with a tired voice and whispered, "Annie, I will tell them hello, and Annie, please don't be sad anymore."

Annie didn't know what to say. She hadn't told anyone of her past and was totally puzzled. In fact, being with the children was something that had made her genuinely smile. How did Lauren know? Choking back the tears, Annie nodded her head, kissed Lauren on the cheek, and then softly stroked her hand against the tiny cheek.

After giving Lauren's mother a hug, Annie and Bridger walked to the elevator. Bridger was still struggling to hold back his tears when he said, "I guess that I really haven't had that much to complain about, have I?"

"It's OK. You didn't know then what you know now," Annie answered after they stepped into the elevator. Then, as if it were the most natural thing to do, she reached down and gave Bridger a hug. "Thank you so much for coming with me today. I don't know what I would have done without you. You were amazing!

As they made their way to the main lobby, they noticed there was a press conference going on and heard someone say it was about the hospital's new wing.

Even though there was a crowd, one of the reporters happened to spot Bridger and shouted, "Hey, it's Bridger Jones!"

Suddenly it was a circus, and reporters came out of nowhere. They started asking Bridger a million questions. "How are you? Where have you been? What are you doing here?"

Annie was proud. He handled it well. You name it, they asked it. Then one of the reporters yelled, "Who's the pretty lady? Do the two of you have any plans? Bridger could tell the attention and the flashing cameras were overwhelming Annie. He tried to sway the press and get their focus back on him, but they wanted to know all about Annie.

It was so hard not to tell the whole world right then and there that Annie was the woman he loved, but how could he do that when he hadn't even told her? And he knew if he didn't say anything about the woman he was with, the press might go wild.

With a cool and calm voice, Bridger answered, "Ladies and gentlemen, I would like you to meet Annie. She is my nurse and thanks to her, I'm finally doing a lot better." Then he thanked the press for their interest and told them that he was very tired, and that maybe in the near future he could arrange for interviews on a more personal level. Annie took the cue and pushed Bridger toward the exit as fast as she could.

Annie was happy to get back in the car and back on the freeway toward home. "That was so crazy! Is that what your life was like?" She asked innocently.

"It could get pretty bad sometimes but it was all part of the deal," Bridger answered. He was thinking to himself that he'd blown it by introducing Annie as his nurse.

"Bridger thanks for what you said, but I think you are giving me way too much credit," Annie said, looking over at him.

Finally

"Are you kidding me? Look how far I've come since you came," Bridger answered looking back at her beautiful blue eyes, wanting so much to tell her he loved her. All he could think to say was, "Look, we've argued about a lot of stuff, but I'm not arguing with you on this one, because this time I'm right!"

Chapter 14

Fall came and went, giving way to winter. The season started out very wet and chilly, and throughout the months since Annie's arrival, Mary, Flora, Bridger, Annie, and Buddy had become a family. Dr. Ray and his wife made the journey from Utah to Washington to spend Thanksgiving with his sister and her family. Everyone, including Buddy had a great time. Dr. Ray and his wife were amazed at the progress Bridger had made, and one of their best moments of the trip was when Bridger turned on the TV to watch a football game that his former teammates were competing in.

Everyone was excited to join Bridger to help cheer on his beloved team. Annie decided she would join the family and watch the game, but she knew she needed to keep her hands busy and so, she decided to work on Bridger's scrapbooks. Annie spread her scrapbook supplies on the coffee table and then got comfortable on the floor, next to the couch where Bridger was lying. As the small group excitedly cheered and anxiously debated plays, Annie divided her time between making new pages, looking up at the game, and watching how the game affected Bridger. Annie found herself wanting to know what was going on, and once she started asking questions, she couldn't quit. At first, Bridger was surprised that she had taken an interest. He patiently and eagerly answered each question, thinking she was just trying to be her sweet self and act like she liked the game just because he did, but that wasn't the case, and the more questions Annie asked, the more excited Bridger became.

During the holiday, Bridger and his uncle enjoyed some time alone and even had some pretty good talks, something they hadn't done in a long time. Ray was very excited to see all of the progress Bridger had made, but most of all, he was happy to see his nephew enjoying life again. During one of their chess games, Bridger tried to get his uncle to open up and tell him what had happened to Annie.

"Hmm," he said. "She hasn't told you yet?"

"No, and by the look on your face, you aren't going to tell me either," Bridger answered.

"You are right, my boy, but, I will tell you this. Like you, she looks and acts so much better than the last time I saw her." Ray paused for a moment before he replied, "She has been through the unimaginable. Just keep doing what you're doing. You're good for her, Bridge. She needs you more than you will ever know."

"But how can I help her, if I don't even know what it is that I'm helping her with?" Bridger answered back.

"Annie is very special to me and I am not going to betray her trust, but you trust me, and believe me when I say this. She will open up to you when the time is right, and I can tell that moment is getting closer," Ray said, trying to reassure Bridger.

"I hope so, Uncle Ray. I hope so." Bridger added.

With a smile on his face, Ray asked, "Have you told her that you love her yet?"

"You don't know how much I've wanted to, but I'm afraid. There are moments when we are talking and I feel like we are getting so close and then just when I think she wants to open up to me, she shuts down. It's like she shuts a door," Bridger answered back.

"Son, I don't think she's shutting a door on you. It's more like she's afraid to open that door, and there are many reasons why. Don't give up, Bridge; just don't give up," Ray replied, hoping he had sounded encouraging.

A few days after Dr. Ray and his wife had left to go back to Utah, Flora decided it was time for her to make one of her authentic Mexican meals.

As the family sat at the table enjoying their meal, Annie said, "Flora, every time you make something new, I swear it's my favorite, and I couldn't like anything as well, and then you do it again. This is delicious."

Finally

"Here, here. I second that!" Bridger agreed.

"And I totally agree with the both of them," Mary chimed in and then added, "I was thinking in the morning, I would have Tom bring all the Christmas decorations down from the attic. I was wondering if anyone wanted to help me decorate." Flora and Bridger both answered yes at the same time, but Annie didn't quite know what to do about Christmas. Of course, she would help them decorate, but she had decided to go home for Christmas and hadn't told them of her plans, and she wasn't sure how to break the news. She took a few more bites of her dinner to buy herself some time. In the silence, Mary worried she'd said something wrong.

After swallowing, Annie smiled and said, "So will we start decorating tomorrow?"

Mary gave an inward sigh of relief; she could ever forgive herself if she did anything to hurt Annie. "Oh, that would be lovely. You know, Annie, we really haven't wanted to celebrate much since Bridger's dad passed away. He loved the holidays so much, but it just wasn't the same after he was gone," Mary answered with melancholy in her voice.

"Do you remember all the fun we used to have, Bridge? Your daddy was always such a big kid at heart," Flora added.

Mary looked directly at Annie, smiled, and said, "You know, Annie, since you and Buddy came to our home, it hasn't felt empty. You've breathed new life into this house."

"You are so very special to all of us, Annie," Flora said as she wiped the corner of her eye with a napkin.

Bridger was watching Annie; she was smiling, but she was also squeezing her eyebrows together. He could tell something was bothering her, and then it hit him. *I'll bet she wants to go home for Christmas and doesn't have the heart to tell us.* Bridger hurried and jumped into the conversation. "Annie, have you talked to your parents lately. How are they? What are their plans for Christmas? I'll bet they're looking forward to you coming home for the holidays?"

Annie almost fell off of her chair. *How did he know what I was thinking?* There had only been two people in the world who had ever known her that well: Alex and Karen. Not knowing quite what she should say, Annie stammered through her words. "Ah, I um, well I really hadn't thought about it yet. I guess I'll call them later and see what they have planned. I don't know. Maybe, I should go home for a bit and check on everyone."

Annie felt terrible when she saw the disappointed looks on Mary's and Flora's faces. Thinking of how she could make things better quickly, she added, "But you know what? We've got a lot to do, with all the decorating and buying presents for our kids at the hospital. Mary and Flora, we have twenty-two kids who need cheering up." After she said the word twenty-two, she thought of Lauren and wished there was twenty three, but she quickly moved on, knowing that Lauren was in a better place and was no longer so dreadfully ill. "You know ladies, Bridger and I are going to need help. There is no way we can do all that shopping by ourselves." It worked. The mere mention of kids and presents refocused Mary and Flora, and they immediately started making plans and looking forward to tomorrow.

After Annie helped Bridger into bed, she told him that she needed to call her parents, but as soon as she was done, she would be back for a game of chess.

It was good to hear her father's voice. "Daddy, what's up?" Annie asked.

"Oh, not too much, your mother's already gone to bed," he answered.

"Oh, I shouldn't have called so late. Is Mom OK?" Annie asked.

This was her biggest worry. What if something happened to either of her parents and she wasn't there with them. How would she ever forgive herself?

"Of course, your mom is just fine. She was just a little tired tonight," he answered back reassuringly.

They chatted for quite a while and caught up. Annie always had to have a moment-to-moment report on what was happening back at home, and her father always wanted to know something new about the famous Bridger Jones. It was weird for Annie to think of Bridger as some famous celebrity, because she had only known him as he was now.

Soon after Annie had settled into her new job, her father confessed that he had followed Bridger Jones's career since his college days. Each time they talked, he would have a new question for her. What's he like? Did you see all of his trophies? Has he ever talked about the game when his team was robbed of the win of the century? During their first conversations, Annie didn't know what to say to her father. She really didn't want to break his heart and tell him that her nickname for Bridger was "The Beast," so she had just muddled through it, but now, it was Annie who talked about Bridger. Bridger and I did this. Bridger and I did that. Now her father just liked the way her voice sounded when she talked about Bridger; she sounded excited and happy.

After a bit, Annie said, "Dad, I think I'll head home for Christmas about the fifteenth. I want to get home and help Mom, and I'll need time to visit everyone."

There was a pause before her father answered. "Annie, your mom and I thought we would spend Christmas at your Aunt Carol's this year. You know, we've really been looking forward to getting to the warmer climate, and Uncle Charlie and Aunt Helen are planning on meeting us there."

"That sounds good to me. I can fly into St. George on the same day that you drive and you can pick me up, and then we can head out to Aunt Carol's together." Annie answered back excitedly.

After a brief pause, her father stammered out the words, "Ah, I guess your mother hasn't talked to you about this, has she?"

"Talked to me about what, Dad?" Annie asked.

"Well, we thought it might be better if you stayed with Bridger for Christmas. He might need you and all," he said.

"I thought you guys might be missing me by now. Don't you want me to come home?" Annie questioned, trying not to sound irritated.

"Annie, it's not that at all. You know you are our world. Look, I'm just going to be honest with you. I don't think," he paused. "I don't think you're ready to come home yet. And besides, your mother and I think that you have a responsibility to Mr. Jones and his mother." her father answered back with a stern voice.

"Dad, you make it sound like I'm eighteen and I haven't stayed away at college long enough to know if I like it!" Annie answered back not knowing if she should get angry or cry, because once again, someone was telling her what they thought was good for her.

"Now you listen here, young lady. I know exactly how old you are. Remember, I was there when you were born. I'm just going to say this; I've never been one to tell you what to do. I might have given a lot of advice, but I always left the decisions up to you. But I can tell by the sound of your voice that you are doing great up there, and I think if you come home now, well, I just don't think you're ready. As far as missing you, there are days your mother and

I can hardly stand it. But then I talk to you, and I hear your voice, and I can tell that you're happy up there, whether you want to admit it or not." When he had finished, he had to fight to hold back his tears.

"Dad, it's just that I really miss you," Annie said crying.

"Don't cry, sweetheart. This is all going to work out, and after Christmas, your mom and I would really like to come up there and see you, and we are very excited to visit with Bridger and his family."

It was so hard to not give in and just tell his daughter to come home, but every bit of his fatherly instinct told him not to. After a further bit of persuasion, Annie agreed to stay where she was and before ending the call, Annie and her father apologized for the way they had talked to each other, and ended the conversation with an I love you.

After she hung up the phone, Annie felt lost. It would be her second Christmas without Alex and the children, and the first Christmas she had ever spent without her parents. Most of all, she couldn't believe she had agreed to any of it.

After her tears subsided, Annie called Buddy and said, "Come on baby, let's go check on Bridger." The moment Annie walked into the room; Bridger knew something was very wrong.

"Are you OK?" he asked with concern.

Annie climbed up on the bed and sat opposite him. Looking down at her hands, she started to cry again. "They don't want me to come home for Christmas. I know they mean well," she sobbed, "but I feel so rejected."

Bridger reached out his arms to her and she accepted his embrace. As he held on to her, he said, "I'm sure they didn't want to hurt your feelings. But, you know what? I'm glad they don't want you to come home, because I know three people who are going to have the best Christmas ever!" Then he gently lifted her chin softly and forced her to look at him. "There's something I've wanted to ask you, and I'm thinking now is as good a time as any." He continued, "The word spread quickly that I'm still alive and anyway, I've been asked to accept an award."

"That's great, Bridge. What kind of an award?" Annie asked as she sniffled and wiped away her tears.

"Well, I'm kind of embarrassed. The word also got out that I spend time at the hospital with the kids and that I give donations to charity, and because of this, someone thinks I need to be given an award. There is going to be a big to-do at the City Civic Center. It's a holiday ball, complete with a big dinner and an awards ceremony. I know that I can't dance yet, but I would be more than honored if you would be my date. It's on New Year's Eve."

Instead of giving Bridger an answer, Annie just sat in silence. Bridger waited patiently, but after a few agonizing moments, he finally spoke up and said, "Annie, um, wow, I'm starting to melt here. Are you going to say anything?"

"Oh, um, I'm sorry. I guess that I was lost in my thoughts," Annie answered. "It's just, well, I haven't been asked to go on a date in a long time. I just don't know what to say. I hope this doesn't sound too stupid, but I was thinking that I wouldn't even know what to wear. I've never been to a holiday ball." After she answered, Annie looked at Bridger and felt bad. He had a look on his face that reminded her of a little boy, who had just asked for his first kiss and then been turned down. Without letting another moment pass, Annie said, "Of course, Bridger, I would love to go with you."

Bridger let out a big sigh of relief and said, "Awesome! It will be a great night! But there is something I want to ask you. You see, there is a reserved suite for us at a hotel next door to the center. It is going to be a late night, and I really don't want to be out on the roads, especially on New Year's Eve! I will be honest. I don't want to chance being on the roads with people who think they can drink and drive!"

"I understand completely. I just have one question. Will there be two beds?" Annie asked hesitantly.

"Of course, and I promise—now, wait a minute, haven't I been a perfect gentleman even though you've helped bathe and dress me from day one?" Bridger replied with a smile and a wink.

"I'm sorry, Bridger. I shouldn't have even asked. You have always been a gentleman," Annie answered back, smiling and yawning at the same time.

"Hey, why don't we skip the chess tonight and you go and get a good night's rest. You're going to need it! I think my mother forgot to tell you that she has a Christmas tree for every room, and I am not exaggerating!"

"Wonderful! It will be fun, and you know what? I think Buddy and I will take you up on that offer," Annie replied with another yawn as she moved off the bed.

After saying goodnight, Annie and Buddy walked to the door, as he watched them leave, Bridger couldn't help but wish they would stay.

When Annie reached the door, she turned back around and said, "Bridger, I think we are going to have a really good time on New Year's Eve! Thanks for asking me." Then she blew him a kiss and went to her room.

Chapter 15

It had been a long time since the Jones's house had enjoyed getting ready for the holidays. Together, Mary, Flora, Bridger, Annie, and Buddy decorated all day and then some. Annie and Bridger helped Tom put up the outside displays and lights. Since Bridger was still in his wheelchair, he was in charge of untangling all the lights. Annie and Tom had to hide behind the bushes and laugh several times when they heard him cussing about the tangled messes they handed him. Most of all, Bridger was shocked to find that his father, "Mr. Christmas," had known how to hang the lights but hadn't had a clue when it came to winding them up and storing them for the next year. Bridger thought the whole arrangement had been unfair, but he was a good sport anyway.

Annie told Mary over and over how beautiful everything looked. She fussed over all the beautiful treasures that Mary had collected over the years, and Mary beamed with pride. There were times, though, as she looked at the Christmas decorations, Annie couldn't help but think of her own Christmas treasures and memories. There were times it took every ounce of her strength not to totally fall apart. A certain smell, a sound, there were so many things that would remind her of other Christmases, and it was at those moments that Bridger seemed to sense her need and without knowing, he would get her through it. Each time she'd think to herself, "I'm going to tell Bridger, just not now, not before Christmas. I don't want him to think of such sadness, especially when he's doing so well. He's so looking forward to Christmas, and I don't want to burden him."

Flora brought back her tradition of Christmas baking and candy making. She seemed to bake from the time she woke up in the morning until the time she went to bed. Mary, Buddy, Bridger, and Annie were the official taste testers. They loved all of Flora's delicious creations, but after a while they started getting a bit worried about who was going to eat all of them. Annie suggested they make baskets for the neighbors, and so Annie, Bridger, and Mary decorated and filled baskets. When the baskets were ready, Annie, Bridger, and Buddy delivered them. The neighborhood was spread out since the houses hugged the coastline, but Annie was amazed at how close the people were. Most of them had lived there all of their adult lives. They had all raised their children together, and now, as senior citizens, they looked out for each other. Annie could totally understand why none of them had the desire to live anywhere else. It was such a beautiful place. Each home had their own little Garden of Eden at the edge of the sea.

Every one of Bridger's old neighbors would insist that Annie and Bridger come in and visit. Bridger had grown up with all of their children and they were all so excited to see him. They shared stories with Annie about Bridger's childhood. And all of the neighbors told her about how they had watched his career blossom, and how proud they were to tell the world that Bridger Jones had grown up right before their eyes. They all shared how they had prayed for Bridger, and more than once she heard, "Would you just look? This young man almost left us, and it's nothing more than a miracle that he's here with us today." The men would pat Bridger on the back, and the women would dot at their eyes, and Annie found herself crying each time the story was repeated.

After sharing things about Bridger's past, they would turn their attention to Annie. "Flora and Mary have said such good things about you." Then they would start to ask questions, "So you're from Milford, the place Mary's brother settled." Annie was OK with simple questions, but then unknowing they would start asking questions that made her feel uncomfortable, and being protective of her, Bridger would quickly draw the attention back to him or suggest they needed to go.

The decorating and the baskets were fun, but nothing was as special, as the presents, they bought for the children at the hospital. They spent many hours picking out the perfect gifts and then wrapping them with candy canes and Christmas whatnots. Bridger and Annie planned and organized a Christmas

Finally

Party at the hospital which included Mary, Flora, and Buddy. All of them wore Santa hats, and Buddy attended in a full, doggie, Santa Suit. Bridger thought that Buddy had been forced beyond the call of duty, but the kids loved it. On the way home, as they talked about how great the day had gone, they all had to laugh because Buddy became the star of the show, and had gotten far more attention than Santa!

Throughout December, Bridger did several local TV interviews and even one for a national sports program. He was excited when his old coach took the time to join him and talk of all the records they had broken together. When he was asked if he missed the game, Bridger had answered, "Of course I miss the game. I was good! But now, I understand that sometimes, God puts certain circumstances in your way. Sometimes you never figure out why, and then other times, it takes you a while to figure out just what he's doing. But it's all OK, because the most important thing that I've learned is that when you stop feeling like God's picking on you, and believe me I did, you start to see the big picture. I know that I will never play football again, but I have found there are so many other things in life for me to do, and they have become far more important to me than football ever was." As they watched the interview on television Mary, Flora, and Annie beamed with pride and wiped tears from their cheeks.

One afternoon during their weekly calls, Karen brought up the subject of Robert again. "Did you get to see him yet?"

"No, I really don't know how to go about it. The way Bridger reacted when I mentioned his name, suggested that they're not on speaking terms, and I totally forgot to ask Dr. Ray about him when he was here. Maybe I'll get around to seeing him one of these days," and then Annie changed the subject. She really wasn't too worried about seeing Robert again. She was quite happy to spend her time with Bridger. "You know, friend, the nights might be long, but the days are really busy. We still have some work to do with Bridger's therapy; he's really come a long way," Annie said.

With deep concern, Karen asked, "So how much longer is Bridger going to need you?"

"I think it's getting pretty close. Dad talked about coming up in February, but to be honest, I think, I'll be headed for home before then," Annie answered with the excitement in her voice fading toward the end of the sentence.

"Are you serious, girlfriend?" Karen shot back.

"I think so. What are you talking about?" Annie asked.

"All I hear is Bridger this and Bridger that. Bridger, Buddy and I went here, and Bridger, Buddy and I went there. I guess if you haven't figured out by now that you're crazy about the guy, who better than your best friend to tell you?" Karen said laughing.

"I'm crazy about the guy? Of course, Bridger and I have become really good friends," Annie replied slowly.

"Yep, you're crazy about the guy," Karen answered with a chuckle.

"Karen, I work for Bridger, and besides my husband has only been dead a little over a year, and I wouldn't even consider thinking about someone else," Annie snapped back at Karen. After she realized how harshly she had spoken, she was angry with herself.

"You just go ahead and be mad at me, but I'm the only one who has ever been totally honest with you, and you know it," Karen answered. "You just think about what I've said, and I'll talk to you later. I love you. Merry Christmas," and with that she hung up.

Annie couldn't believe what Karen had just said to her, and she couldn't believe that she had just hung up on her like that. *I'm so glad that I'm not going home,* Annie thought. *They are all driving me nuts! Same old stuff—they think they know me better than I know myself.* She was glad she hadn't mentioned her date to the Holiday Ball, because she knew that Karen would make far more out of it than necessary.

Christmas Eve turned out to be a very cold and rainy night, but they didn't seem to notice. They shared a wonderful dinner that Flora had prepared and then watched their favorite Christmas movies. They had decided to open their gifts on Christmas Eve, because Mary and Flora were worried about getting to church on time in the morning. Annie was feeling like she used to feel when Alex spoiled her by piling gifts around her. Although they had bought her too many gifts, she knew better than to say anything because she would have broken their hearts. Bridger insisted that Annie open his gifts last and so she waited patiently. Even Buddy had quite a few presents under the tree, but he didn't seem too interested in them. He was perfectly content to lie near the fireplace and chew on the hambone he was served at dinner. Annie's mother had made afghans for everyone, including Buddy. Her father had sent Bridger a large box of pine nuts that he had picked and roasted himself, and Annie was happy to see how excited Bridger was about the gift.

"I see you've had pine nuts before," she said.

"I've even been pine nut hunting, back when I was a kid. I used to go with Uncle Ray," he said with a mischievous grin.

Annie had asked Bridger to help her with her gifts for Flora and Mary. Secretly, she had asked Bridger to find childhood photos of Mary and Flora. Then she had made scrapbooks for each of them. As they both fussed and carried on over her gifts, she told them she would love to add to them if they would just supply her with more photos. Both were very excited and agreed to the offer, and they thanked Bridger for his detective work.

Annie was sitting quietly admiring her gifts of books, sweaters, and pajamas from Flora and Mary when Bridger wheeled himself over to the table where he had placed his gift for her. Then much to everyone's surprise, he stood up, picked up the beautifully wrapped box, and walked very slowly with the help of a cane to where Annie was sitting.

"I hope you like it!" he said with a grin from ear to ear.

It was hard to tell who was talking, because all three women started talking at once.

"Thank you, thank you, Jesus," Flora kept saying over and over.

Mary almost fell off the edge of her chair. "Bridger, you're walking. I can't believe it. Thank you, God. Thank you, God!"

But it was Annie's words that he waited to hear. With tears in her eyes, Annie said, "I knew you could. I knew you would!" And then she jumped up and gave him a hug that lasted a very, very, long time.

After moving to sit on the sofa together, Bridger smiled at Annie and asked, "Aren't you going to open my present?"

"Oh my gosh, Bridger, I just got my present! When did you start walking? I'm supposed to be your physical therapist. This is so wonderful!" Annie answered smiling. Bridger smiled back and then turned his attention back to the present. Still stunned, Annie moved her attention to the gift he had just handed her. "Well, I don't think I've ever seen such a beautifully wrapped present. It's almost a shame to open it!" After taking a few more moments to admire the gift, Annie slowly started to unwrap it. At first, she was speechless, and then she exclaimed, "Bridger, it's beautiful."

Without the help of his mother or Flora, Bridger had purchased Annie a designer gown and shoes. The floor-length gown was simple yet elegant, and most important to Bridger; it was the exact color of Annie's eyes.

Mary and Flora went on and on about how beautiful the dress was while at the same time thinking how unbelievable it was that Bridger had picked out something so exquisite!

Unable to contain his excitement, Bridger spoke up and said, "I thought you might need a new dress to wear on New Year's Eve." When he and the designer had gotten together, it had only taken Bridger seconds to show him the color he wanted. The designer had stewed and worried whether the color was right, but Bridger knew the exact shade of her eyes and hadn't doubted his choice for a moment. Oh, how he loved to look at her eyes.

"I love it. I can't wait to go. I've never worn anything like this," Annie said as she brushed her hands across the material of the dress.

"You will be the most beautiful woman there," Flora announced proudly and then added, "And my Bridger will be the most handsome man. Everyone will think you are the prince and princess."

"I'll bet we're more in the age range of the queen and king! But I'm so excited. Thank you so much!" Annie said, reaching over to give Bridger a kiss on the cheek, but he couldn't stop himself this time and turned his face to kiss her on the lips. She didn't pull away like he thought she might. Even though the kiss only lasted a moment, Flora and Mary could see it lasting a lifetime.

After opening the presents, Annie and Bridger scooted Mary and Flora off to bed and then tidied up the room. By the time Annie helped Bridger into bed and had got him his night meds, they were both yawning.

"You're still in a lot of pain, aren't you?" Annie asked.

"Yeah, but someday, it will all be worth it," Bridger answered.

"That day is getting closer and closer," Annie said.

Bridger quickly changed the subject. "I have one more present for you, but I wanted to give it to you when it was just you and me." Then he reached into the drawer of the nightstand.

"Bridger, you've done way too much for me. I feel like I should have done more for you," Annie said with protest.

"I love my new video games, and the Bible is beautiful. It's the best present I got. I just thought this would look real pretty with your dress," Bridger said as he handed Annie a small box. Once again, she unwrapped the present slowly, and when she lifted the lid, her beautiful eyes seemed to grow even larger as she gazed at the diamond tennis bracelet. He'd wanted to get her a necklace, but he'd figured out soon after she came that she never took the locket off. He knew it had something to do with the past, so he had picked out the bracelet.

"Bridger, you shouldn't have done this," Annie said as she looked at the gift. "It's gorgeous!"

"I wanted to. There really isn't anything that I could possibly do for you or buy for you to really show you how grateful I am for what you've done for me," Bridger said as he reached for the bracelet and placed it on her wrist.

"Again, thank you so much," Annie said. "But I think you give me far too much credit, Bridge. I wish I could begin to tell you how much you've done for me." In between her words, Annie paused and then started to cry. In between her tears, she added, "And I promise, one day, I will tell you."

Bridger reached out to take hold of her. "Remember what I said. I'm here when you're ready to tell me."

Annie liked it when Bridger held her; it felt so right, and then she thought of Alex. Bridger had gotten so he could tell when something was pulling her away. He didn't want to force her, and so he looked at her and said, "I guess I'd better get some sleep if I'm going to make it to church on time. Would you mind helping me get ready? I kind of wanted to surprise Mom and Flora. They'll probably both faint when they see I'm going to church. It's been so long, I'm afraid the walls might fall down. I'm just warning you; let me go in first so you guys don't get hurt," he said smiling, while at the same time anticipating the expressions of complete shock on his mother's and Flora's faces.

"Bridger, I'll be in at eight, and by the way, you don't have to worry if the church falls down because I really do know CPR!" Annie said smiling. Just as she went to stand up from the bed, Bridger gently pulled her back and gave her a kiss goodnight.

They all headed for church, leaving Buddy to hold down the fort. Mary and Flora beamed as they walked into the church behind Annie and Bridger.

Chapter 16

Annie planned and packed everything she could possibly think she or Bridger might need for one night.

Bridger laughed when he saw Annie packing the suitcases and asked, "Are we going for a night or a week?"

"My mom always said that you can never be too prepared!" Annie replied. After taking a second to think about what she had said, she added, "Wow! I just sounded exactly like my mother!"

"I can't wait to meet your mom and dad. Are they still planning to come and see us in February?" Bridger asked.

Without answering, Annie busied herself and checked the locks on the suitcases to make sure that they were secure.

"Annie, I know you're acting like you didn't hear me, and I am not quite sure why that question bothered you. But I do know that when something bothers you and you don't want to talk about it, because you squeeze your eyebrows together like this." And then Bridger did his best to mimic Annie's expression.

As Annie listened and watched Bridger, cold chills ran up her spine. Alex used to do and say the very same thing. She didn't know whether she should laugh or cry. She laughed.

"So you think that's funny! Come on, are you going to tell me why that question made you do your funny eye thing?"

"Well, um," she sighed.

"Annie, come on. Just tell me," he pleaded.

"OK, then. I'll be completely honest with you. I don't think you're going to need me in February. You're doing really well, Bridger. The only thing that I help you do now is your physical therapy. Every day you are doing more and more for yourself. So I think that I will be done before February."

"Hmm, but what if I think that I still need you?" Bridger asked.

Before Annie had a chance to answer, Mary and Flora bustled through the door and announced that Tom was coming to get their bags and that the limo driver had arrived.

Not knowing how she would have answered Bridger's question, Annie was thankful for the interruption. Bridger, on the other hand, wanted Annie to know that their conversation wasn't finished. Before Annie could head for the door, he took hold of her arm gently and said, "We will talk about this later."

When they reached the front door, Flora could sense Annie's apprehensions about leaving Buddy. She looked directly at Annie and said, "Don't you worry, dear, we'll take real good care of our little Buddy."

"Oh, I know. It's just that I haven't left him overnight for a while," Annie replied as she reached down to give Buddy one last kiss and scratch behind his ears.

Bridger was already sitting in the back of the limousine and was feeling very satisfied that he had managed to get in all by himself. After Annie had said her good-byes, she hurried to join him in the limo, and they were on their way.

After settling in, Annie looked at Bridger. "I've got to confess, I've never been in a limo before. It's beautiful, and I am so glad that I don't have to drive. I really don't mind driving, but after having lived in Milford for most of my life, I just haven't had to do much city driving."

Shaking his head, Bridger laughed and said, "Now you tell me!"

"Hey, I got you where you needed to go!" Annie answered, laughing as she gave him a little slap on the leg.

Bridger took hold of Annie's hand. "I hope you have a good time tonight."

"I'm just hoping that I don't disappoint you. I really haven't had much experience going to fancy parties either," Annie admitted as she looked down at the bracelet Bridger had given her.

Bridger lifted Annie's chin softly so that she would have to look at him. "It should be the other way around. I hope I don't disappoint you." After he had finished speaking, Bridger couldn't stop himself from giving Annie a kiss.

Finally

With their faces just inches apart, Annie smiled and said, "We're going to have a wonderful night."

The hotel and suite seemed like another world to Annie. She left Bridger with the hotel attendant and hurried to inspect their rooms. Bridger had to smile when he heard her call out, "Wow! This is gorgeous! Look at this bar! It's fully stocked, and I'm not talking about a mini fridge!"

Making his way into the room, Bridger said, "I guess it would be pretty hard for me to try and give you a sob story about how I lived out of a suitcase for nine months out of the year. But now that you've seen the kind of places I used to stay, I want you to know, I had to pay my dues before I did."

Moments later, the concierge knocked at the door and wanted to introduce himself and apologize that he had not been there to greet them and escort them to their room personally. "I have taken the privilege of chilling a bottle of champagne for you. If you would like, I can unpack your bags, arrange for some lunch, or if you would like, I can arrange for you to have a couple's massage. I just want you to know that I am here to make your stay with us comfortable."

After giving the man a chance to do his thing, Bridger thanked him and told him that they would call him if they needed him.

As soon as Annie heard the door close, she let out a little chuckle and said, "I guess, I'm just not used to someone putting away my things. You know, maybe we should have had him bring us something to eat. I'm kind of worried about you. You look so tired. We could have a little lunch, a nap, and by then, it will be just about time to get ready."

"That doesn't sound like much fun. Don't you want to go and see something?" Bridger asked.

Taking hold of the wheelchair, Annie knelt down so that she could be face to face with Bridger. "We didn't come so that I could go sightseeing. This is a big night for you, Bridge, and I'll feel better knowing you're ready and rested."

Annie and Bridger shared a fruit plate and a salad for lunch so that they wouldn't spoil their appetites for the banquet. After lunch, Bridger decided Annie was right and that he had better lie down. His eyes were closed as soon as his head hit the pillow. After covering him with an extra blanket that she'd found in the dresser, Annie turned and tried to walk away from the bed quietly. She hadn't even made a full turn when she felt Bridger take hold of her hand.

"Don't leave me." But as soon as he'd asked, Bridger knew that he had made her feel uncomfortable. "I just want to hold you. Please?"

Not sure of what she should do, Annie gave into the coaxing of Bridger's gentle pull. After lying down on the bed, she turned on her side and felt Bridger's strong arms pull her closer.

Two hours later, Annie was shaking Bridger, saying, "Bridger, wakeup. You have to get ready first. I'll help you, and then it might take me a while to get ready. I think the only two times I've dressed up this fancy was for my senior prom and my wedding," Annie said without even realizing that she'd mentioned that she had been married.

Bridger thought to himself, *Uncle Ray was right when he said that Annie would open the door when she was ready.* He was thankful even if it was just a crack."

Annie hurried to lay Bridger's tuxedo out on the bed. As she was fussing over things and making sure everything was ready, she said, "You're going to look so handsome. I'm afraid the ladies are going to steal you away from me tonight."

"Couldn't happen in a million years," Bridger replied.

"What couldn't happen in a million years?" Annie asked as she continued with her busywork.

"Ladies couldn't steal me away," he said.

Annie smiled as she walked toward him and then reached down and gave him a kiss on the cheek.

"I have a surprise for you," Bridger said taking hold of her hand.

Annie smiled, placed her hands on her hips, and replied, "More? I think you have done enough."

"I can never do enough for you. And you don't have to worry about me because I have arranged for the concierge to help me get ready, and I have arranged for you to go to the hotel spa to get a massage. Then there is a hairdresser, who will do your hair, and someone will be there to give you one of those manicure things," Bridger announced proudly and then added, "After all, you should be treated like royalty."

Annie sat back on the bed next to Bridger and gave him a kiss. Their kisses had always been simple, but this one was different. With their eyes fixed on each other, Annie smiled and said, "You are a very sweet and amazing man, Bridger Jones."

Finally

Annie made it back to the suite by 7:30 and made the concierge promise that Bridger would keep his eyes closed until she was in her bedroom. As Bridger waited patiently for her to walk through the door, he felt as if he were sixteen years old again. He had to give an acceptance speech in less than three hours, and all he could think about was Annie.

When she finally walked out of her room, Bridger knew there had only been one other time in his life he'd ever seen anything as beautiful. "Annie, you look so beautiful. I feel like I'm in a dream. I just can't believe you're really here with me. After all this time, you are really here with me."

With a radiant smile across her face, Annie walked toward Bridger and said, "Thank you for your compliments, and yes, I am really here with you, but if we are going to be on time, we had better get going."

As they made their way to the private elevator, Bridger looked at Annie and said, "Remember earlier when you said that one of the ladies would steal me away. I think it is going to be the other way around!"

Annie gave Bridger a sweet smile but deep down, she couldn't help feeling overwhelmed about meeting and mingling with Bridger's friends, and it didn't help knowing that many of them were celebrities from the world of sports. On the walk over to the hall, where the ball was being held, Annie did her best to stay a step behind the wheelchair just in case she was squeezing her eyebrows together. The last thing she wanted to do was cause Bridger to worry about her or do anything to ruin his big night.

As soon as Bridger and Annie entered the hall, a man spotted them and hurried over. After a quick man hug and several pats on the back, Bridger turned toward Annie. "Annie, I want you to meet my old friend, Dave Bennett."

Dave had looked so familiar, but it wasn't until he shook Annie's hand that she realized why. The man holding her hand, was the same man that she had looked at every time she had walked into Jack's bedroom. Dave had been Jack's idol, and he had decorated his room with picture after picture of Dave. Annie was able to hold it together during the conversation, but in her mind, she kept repeating over and over, *Oh Jack, this should have been you!*

After an hour of socializing, it was time to be seated in the banquet hall for dinner and the awards presentation. Following the dinner, everyone was to meet in the grand ballroom for the New Year's Eve celebration.

Annie had never seen or eaten such elegant food. Along with her other worries, she'd fretted over her table manners. But after watching the big, hungry, football players enjoy their meal, she decided she would do the same. Bridger continued to enjoy his time with his friends, but Annie was still the center of his attention. Many times throughout the dinner, he would reach over and whisper in her ear, telling her how beautiful she looked or question her to see if everything was OK.

Everyone had just about finished eating when the master of ceremonies started to present the awards. Several smaller awards were given out, and then Michael O'Conner, who just happened to be one of Annie's favorite pop singers performed.

"How cool is this? He's one of my favorites!" Annie said as she reached for Bridger's hand. "It's almost your turn. I'm so excited for you."

Each time Bridger looked at her, it seemed she grew more beautiful.

Once the entertainment was finished, the MC introduced Ed Summers. Ed had told Bridger and Annie earlier that he had been very excited when he'd been asked to present Bridger with his award.

"Folks, it is such an honor to be here tonight. When I was asked to give this award tonight, I can't tell you how much it meant to me. I've been a friend to this man for almost fifteen years. It was his second year of college, and he'd blown everyone's socks off by breaking every record set by any collegiate player. I had made it a point to get to watch him in action, and the first time that I watched this young man play; he broke two of his own records. It was totally amazing! No one could stop him, and as I watched him that first day, I knew the game of football would never be the same. This young man had more determination and more talent than any player I have ever witnessed." Ed paused for just a moment and reached in his pocket for a hankie. "After the game, I asked him to join me for dinner, and I've got to tell you, I was just as impressed with this young man, as we sat and ate dinner, as I had been watching him on the field that day."

Annie was feeling so excited for Bridger and proud to be with him that for a moment, she wished she had known him and been able to see all the wonderful things he'd done. But then the voice in her head shouted, *"That's stupid! If you'd known Bridger, how would you have known Alex?"* Deep down, she knew Alex would want her to be happy. He wouldn't want her to be sad and alone. Many times, she'd tried to think how it would have been if things had been the other way around and Alex had been the one left behind. She loved Alex, and she would have wanted him to be happy and go on with his life. But even when she could somehow come to accept that aspect of the situation, she would hear the voices start asking, "How could a mother who had truly loved her children possibly allow herself to go on without them?"

The touch of Bridger's hand brought her back from her own thoughts. She was thankful he hadn't noticed that she had drifted off. Annie was mad at herself for not listening to what Ed had just said. She forced her mind to listen to his voice, instead of the voice in her mind.

"And not only has he been an example on the field, but off. Bridger is responsible for organizing and making sure underprivileged children all over this county have attended summer camps. This man has shared his wealth by donating millions to charity. Bridger has always wanted to come across as a tiger, but I'm telling you, this guy is nothing but a teddy bear," Ed said, fighting back his tears. "A little over a year ago, I got a telephone call telling me that Bridger had been in a terrible accident. They didn't think he was going to make it. But you know what I said to myself? 'It's not his time.' And then I began to pray, just like I know all of you did, and today, I thank God every day for sparing the life of my good friend."

The audience remained captivated as they gave Ed a moment to pause. Then he reminisced with the audience again about some of Bridger's football days. "You know, it would take a man like Bridger to be able to walk again, when in all reality, he really shouldn't even be alive. This is a man of courage, determination, and charity. The first time he went out in public after many months of rehabilitation and seclusion, he chose to visit terminally-ill children. He truly is unbelievable. Folks, I proudly give this lifetime achievement award to Robert Bridger Jones. Come on up here, buddy."

Shit! Why in the hell did they use his given name? Nobody had called him Robert Bridger Jones since the day he graduated from high school. He was so worried about what Annie was thinking that he forgot to get up. When he looked over at her, he knew exactly what she would be doing, and, sure enough, she was squeezing her eyes together.

"Are you coming up here, or am I going to come to you?" Ed asked after a moment of waiting for Bridger to stand and make his way up to the stage. He tried to make it sound like a joke, but at the same time he was wondering what was taking Bridger so long.

Bridger needed to talk to Annie. He was worried about what she was thinking, but the crowd was cheering,, and he knew he had to go and accept the award. He would just have to explain everything later. Bridger stood, and Annie instinctively took his arm and gave him his cane, along with a kiss. It was slow-going for him as he made his way through the crowd, up the four stairs to the stage, and across the stage to the podium. As he did, the crowd gave him a standing ovation, and Annie proudly stood and joined them.

As she watched Bridger and clapped, she was trying to figure out what Ed had just said. *Robert Bridger Jones, Robert Bridger Jones, Robert Jones. He's little Robert. Why did I think Bridger was Robert's cousin? He's little Robert! Why didn't I know that? I am such an idiot!*

By the time Bridger made it to the microphone, he'd forgotten everything that he had planned to say.

"I really have never been one for speeches, and I know that must sound so cliché, but it's so true at this moment," he said, embarrassed by all the fuss. "I really want to tell you that I do appreciate the fact that you want to honor me like this. You know, football really was my life. When I was about fourteen, I was really struggling to find where I fit in. My dad figured I needed to get myself focused on something, so he gave me a football, and it didn't take me long to figure out that I wanted to be a quarterback. Not just any quarterback, I wanted to be the best quarterback. I would set a goal, reach it, and then go for the next one. I know that I was blessed with talent, but my dad taught me the game. He spent every spare moment of his life helping me. Looking back now, I know that the best part of all of it was that through it all, my dad became my best friend. My dad, mom, and my dear Flora were there to support me through every game. They were the greatest fans ever. Unfortunately, there came a point in my life where the game took over, and nothing else mattered! If I had only known then, what I know now. My talent was a gift from God, and because of his blessings, I've seen and done more things than I could have ever dreamed of, and given far more than I ever deserved. But I have to be honest with all of you; all of those wonderful things that Ed just said about me aren't exactly the truth. My agent and manager took care of the donations and the publicity that went along with it. He said it was important for me to look good to the public.

I'd show up, take a picture with some little kid, and then I'd get out of there as fast as I could. I really didn't care what was lined up as long as I didn't have to give up any valuable practice time. The only thing that mattered to me was the next game, the next season, and getting to the Super Bowl. But as I said before, I only wish I could have known what I know now. I would have been a better role model for my younger fans. I would have appreciated what I had been given. I would have given more of myself."

Bridger paused to wipe his hand across his face and wipe the tears that had fallen from his eyes. Then he looked at Annie and said. "The day my dad died, I was clear across the country playing in a playoff game, and you know what? We didn't even win. Now every day, I wake up, and I ask my dad to forgive me. And then, close to a year ago it was a given. I was going to the Super Bowl. The thing I wanted the most was just about in the palm of my hand. Every sportscaster in this country said it was a given. With Bridger Jones as the quarterback, my team had it. No contest! And then one night, I was just driving home, minding my own business, and along came a guy who'd had one too many beers. All I can remember is that suddenly, there were bright lights in front of me, and then I heard the sound of glass breaking.

The doctors told my family that they didn't think I'd make it, and you know what? I didn't give a damn if I did, because if I didn't have football, I didn't have a reason to be here. But God pulled a fast one on me, and he wouldn't let me die, so I sat in my chair and cursed him. Now you'd think he'd get tired of all the bad things that I had said, but you know what? He continued to love me despite myself. He loved me so much that he sent me an angel, and that angel's name is Annie." Bridger continued looking directly at Annie. Everyone in the audience turned to see his angel, but Annie didn't notice because all of her attention was on Bridger. After he cleared his throat, Bridger continued, "I was a mean, angry, Son-of-a-Gun. I went through just about every nurse in the Seattle area, and I would truly like to say at this moment that I am so sorry to all of those poor men and women for the way I acted. I am so sorry for the way that I treated anyone who had to have anything to do with me. Anyway, back to my angel. One afternoon, my mother told me that she and my Uncle Ray had arranged for a nurse from a little town in Utah, to come and try to help me. I'm telling you, I was no teddy bear. But Annie said that she had come to do a job and wasn't leaving until it was finished. All I know is one day, I was sitting in a chair feeling sorry for myself and the next thing I knew she had me going on picnics, decorating for Halloween, hanging Christmas lights, and visiting sick kids. I guess what I'm trying to say is that you can pat me on my back for playing a good game of football, but it is people like, Annie, who should be recognized and given the awards. The day the press saw me at the hospital, I had no idea that Annie was taking me to spend an afternoon with a bunch of sick children. To tell the truth, I wanted to turn and run the other way when I found out where we were going, but I couldn't run."

The crowd chuckled a little.

"Friends, just remember, it's OK to play football, but in the end, it's just a game. I dedicate this award to all the angels in the world, to those people who love and give of themselves unconditionally, and to those who know what life is really about. My friends, I just hope that we can all reach deep and try to make this world a better place by finding the angel within ourselves, and remember to take the time to tell the people you care about that you love them. Spend time with them because you might not be given another day."

Bridger held up his award and said, "This is for my dad, for my mom and Flora, and for my angel, whom I'm deeply in love with. Thank you! Thank you everyone!"

The audience again rose to a standing ovation. There were tears and shouts of admiration for Bridger as he made his way back to the table. Everyone wanted to congratulate him, but all he could see was the woman he loved, and the only thing he could think about was that he had loved her for as long as he could remember.

Annie's heart was torn. Bridger's words had touched her deeply, and as much as she wanted to dwell on the words, she could tell by looking at his face that he was in pain. She wanted to get to him and help him, but she held herself back, knowing he had to do this on his own. It seemed like it took forever for him to reach her. As soon as he reached her, their arms reached for each other. Bridger held her tight and had tears in his eyes when he said, "I meant it. I love you, Annie,"

In an instant they were surrounded by the crowd. Annie smiled graciously as she welcomed each of Bridger's friends and acquaintances, but at the same time, she continued to mull things over in her mind. She still couldn't believe she hadn't known he was Robert and wondered why he hadn't told her. Most of all, her heart was filled with emotion as she thought of his confession of love for her. Both Bridger and Annie wanted and needed to get away from the crowd. Thankfully, Bridger's football knowledge gave him the edge, and as soon as he saw a break, he took Annie by the hand and led her through the crowd and out to the balcony.

"Annie, come here and let me keep you warm," Bridger commanded gently.

It felt right to surrender to him. She sat on his lap, and he gently wrapped his coat around her and then his arms. The comfort of his arms felt right.

"I'm so sorry that I didn't tell you," Bridger said.

"Why are you sorry? I feel so stupid. Why did I think Robert was your cousin?" Annie asked.

"I don't know, but when I figured out you didn't know that I had been that pathetic, little, skinny runt who followed you around, I just figured I didn't need to tell you." He laughed then took on a more serious tone. "I know you're not ready to love me, but I meant what I said. I love you. I've loved you since the first day I saw you. You and your friend Karen were sitting with your feet dangling in the swimming pool."

Annie didn't say anything. He could see that she was trying to remember.

Bridger continued, "Uncle Ray dropped me off at the pool. He told me that I'd have a great time with all the kids. He told me how friendly all the kids in Milford were. You and Karen were the first two kids that I saw, and Darwin the Bully was the next. To be honest, I had my eyes on both of you, but when Darwin started picking on me, and you told him he'd better leave me alone or he'd have to deal with you, I was a goner. I was so impressed that a little skinny girl could scare a big kid like that. I probably drove you two nuts those two summers that I followed you around like a puppy," Bridger paused.

Annie looked into his eyes and once again saw the shy, little boy. "No, you didn't drive me nuts. We had fun," Annie said as she started to remember her carefree childhood days of summer.

"I was so mad at my mom and dad the next two summers. They wouldn't let me go visit Uncle Ray because I'd failed math and reading. They insisted that I stay home and attend summer school. It took me two years to figure out that I'd better work hard in school if I was going to get to see the girl that I loved," Bridger said as Annie turned to face him. "But by the time that I got back, you'd forgotten all about me and by then I was way too self-conscious to even say hi. So, I'd just sit at the pool, or the softball games, and wherever else I could get the chance to see you. I guess nowadays, I might even be considered a stalker. A couple of times, I talked myself into approaching you, and there would be this kid named Alex right by your side. I went every summer just to look at you. I even went to your senior prom. I took that poor girl; I think her name was Stephanie."

Finally, Annie said, "I remember. I tried to talk to you that first summer you came back, but you kept your head down, and you scared me. I thought you didn't want me to talk to you."

"I had a bloody nose, and I had toilet paper up one of my nostrils. There was no way that I was going to let you to see me like that!" Bridger laughed.

"I remember you at the senior prom. I do, but I didn't even think you knew who I was," Annie said.

"That poor girl, Stephanie, all I did was look at you. There was one moment when she went to the girls' room with her friend, and I saw you sitting all by yourself. I was two steps behind you and ready to ask you to dance."

Annie interrupted and finished Bridger's story. "And then, Alex borrowed the microphone from the lead singer and asked me to marry him."

"Yep, I just about melted right where I was. I left that poor girl at her senior prom. I went back to Uncle Ray's house, sat on the back porch, and cried like a baby. That was my last chance, and it was over. Needless to say, I've never been back to Milford."

"When my mom said that Uncle Ray had a friend who was a nurse, who needed something different, I just figured that I'd treat you like the rest and send you packing back to good old Milford. And then when you walked in my room, man I was so pissed. Of all the nurses in the world, I never figured it would be the girl, who broke my heart. That first day, when you got in my face, and I looked in your eyes, I felt like I was ten years old again." Bridger paused. "Annie, I know this is a lot to take in. Maybe we'd better go in. We can finish talking about this later." Bridger said, looking at his watch "It's just about time to ring in the New Year."

Annie had been very quiet as she'd sat listening to Bridger. She wondered if it was all real. As they reentered the ballroom, a slow song was playing. "Bridger, I'd love to dance with you," Annie said and then added, "If you feel like you can."

Finally

Bridger smiled as he pushed himself out of the wheelchair. Standing next to Annie with his arms around her he said, "Well, I'm not going to miss my chance this time around!"

As the music played, they held one another in a deep embrace. The large clock, which had been placed at the top of the stage, chimed loudly above the music. Though the crowd began shouts of revelry and began to sing a chorus of, "Auld Lang Synge," Bridger and Annie danced and remained lost in their embrace, oblivious to all the others. Bridger lowered his face to Annie's and together they welcomed the New Year with a deep and passionate kiss.

Chapter 17

Annie and Bridger were both happy to be back in the quiet of their suite, even though they were both feeling a bit awkward—Bridger for all of his confessions, and Annie because she needed time to absorb everything. In silence, Annie helped Bridger change and get into the bed. As she picked up a few of their things, she tried to think how she was going to get out of her dress. It was late, and she really didn't want to bother anyone in housekeeping. After giving the situation some thought, she decided she would just have to ask Bridger to help her.

Annie sat on the edge of the bed and with a shaky voice, said, "Bridger, would you mind unzipping my dress?"

Bridger reached and began to carefully pull the zipper down. His heart began to race as he gazed upon the bareness of her back. It was probably one of the best things he had ever laid his eyes on, while at the same moment, it was the worst. He knew she wasn't ready, and if he pushed her too fast, it could be the end of his dreams.

Annie continued to sit on the bed with her back exposed to him and her arms crisscrossed in the front to hold up the dress. She lowered her head and said, "I did marry Alex."

It wasn't exactly what Bridger had wanted to hear at the moment, but at least she was talking.

"I know. Uncle Ray was talking to my mom shortly after your wedding. I heard him tell her that you were the prettiest bride he had ever laid eyes on and that you were like the daughter he'd never had."

"So what else do you know about me?" Annie asked.

"That's about all that I could handle, and that's about the same time that I really threw myself into football. I didn't want to know any more. I didn't even go to any of my cousins weddings for fear that I would run into you," Bridger confessed as he traced the line of Annie's spine with his fingertips.

Responding to his touch, Annie turned to face Bridger. He stroked her face and ran his fingers through her hair. He was unable to stop himself and he reached over to kiss her. The kiss was passionate and for just a moment, Annie let herself go. It felt right; it felt good; but the feelings of guilt rushed in and stole away their passion. Annie started to cry and her body began to tremble. She was sorry that she'd ruined the moment; she was sorry that she'd betrayed Alex.

"Please don't cry, Annie. I won't push you. I won't hurt you, Annie, I promise," Bridger said, trying to reassure her. "Here, let's get my shirt on you." Bridger tenderly covered Annie's shoulders and buttoned it until she was covered. I'm going to order us some hot cocoa and we can watch a movie. It's been quite a night, and I know that you're tired."

Annie looked down at the way Bridger's shirt fit her and she thought of the many times that she'd slipped into Alex's shirts. What was Alex thinking of her? Silently she prayed, *Oh, God, please make this stop. I can't handle this battle in my mind anymore. Alex isn't here. Why can't I just go on?*

Bridger reached for the phone to order room service.

Annie stopped him by placing her hand on top of his. Then she took a deep breath and said, "Alex and I were married that summer, and then we moved to Salt Lake City. We lived there for about four years. We were the typical, young, married, college students, very poor, but very much in love and through it all, we learned to depend on each other." Annie paused for a moment as her mind took her back in time.

Bridger's heart was heavy as he thought, *why couldn't it have been me?*

"Alex graduated from the university with a teaching degree, and I graduated from nursing school. We were both so excited when he was accepted as

Finally

the English teacher in Milford. We wanted to go home, since neither of us had caught on to city life, and it wasn't long after we moved home that we had our first baby, our son, Jack. The day that I became a mother was the best day of my life. I loved everything about that little boy. Sometimes, Alex and I would just sit for hours and watch him. I can still remember how I couldn't believe that something so perfect had come from my body," Annie said.

As he listened to the story of her life, his mind became filled with the same questions that he'd had since she'd arrived, "Why wasn't she with them? Where were they?" Bridger held her hand as she continued to talk. She started talking about a morning that she and her family were having breakfast, and then she broke down. "I can't, I can't do this! I don't want to talk anymore," Annie's body began to tremble, and she was crying hysterically.

"It's OK. It's OK, Annie," Bridger said as he pulled her closer and wrapped his arms tightly around her. He held her until she fell into a troubled sleep, and he didn't let go until the morning. It was around eleven when Bridger woke up. Lying quietly by her side, Bridger watched as Annie slept. When she woke up, she seemed to be quiet and withdrawn from him. Now, he wasn't sure if he was glad that she'd opened the door or not. He sensed that she needed space, and so he gave it to her.

"I guess that we'd better get ready and head back home. I think you need to see the Bud Dog," Bridger said, trying to think of something that might cheer her up.

"You know me so well. I'm sorry, Bridger, last night was so great, and then I ruined it," Annie said as she started to get off the bed.

Bridger pulled her back and forced Annie to look directly into his eyes. "I meant what I said last night. All of this would have meant nothing without you."

Annie didn't speak but nodded her head and fell into Bridger's embrace. She needed his strength. As she lay in his arms, she thought of everything that had happened. It wasn't fair to Bridger if she couldn't give herself completely to him, and at that moment, she didn't know if she'd ever be able to do that.

It didn't take them long to get packed and get on the road for home. Bridger felt some hope when Annie decided to sit next to him in the limo. He placed his arms around her shoulders, and she moved closer to him and laid her head on his shoulder as they rode in silence.

She just needs more time, and then she'll be able to tell me what happened, Bridger thought to himself.

Bridger and Annie found two notes taped to the door when they got home. One from Flora telling them that she'd gone shopping to find something special for dinner, and one from Mary that said she was playing bridge at a friend's house. Both of them were excited to hear how the trip went, and they would be home as soon as they could. Annie was relieved that they were gone because she really wasn't up to facing anyone at the moment, and she knew that Flora and Mary were expecting to hear something totally different from what had happened.

It was a wonderful night, and I did have a great time, Annie thought to herself. *But why can't I let go?*

The moment Buddy heard the door open, he jumped from the chair he'd been resting on and made a mad dash for Bridger and Annie.

"We missed you, too, Buddy Boy," Bridger said as he reached down to scratch Buddy's ears.

Annie reached down and gave Buddy a hug too, but it didn't take long for the little dog to sense that something was wrong, and he began to follow Annie's every move.

After the driver had brought their bags in and Bridger was settled in a chair, Annie said, "Bridge, I really need to go for a walk. I need to think. Will you be OK if I go?"

"I'm fine. It's you that I'm worried about. Are you going to take the trail? I could go with you. I promise, I won't say a word," Bridger answered as he started to raise himself from his chair.

Annie walked toward the chair and gave him a gentle push so that he had to sit back down. "I think you need to rest. You pushed yourself pretty hard the last few days, and I'll be fine, really." Then she gently traced her fingers over his lips and kissed him good-bye.

Bridger had never felt so helpless. His mind kept replaying the picture of Annie as she walked out the door, and each time his heart felt as if it was being ripped apart. The first hour she was gone, Bridger thought he was going to lose his mind. He flipped the channels on the television one way and then the other. "How did I sit and watch this crap?" he asked himself out loud. His nerves had gotten the best of him, because when Annie's cell phone rang, he jumped a mile. Bridger wasn't sure if he should answer it, but he decided to take the chance.

"Oh my gosh, is this the famous Bridger Jones?" He heard the voice on the other end ask sarcastically.

"Speaking and I'll bet this is the World's Best and Greatest Friend, Karen," Bridger shot right back, trying to mimic her tone of voice.

"So how's it going up there, Robert?" Karen asked.

Bridger almost fell off out of his chair. Since she had left her phone behind, there was no way that Annie could have talked to Karen and told her what had happened. "If you've known all along that I was Robert, why didn't you tell her?" he asked.

Karen laughed and then answered, "Believe me, I gave her enough hints. I kept asking if her if she had seen her old friend, Robert? I can't believe that Annie didn't figure it out, and to be honest, I don't know why I didn't tell her. I guess that I just figured you would tell her when you were ready. Annie didn't have to watch sports like I do, because Alex wasn't into sports, unlike my husband. But I've just got to tell you that you're Matt's favorite sports hero. I've followed your career for years. I can't believe that Annie didn't at least remember you from your underpants commercial. I've just got to tell you—you did look awful good in those shorts! All kidding aside, Robert, I do want you to know that you've been in our prayers from the moment that we heard about your accident. Our entire church congregation prayed for you. In fact, we were saying a lot of prayers for Annie at that time, too. Isn't life weird sometimes? So tell me, are you still madly in love with my best friend?" When Bridger didn't answer, Karen didn't know what to say. "Oh, come on, don't be such a grump," Karen coaxed as she tried to get Bridger to say something.

Finally, Bridger answered, "You tell me what happened to Alex and Annie's children, and I'll tell you how much I love her."

"You know that I can't do that, and I can't believe that she hasn't told you. What am I going to do with her?" Karen said while at the same time trying to figure out how to help her friend. "You know she loves you too! Bridger, believe me, she is just scared. If I were in Annie's shoes, I don't think that I could have done what she's done."

Bridger was just starting to think that he liked Karen, when she turned the conversation around and said, "So I hear that she's turned you into a champion scrapbooker! I hear that you two made some great books. Sounds like fun!"

"Are you serious—scrapbooks? You're really helping me here!" Bridger growled, unable to control his irritation.

"Bridger, I really am trying to help you; if only you would listen to what I'm saying. Think about it. Why would someone just suddenly be an expert at making scrapbooks? Wouldn't she have to have some experience? Wouldn't she have to have some scrapbooks of her own?" Karen retorted with her own frustration.

"You are crazier than I remember," Bridger commented, remembering how much Karen had bugged him when they were young.

"And you know what, Robert? You're a lot dumber than I remember," Karen growled back. "I just want you to know that I wouldn't even be wasting my time on you, if I hadn't figured out that Annie loves you so much. I can't betray my friend's trust, but if you will try and clear your marshmallow head, I'll try and give you a few more hints as to how you might be able find out about what happened to Annie. I'll just bet that if I looked at your scrapbook, I would be looking at the story of your career, your life! And one more thing—did you know that sometimes you have to open a door to look in a scrapbook. I really don't think I can make it any clearer than that!"

Karen wanted to scream, and at the same moment, Bridger was wondering why such a sweet woman like Annie had stayed friends with such an obnoxious person. He was also wondering if everyone from Milford, gave advice about life that included an analogy about doors. First, Uncle Ray and now Karen, and then it hit him!

"Annie has scrapbooks in her room? Is that what you are saying?" Bridger asked. He suddenly felt ashamed of himself for the way he had just spoken to Karen. He was starting to understand that she really was trying to help him. "I can't just go snooping about in her room."

Finally

Karen quickly replied, "You can, if you really love her and if you really want to help her. Look, I have to go. I'm praying for the both of you."

Then before Bridger could say anything else, she hung up. Bridger couldn't get to the second level fast enough. He quickly found the master set of keys his mother used when the house had been a bed-and-breakfast. The keys weren't marked, and so he worked quickly and tried each key to see which one would open Annie's door. His heart filled with disappointment when he reached the last key and the lock didn't turn. In frustration he hit his hand against the door, and it opened. "You idiot; it wasn't even locked," he shouted out loud and then hurried into the room to look for the scrapbooks. His eyes quickly scanned the room. It was exactly as he remembered except for the photos. The first photo that caught his eye was of a handsome little boy who looked exactly like Annie. It had to be Jack! Then there were photos of two beautiful little girls. The older girl was beautiful and reminded him of Alex, and the little one's smile tugged at his heart like no other smile ever had. But when he looked at the wedding photos of Annie and Alex, his heart filled with jealousy.

"If you loved her so much, where are you, Alex? What have you done to make her so afraid to live, to love?" Bridger asked out loud. Bridger knew he needed to focus, and he knew he wasn't helping Annie by standing in her room yelling at a photo of Alex. His heart started to pound even faster when he thought of what she might do if she caught him in her room. It was at that moment, his eyes caught sight of the opened closet door and the scrapbooks that lined the shelves. He maneuvered the wheelchair closer and then held onto the wall. He let his body slide down to the floor. He couldn't believe how many books she'd made. He began to run his finger over the back of the books as he hurried to read each title. He picked up the one that was titled, *Annie and Alex* and underneath their names she had written, January-September, 2004. "This has to be the one!" he said out loud.

He scanned through the pages quickly, each page only a reminder of things that he had only dreamed about. "Why do you have to be so selfish? This isn't about you; now get on with what you have to do," he said to himself. Bridger's frustration grew because the only thing he could figure out was that Annie's life had been picture perfect until he turned the next page.

Tragedy for the Little Town of Milford, Utah:
Overloaded Semi Kills Five
Semi Driver, Father, Son, and Two Daughters

Bridger had to force himself to take several deep breaths to keep from throwing up. He couldn't believe it. The sorrow in his heart was almost unbearable as he cried, "Oh Annie, I'm so sorry. I'm so sorry."

"What are you doing, Bridger?" Mary asked.

Mary had returned home to find Bridger and Annie's bags left at the door. Instantly she knew something was wrong and began to look for them.

"I had to, Mom," Bridger answered in despair. "She tried to tell me, but she couldn't, and none of you would tell me. I thought if I could find out what had happened to her, I could help her. I've been so selfish. I was so happy that fate had brought her to me. Annie is such a good person. She didn't deserve this, Mom. I love her so much. What can I do to help her?"

Mary gently took her son's face in her hands and lifted it so that he would have to look her in the eyes. "You know, Bridger, your father and I always worried that you didn't understand what life was really about, but seeing you right now, I could leave this earth and I'd know that you'd be just fine. I just want you to know that I'm so proud to have you as my son and that I love you so very much," Mary said as she reached to embrace him. Then she pulled away and said, "Bridge, I've been here long enough to know, we're not supposed to try and outguess why God does what he does or doesn't do, but when Ray called and said Annie was coming, I thought that it was because you needed her, but now I understand. She's here because she needs you."

Mary helped Bridger to his chair, and then they hurried down to the first floor. By the time Bridger got to the ramp, his mother and Flora were waiting with for him. The sky was now filled with dark heavy clouds and a chilly wind had come up. Flora was holding a bag filled with a flashlight, blankets, and a thermos of hot cocoa. Bridger's heart swelled with love when he looked at their faces. He would never understand why God had blessed him with such wonderful mothers, but one thing he knew for certain, he would always be grateful. "I'd better hurry," Bridger said as he reached for the bag.

Finally

Flora hurried to give him a hug. "It's going to be OK, Bridge. I knew the moment Dr. Ray called and said that she was coming that everything would be OK."

His mother followed right behind Flora. After giving her son a hug, she told him that she had put Annie's cell phone in the bag, and if he needed anything, they'd be waiting by the phone.

Bridger headed the chair in the direction of the walking trail. He just knew that's where he would find her. As he made his way down the trail, he prayed that God would keep her safe. When he reached the picnic area, his heart sank. He couldn't see her anywhere. The sky was getting darker and the wind was getting colder. He moved the chair to the edge of the pavement and scanned the rocky shoreline. It felt like an eternity, but in reality, it was only seconds later that his eyes caught sight of a little black figure. Buddy looked toward him but didn't make a sound. Bridger frantically scanned the area near Buddy and finally caught sight of Annie. She was sitting with her back against a rock, her legs were drawn in, and her head down. He knew if he was going to reach her, he would have to walk. The unevenness of the sand and the gusts of wind made it tough for him to maneuver as he made his way across the beach, but every step was worth it when she was in his grasp.

Annie didn't even look up. She needed him, and she knew he would come. As soon as Bridger touched her shoulder, she scooted forward to make room for him. Bridger lowered himself until his back was against the rock, and then Annie moved back until her body fit tightly against his.

Bridger threw the blanket over his shoulder and then wrapped his arms around Annie. He let go for just a moment to pour a cup of hot cocoa. Huddled together, they watched the sea as the wind hurled the waves against the shoreline, and in silence they took turns sipping the cup of cocoa. Knowing his beloved Annie was safe in the arms of the man who loved her, Buddy decided to head for home.

Annie was the first to break the silence, though her voice was hardly audible. "It was my fault. All of it was my fault, Bridge."

Bridger couldn't understand. Why would Annie blame herself? She wasn't even with them. Every one of the articles had said that the cause of the accident had been an overloaded truck.

"You see, it was my birthday. They had gone to Cedar City to get presents for me. If they hadn't gone to Cedar, they wouldn't have died. Do you understand? It was my fault! Oh God in heaven, it was my fault!" Finally, Annie let go and told Bridger every moment of that fateful day and continued to tell him about the rest of her life up until the day she had left to come to the Northwest.

When Annie ran out of words, Bridger held her closer, knowing that he had no words of comfort to give her that she hadn't heard before, and then he did something he had never done before. He prayed for her out loud. When he was finished, Bridger said, "Annie, do you remember when you told me that you believed with all your heart that God didn't waste anything?"

Annie nodded her head several times to answer yes.

"As long as we're alive, we'll never know why God chose to take your family home, but I know with all my heart that he has brought us together because he loves us, and I know with all my heart that I love you, Annie. I have always loved you, and I know that I love you more than life itself, because if God would take my life in exchange for Alex and your children, I would do it in a second. I would do anything to have spared you this pain."

As Annie listened to Bridger, her heart ached when he told her that he would have given his life so that she could still be with her family, and it was at that moment, she realized just how much she loved Bridger. Admitting that she loved him sent terror through her body.

"Annie, talk to me. Tell me what you're thinking," he pleaded.

"I'm so scared Bridger. I'm scared to love you. What if something happens to you? Don't you understand? I couldn't take it if something happened to you! I couldn't go through that again," she cried.

So that was it. Not only was she blaming herself for her family's deaths, but she was afraid to love again. Bridger knew that he couldn't promise Annie that nothing would happen to him, but he understood her fears. "Annie, you know that I can't promise you that something won't happen to me. All I can promise you is that I will spend every minute of the rest of my life loving you."

At that same moment the clouds opened up and the raindrops began to fall. Bridger pulled the second blanket over their heads. Annie didn't say anything but instead of taking her silence as rejection, he gave her time to think things out.

"Bridger, I need to go home," Annie said quietly.

Finally

"OK, if that's what you want to do. We'll head back," Bridger said reaching for the rock to standup.

Annie pulled him back. "No, what I mean is that I need to go home, to Milford."

"What? Why?" Bridger asked, trying not to lose it and at the same time thinking to himself, he was going to lose her again.

When Annie turned around to face Bridger, she could see the fear in his eyes. She lifted her hand to touch his face and said, "I have to be honest. I left everything in my life just as it was before the accident, hoping that when I returned everything would be just as it was before. I know I have lived through hell on earth, but today, you helped me to see that it's time for me to stop living that way. I'm still alive. Things are never going to be as they were before, but now that I understand that, I need to go home."

Before Annie could finish, Bridger interrupted her and pleaded, "I'll go with you."

"No. I..." She tried to say more, but Bridger interrupted her again.

With tears in his eyes, Bridger said softly, "I've told you that I'd be here when you were ready, but if..."

Annie moved her hand from his cheek to his lips and said, "Bridge, please, let me finish. There are things I have to do, and if you can't wait, I will understand."

"Annie, haven't you heard a word I've said? I have spent my whole life loving you, and as crazy as this sounds, I didn't even realize it myself until I saw you again. I've compared every woman that I ever tried to have a relationship with to you, and I'll wait the rest of my life if that's what it takes."

It felt completely natural when Annie leaned forward to kiss Bridger. The kiss was long and passionate, and it felt so right.

Annie took hold of Bridger's hands and said, "I still have to go home, and it wouldn't be fair to you if I asked you to come with me. Bridger, if I'm ever going to be able to love you the way you deserve to be loved, I need to let go, and I can't do that if I don't go home."

Chapter 18

It didn't take Annie long to decide that the sooner she went home, the sooner she could think about coming back, and it was only a matter of days before she was ready to go. On the morning of her flight, Annie got up extra early and quietly made her way to the kitchen to get a cup of tea.

Just as she was walking through the doorway, she heard Flora's sweet little voice say, "Annie, I was hoping you would come for your morning tea. Come and sit at the table and have your tea with me."

As she watched Flora fix the tea, Annie couldn't believe how much she had grown to love Flora and Mary, and as she looked around the kitchen, she was amazed at how much the house felt like home.

"Annie, I want to tell you something before you go," Flora said as she pulled the chair out to sit on. As soon as she sat down, she took Annie's hand and continued. "Did you know that I was married for almost twenty years? I was only fifteen when I fell in love and married my Tony, but that was OK, because it was different then. My Tony and I had our own farm in Mexico. I was a momma too! God didn't bless me with my Arturo until I was almost thirty. Oh my, he was a beautiful baby. Everyone who saw him would stop and fuss over him, and oh my goodness, he was such good baby. We were so very happy on our little farm. But like you Annie, God took my family home. One night, I waited for Tony and Arturo to come home. They had gone to town to get a part for a broken water pipe. The later it got, the more scared I became. I knew something was very wrong. It was too late for my Tony to be out. You see, he did not see very well in the dark. I waited and I waited, but they didn't come home. They too were in a bad automobile accident. When Mary told me your story, I almost felt as if my heart had been ripped again from me, oh, to know such pain." Flora paused to wipe the corner of her eyes with the back of her hand.

"I know you have to go home, but your Flora wants you to choose to love again. Don't be afraid, my beautiful friend. Don't do like I did. Now, don't get me wrong. I love this family, and I thank God every night for the missionaries who told Dr. Ray about me. I have been very happy here. But late at night, I often think of the man who loved me after my Tony died. He was such a sweet man, but I was too afraid to give my heart. You understand, don't you? Don't be like me, Annie. Don't be afraid to love. You will miss too much. Some people are meant to be alone. You, my friend, are not. You are meant to love and to be loved!" Flora placed her hands gently on Annie's cheeks and forced her to look directly into her eyes. "You and Bridger, you'll be fine. I pray for both of you. It is so wonderful to see what God has done already."

Through her tears, all Annie could do was smile and say, "Thank you, Flora."

The next few hours passed quickly, and the taxi pulled in at 10:00 a.m.—right on time. Mary, Flora, and Bridger had tried and tried to get Annie to let them take her to the airport, but she insisted that she and Buddy would be fine. "Good-byes are hard enough at the front door," she had told them.

Bridger had argued for days that he could arrange to have a private jet take her home, but Annie wasn't having anything to do with that idea. In her argument, she had told him over and over that the runway at the little Milford Airport was only made for small airplanes, and there was no way she was going to fly to Milford in a Learjet and then crash because the runway was too small!

Buddy looked forlorn in the pet carrier when Tom carried him to the taxi, and Bridger walked behind them carrying one of Annie's bags. But as sad as Mary and Flora were feeling about Annie's departure, they were overjoyed at the fact that Bridger was walking more and more each day. After Bridger had put the bag in the trunk, they all stood by the opened door of the taxicab, though no one made any attempt to say good-bye. Bridger reached through the carrier and scratched Buddy's neck, hoping to give him some encouragement about his situation. "You're quite the dog, Bud. Sometimes, I swear you're more human than you are canine. You look after our girl, OK? I'm depending on you."

Right on cue, Buddy lifted his head and let out a little bark as if to say, "Of course!"

Finally, Annie said her good-byes to Tom, Flora, and Mary, and then she turned to Bridger. The two stood facing each other, and even though the others were circled around them, it felt like they were the only two souls in the universe. One was about to say, "I'm going with you," and the other, "Come with me," but in the end, they both kept their words to themselves. Bridger knew that she needed this time, and Annie thought it would be cruel and unfair to ask Bridger to watch her say good-bye to the past.

Bridger took hold of Annie's hands, "I'll call you," he said.

"I'll be waiting," Annie answered, trying to smile.

Taking her face in his hand, Bridger reached to kiss her. When the kiss ended, both reached to wipe the other's tears away.

"I can't believe how much I've cried since I met you," Bridger said as he cleared his throat.

Doing her best not to break down, Annie said, "They say it's good for a man to cry."

"Why?" he asked.

"Oh, heck, I don't know. It's just one of those things they say, whoever they are," Annie said as she buried her head in Bridger's chest.

"I love you, Annie. Pease remember that," Bridger whispered in her ear.

Closing her eyes, she nodded to gesture that she would. When Annie opened her eyes, she could see that the cab driver was getting anxious, and she knew that she had to go or she would miss her flight. Annie gave Bridger one last kiss and then she left.

Flora took hold of Bridger's arm and said, "You know, she left her scrapbooks here. I just know that she will come back to us."

After a two-hour layover and a thirty-minute delay in Salt Lake City, Annie was glad to hear the announcement that the passengers who were traveling to Cedar City, could board the plane. After quickly making her way to her seat, Annie looked out the window and began to watch for the luggage cart. She felt instant relief the moment she saw the little tan cage being loaded onto the plane, seconded by a strong feeling of guilt. *Poor Buddy, I'll have to make this up to him,* she thought.

Just after the plane took off, Annie closed her eyes, thinking she would rest for a moment and was very surprised when she woke up almost thirty minutes later. Feeling restless and wanting the flight to be over, she rummaged through her backpack several times to pass the time. Annie was thankful when the captain made the announcement that the plane was going to begin its descent and that they would be landing at the Cedar City airport in fifteen minutes. She even got a little tearful when he mentioned that the little town to the right of the plane was Milford, Utah. Looking out the window, Annie's heart warmed when she looked below and saw home. A shimmer of light caught her eyes, and she knew instantly that the light had come from the old water tower. Even though the tower was now empty of water and retired, it stood proud and tall over its sleepy little town. It had always reminded Annie of a lighthouse, only the desert was its sea, and just like a lighthouse, its reflection was a beacon to guide and welcome you home from any direction.

After the plane landed, Annie waited patiently for the other passengers to make their way to the exit. She took advantage of the moment to stretch before she retrieved her bags. As she stepped from the plane, the south wind rushed to greet her. Annie couldn't believe how mild the temperature felt. Her father had mentioned to her during their telephone conversations that it had been a mild winter, but this was far warmer than she'd been expecting. Standing at the bottom of the steps of the plane, Annie removed her jacket and tied it around her waist while she waited for the crew to get Buddy. She let go a sigh of relief when she saw his carrier. The moment Buddy made eye contact with her; she could see his little body shake with excitement.

As Annie walked toward the gates, she looked at the large windows, and her heart filled with joy when she caught sight of her parents. They were standing next to Joe, Gladys, Karen, her children, Sherri and the boys—all lined up to meet her. The instant she walked through the door, she was greeted with hugs and kisses. Taking a moment to step back and get a good look at everyone, Annie was amazed at how much all the kids had grown. Unfortunately, there was no time to visit, because Annie's father started to usher everyone to the front door, while at the same time, announcing that there would be plenty of time for catching up while they ate lunch at Annie's favorite pizza parlor.

Finally

The next two hours seemed to fly by as the group of friends and family enjoyed eating and visiting with each other. They decided it was time to leave when the waitress started clearing her throat every time she cleared the tables that were next to theirs. As excited as everyone was to see her, everyone understood that Annie was anxious to get home, and they quickly said their goodbyes along with promises to visit soon. After Annie and Buddy were settled in the back seat of her father's car, Annie spent the first five minutes of the ride home apologizing to Buddy.

Laughing, her father joined in the conversation, "Well, if you'd have taken Bridger's offer to fly home in the private jet, Buddy could have flown in a recliner!"

"Yes, but we aren't going to tell Buddy that, are we, Dad?" Annie added with laughter.

After the laughter subsided, her mother spoke up and said, "Annie, I know you told us that you want to stay at your own house, but honey, do you really think that's such a good idea?"

Annie took a deep breath and answered, "You know, Mom and Dad, I'm torn. I really want to stay with you guys. I've missed you both so much, but on the other hand, I want to stay at my house because honestly, it's going to be the last time that I will call that house, my home."

"What are you saying, Annie? Are you planning on selling your house?" her father asked.

"Let's just put it this way: I am going to make some changes and I promise as soon as I get things worked out, you two will be the first to know the details," she answered.

"OK, if that's what you want," her father said as he glanced into the rearview mirror. "You know, I didn't get a chance to tell you how great you look! And one more thing, I've just got to say, it is so good to see my little girl really smile again!"

"The same back at you, Dad. It's been awhile since I've seen a smile like the one on your face," Annie answered back with a smile and a wink.

After the accident, Annie and her parents had developed a habit of avoiding the Minersville Highway and the accident site when they needed to travel south. It was less painful for them to drive to Beaver and take I-15 South, even if it took them an extra twenty minutes to get to Cedar City, but just as her father was about to exit to I-15 N, Annie asked her dad if they could take the highway home.

Her father and mother were both hesitant but decided to do as Annie asked.

As they neared the mountain pass, Annie's mother asked her if she wanted to stop.

"No, I don't think so," Annie answered, holding Buddy a bit tighter for support.

Shortly after the accident, Karen had made five white crosses and had placed them near the milepost where it had happened. When they were almost to the accident sight, Annie's father released his foot from the accelerator and slowed down to forty miles an hour. As they passed, she was able to read each name; Alex, Jack, Kara, Molly, and Ty. Annie's body filled with relief when the images that flashed through her mind were not bodies scattered among a tangled wreck but that of her family as they had gathered happily at the kitchen table.

She whispered, "Thank you Lord."

After passing through the little town of Minersville, Barney said, "I hope we don't have to wait for a train."

"Oh Dad, you always say that," Annie said.

"Besides, nobody has to wait for trains anymore since they built the overpass," Lil added as she reached to affectionately pat her husband on the cheek.

After crossing over the overpass, Barney decided to head down Main Street and up Center Street before proceeding to Annie's house. Barney turned left at 700 South and pointed over at the hotel and diner. "Guess what I heard yesterday, when I was getting the mail. The news around town is that there's a big-time New York reporter staying there. She's here doing a weekly newspaper article on the Bennett twins. She's going to write about their lives while she tags along with them at the ranch, and then she is going to travel the rodeo circuit with them. They say she used to write a column about New York socialites and fashion. She's supposed to be here a year but the bet is that she won't last a month. All the guys said that she's a real looker and that Spruce and Cooper both got it bad for her. Then someone, I won't say why, piped up and said that he can't understand why because she's such a bit—ah, I meant witch. She's only been here two weeks, but she has managed to offend everyone that she's come close to. I just don't understand it, a fancy girl like that trying to write about those two cowboys."

"Barney, you have no right to talk like that about a young girl that you've never met! Besides, you silly old men should not be yapping about things that are none of your business. Poor girl doesn't stand a chance. I'm sure she's suffering from some real culture shock if she's from New York," Lil snapped back as she rolled her eyes and turned around to look at Annie for support.

At the moment, Annie had wished her mother hadn't stopped her father from sharing the talk from around town, because the closer she got to the house, the more anxious she began to feel. The small talk had been keeping her mind from thinking about the things she had to face. Buddy must have been feeling the same way, too, because the moment he recognized the neighborhood, he began to wiggle and bark excitedly.

After pulling into the driveway, her father reached for her garage door opener that was on the dashboard.

Before they opened their doors, Lil said, "Gladys and I put a few fresh groceries in your refrigerator and pantry for you. We figured you might need a few things."

"As always, Mom, you're the best," Annie said staring as the garage door opened.

Turning around to face her daughter, Lil said, "It's so good to have you home with us, honey, even if it's for just a little while."

"Here's your opener, sweetheart. I had the truck tuned up, and she's running great, but you know, if you want, I'd be glad to drive you around when you need to run your errands."

"Thanks, guys, for everything," Annie said and then reached to pat both of their shoulders.

They all turned to open their doors at the same time and then headed into the house. After turning the doorknob and taking two steps into the main hall, Annie was unable to move. She thought that she had prepared herself for the moment, but she hadn't. The moment she walked through the door and took in the familiar scent of her home, her mind and body was filled with a deep longing for her husband and children.

In an instant, she broke down, "Oh, I miss them so much."

"We know, we know, sweetheart," her mother said, reaching to hold her.

"Annie, I know we've already asked you this, but are you sure that you want to stay here?" her father asked again as he wrapped his arms around his wife and daughter to complete the hug.

It felt so good to have her parents' arms around her. She had missed them terribly but their hug was cut short by the ringing of Annie's cell phone. Both her parents jumped but Annie wasn't surprised at all. She was sure it was Bridger, and she couldn't wait to hear his voice. She needed to hear his voice.

With her parents still circled around her, Annie reached in the pocket of her jacket to get her phone and attempted to try and compose herself. She took in a deep breath and hurried to wipe the tears from her face with her sleeve.

"I knew it was you!" she answered.

Looking at her parents as she listened to the voice on the other end; she nodded with her head to let them know that she was all right and mouthed the words, "its Bridger." Barney and Lil wanted to give their daughter some privacy, so they hurried back to the garage to get her bags.

Bridger's voice was heavy with concern. "I should have come with you. I can tell by the sound of your voice that you've been crying."

"I knew this was going to be hard, but I guess that it was harder than I expected. We just barely walked through the door and to be honest, I was overwhelmed, but now that I've heard your voice, I'm going to be OK," she answered.

Not wanting Annie to have to end her conversation with Bridger, Barney and Lil whispered that they would stop by later as they headed back to the garage.

"How was your flight, and how did the Bud Dog do? Is he through sulking?" Bridger asked teasingly.

As if he knew someone was giving him some sympathy, Buddy walked around the corner right on cue, with his little nose sniffing everything in sight. Annie bent down to give him a scratch on the neck as she answered Bridger with a chuckle, "Oh, we both survived but I think Bud is going to milk this one for all he can. And I really don't think that I can blame him."

"What time are you going to head over to your parents' house?" Bridger asked before he added, "You're still planning on staying at your parents' place, aren't you?"

Finally

"It's so crazy that you should ask but during the flight, I got to thinking that if I stayed here, I could get a few things started tonight. Now, I don't want you to worry; because I'll be just fine. After all, I've got the Bud Dog with me," Annie answered trying to reassure Bridger.

"Ah man, it hasn't even been a day and I feel like you've been gone forever," he added.

Tired from leaning against the wall, Annie let herself fall until her bottom landed on the carpet. "Well then, now I know that I have made the right decision. Her voice started to sound more enthusiastic as she continued with her news. "Oh, I've got something to tell you. When we were having lunch, Gladys told me that my oldest niece, Courtney, is going to be getting married this summer. I think, I've told you about Courtney and Cole. Alex always had such a soft spot for Courtney."

Bridger couldn't believe how excited Annie sounded as she talked about her niece and the wedding, but he couldn't help feeling disappointed that she hadn't mentioned anything about the fact that he had said that it had felt like forever since she'd been gone.

"Cole has been hired to teach the sixth grade, and they have been looking for a place to live," Annie was talking so fast now that she could hardly keep up with her own words. "It got me thinking about when Alex and I moved back home and how hard it was for us to save up for the down payment on our house. You know what? I don't need this house anymore. I've decided that I'm going to give my house to Courtney and Cole. Well, that is, if they want it. I want to leave most of the furniture, but I am going to have to go through everything. I need to share some things with my family and friends. Of course, there are things I'll want to keep. Oh, Bridge, I know that I am rambling, but this feels so right. It's been so long since I've felt like this. Oh, and before I forget, there is something I wanted to ask you. I was wondering, if it wasn't too much trouble, if you would check into finding me a storage rental that is close by your mother's house. I'll need somewhere to keep my stuff until I get things figured out."

She wants me to find a storage place close by. She's coming back! She's really coming back! Bridger thought to himself as Annie continued to talk. He could hardly believe what she had just said to him. When his mind caught up with all that she was saying, he had to interrupt, "Don't you mean, when *we* figure things out?" As soon as he said it, he was angry with himself. Bridger thought his heart was going to stop as he waited for her to reply. His knuckles were gripping the phone so tightly that they turned white. *What did you say that for? Why are you pushing her?* He asked himself.

"I am sorry because that is exactly what I meant," Annie answered. The words she'd said were totally unexpected; yet he didn't quite get what she was trying to say to him.

"Bridger, I, ah, I," Annie stammered again.

"Annie, I'm so sorry. I shouldn't push you like that. I don't mean to. It's just that I love you so much," he added quickly.

"Bridger, you have to listen to me. I have so much to tell you. You don't have to apologize for anything. It makes me very happy to hear you say that we'll figure things out. There are times when I feel so sad, so confused. I've asked over and over, why? Why did God do this to me, to my family? Alex was the kindest, most giving person. My children were sweet innocents. We didn't deserve this. When I took that first step through the door today, my mind was flooded with memories and I wanted it all back. I wanted it to be the way it used to be and then, all those old feelings of sadness, longing and anger came rushing at me." The excitement in her voice had slipped away. Taking in a deep breath, she cleared her throat, allowing herself time to collect her thoughts and words. She wanted so say the right words. "What I'm trying to say is that I had no right to tell you there is a reason for everything that happens, when I really haven't accepted what had happened to me. Bridge, every day since they left me, it hurt just to breathe, knowing that each breath I took reminded me that I was still alive. I had to live on without them. I've felt as if I was sentenced to hell here on earth and then you came into my life. When I'm with you or just thinking about you, I can breathe. Bridge, I can breathe again and it doesn't hurt. I know, I've still got a lot of bad days ahead of me, and I can't just pretend this didn't happen, but I really want to breathe again, and I want to breathe with you. I love you. I love you. I love you."

Was he dreaming? Was this really happening? Bridger couldn't believe it. After all the years, his first love, whom he'd loved and wanted his entire life, loved him back.

After wiping away his tears and taking a long breath, Bridger confessed, "This is killing me, I want to hold you. I want you in my arms right now."

"Me too," Annie whispered through her tears. "When I get back, we will have the rest of our lives to hold each other, and as much as I need you and want you, I need to do this, Bridge. It's time for me to let go, and I promise that I am going to hurry and get everything taken care of, because the sooner things are done here, the sooner Buddy and I can head for home.

The next few days were extremely busy. Annie talked to Courtney and Cole about her idea and they were thrilled. Courtney confessed that Annie's idea was an answer to their prayers. Annie was amazed herself at all the prayers that were being answered. Everything seemed to fall into place. When she began the task of sorting through things, she knew instantly, who she was going to give it to or if she was going to keep it.

After three weeks of sorting, cleaning and visiting with family, Annie's job was almost complete. She and Karen had spent the last afternoon together making sure the house was ready for Courtney and Cole. They even decorated the bedroom, leaving a bucket of champagne, candles and an iPod loaded with romantic music. It was hard to say good-bye to Karen again but she knew as much as she would miss her family and friends, she couldn't wait for the morning to come so she could get on her way back to Bridger. Before leaving to spend the night at her parents, Annie started to take one final walk through the house. Thinking to herself as she neared the back door, she realized it had been nothing less than a small miracle how fast she had been able to take care of things. A strong feeling of excitement raced through her body as she imagined the surprised look on Bridger's face when she walked in the door tomorrow night. Before locking the back door, she stepped out on the deck and took a moment imagined to admire the night sky that was now filled with millions of twinkling stars.

With her hand holding the locket, Annie whispered to the heavens, "Oh, Alex, my babies, I know you are happy. You're in paradise, and nothing on earth can compare to that. All along I knew that, but now it is more than just knowing. I can feel that you're happy and I know that you know that I'm happy, too. Just promise me that you'll always remember how much I love you."

Chapter 19

The quietness of the evening was interrupted when Annie heard her cell phone ring. "Hello handsome!" she answered.

"How did you know it was me?" Bridger asked.

"Oh, I just knew or maybe it was the caller ID," Annie answered back with a giggle.

"I miss you. Are you about done? Did you figure out what day you're coming home yet?" Bridger asked.

"Not yet, but I am getting close. I've just got a few more things to do. I was just locking up and then I was going to head over to Mom and Dad's to spend the night," Annie replied.

"How come you're sleeping at your parents'?" Bridger asked.

"Oh, I guess I forgot to tell you. I just thought I would spend a few nights with them. I just wanted to have a little more time with them before I left." Annie said trying to sound convincing so that Bridger wouldn't figure out that she was headed back. They talked for a few moments, and then Annie figured that she had better say good-night or she might say something that would give away her plans.

Taking one last look at the night sky before heading in, Annie thought of Bridger. Shivers of happiness ran up and down her body. Over the past weeks, she had found herself smiling and talking constantly about him. Karen had loved teasing Annie about the way she was acting,, but truthfully she had thanked God every night that her dear friend had found love and happiness again.

Just as Annie was about to close the screen door, she looked up and watched two small jet airplanes fly over the house. As low as they were flying, she knew that they were heading toward the airport for a landing.

"The only jets that look like that and land at the Milford airport are Life Flight. Two of them must mean that something bad must have happened. I'd better see if I can help. After all, I am still an employee," Annie spoke out loud as she hurried and dialed the hospital.

A young lady on the other line answered, "Milford Hospital, this is Chloe, can I help you?" Not knowing Chloe, Annie tried to explain who she was and that she could come in and help out if they needed her.

The aide seemed to be a bit confused. "Did you say your name was Annie Davie?"

"No, Annie Davis," Annie repeated.

"Oh, Annie Davis, oh yeah, I've heard a lot about you. I've only been here about two weeks, but your name is very popular around here. You are the one that…"

The sound of Chloe's unfamiliar voice was interrupted by one that was more familiar. "Annie, is that you?" Dr. Ray asked. "What's up?"

Annie explained again how she had thought the two jets were Life Flight and apologized for bothering everyone.

"Thankfully, they are not landing for us, and I don't want to hear you apologize for caring. You know, I've said it before, but your ability to care about others is one of the things that I love most about you. As far as the jets go, I'll bet that they have something to do with the corporate hog farm or a mining company. Both of those companies have had a lot of the big corporate guys flying in here lately." Then Dr. Ray quickly changed the subject. "It's too bad that we didn't get to have lunch, but I have a few minutes, so maybe we can talk now."

Annie was able to catch up on a few of her favorite geriatric patients, but then, just like always, Dr. Ray was called back to the floor.

Annie hurried to finish up with a few more things that needed doing around the house, and then just as she was turning out the lights, she was surprised to hear the front doorbell ring.

"Who could that be?" Annie asked out loud as she turned and walked toward the front door. As she walked by the front window, she noticed Dr. Ray's car parked out front. *Dr. Ray—that's impossible! I just talked to him, and he was at the hospital,* she thought to herself as she opened the door only to find that it wasn't Dr. Ray but Bridger. "Bridge, it's you! It's you." She couldn't get her arms around him fast enough. "Oh, I've missed you so much. What are you doing here? I just talked to you on the phone."

It was totally unbelievable how wonderful it felt to be in his arms again. In between the kisses, he answered, "I couldn't wait another day. I've waited a lifetime for you, and I just couldn't wait any longer."

Taking Bridger's hand, Annie led him to the couch, "You'd better sit down. I'll bet your legs are tired."

As soon as Bridger sat down, Annie jumped in Bridger's lap, wrapped her arms around his neck, and began kissing him again. Buddy had been sleeping in the rocking chair when the doorbell ring had hurried to catch up to Annie. He was just as excited as she was when he saw Bridger. As soon as they sat on the couch, he hurried and joined them.

"I missed you too, Buddy!" Bridger said as he reached to scratch his neck.

Annie learned back and with a big smile across her face and said, "Well, I guess you're not going to get your surprise now."

"Surprise, oh come on, that's not fair!" Bridger said and then tried to look as if he were pouting.

"I couldn't stand to be away from you a moment longer, so Buddy and I were going to fly home tomorrow. Gosh, I can't believe how much I've missed you. How did you get here?" As soon as the words left her mouth, Annie figured it out. "Oh, I guess, I was wrong. Our little airport runway here in Milford can handle those big fancy jets after all. But, why did you bring two? What did you do, bring your posse with you?" She asked with a giggle.

"Sort of," Bridger confessed. "But first, you are going to have to let me stand up for just a minute."

Annie wasn't too crazy about letting him go, but she figured his legs must have been hurting. "OK," she said as she scooted over so that he could stand up.

Bridger stood up for just a moment, stretched, and then holding onto the arm of the couch, bent down on one knee and faced Annie. Then he gently embraced her face with both of his hands and said, "Annie, I love you with all of my heart and soul, and I don't want to spend another minute without you by my side. Annie Davis, will you do me the honor of becoming my wife?" Then he reached onto his pocket and pulled out a beautiful diamond ring.

Her hands instinctively reached to wipe his tears and answered, "Yes, Bridger Jones, I will!" After a kiss to seal the deal, Bridger took hold of Annie's left hand gently placed the ring on her finger.

With a smile so big it hurt, Bridger looked at his beloved and asked, "How about tomorrow?"

"Tomorrow, as in tomorrow," Annie asked, smiling back? "What about your mother and Flora. We can't get married without them."

"We won't have to," he said, still grinning.

"What do you mean we won't have to? Are they here? Did you bring them with you? Where are they? I can't wait to see them. But Bridge, how could we ever figure out a wedding in one day?" Annie asked while at the same time thinking how everything could be worked out.

"Well, you have been gone three weeks, and I've had quite a bit of time on my hands. No one to make scrapbooks with, no one to play chess with, no one to kiss," he teased. "The moment, I started planning the trip, I knew that if I came here, I wouldn't be able to wait if you said yes, and I am thankful that you said yes, because I brought the wedding with me. Well, at least the things your mom and Karen told me to bring. Oh and I forgot to tell you that Mom and Flora are at the motel waiting for me to call them."

"You all must have been pretty sure that I was going to say yes," Annie said winking. "Sounds like you've thought of everything."

"Yep, and I was pretty sure," he answered, making his way back to the couch and pulling Annie back onto his lap. "You know, your family and friends are amazing. I can't believe how much they have helped me. Even Joe and Gladys helped. I can't wait to meet everybody."

"I know they are all going to love you, but no one will ever love you as much as I do," Annie said as she reached to kiss him.

With each kiss, their embrace became more intense. "Annie, I um, I think we had better head over to your parents' house, because if we don't stop doing what we're doing right now, our honeymoon night, which is supposed to be tomorrow night, is going to be tonight," Bridger said frowning as he gently pulled away. "I always thought training for a game took a lot of endurance, but I want you to know this is the hardest thing that I have ever done."

Annie let out a sigh. "You're right," she agreed. After moving off the couch, she offered Bridger her hand. "Come with me. I want to show you the house."

Walking hand in hand, she gave him a tour of each room and shared some of the memories that had made the house a home. Annie was glad Bridger was there with her. Now that he was, she couldn't imagine how she thought she could have taken her last walk through the house by herself. When it came time to close the front door and turn the lock, Annie prayed silently. "Lord, as hard as it is to close this door, I know now there are new ones for me to open. Thank you."

Just before they separated for the drive to Annie's parents, Bridger was standing on the sidewalk next to Annie. His hands were in his pockets and he was fidgeting.

"What's wrong, Bridge? Annie asked.

"This is probably going to sound so stupid, but now it is so easy to see that Alex was such a good husband. What if I can't be like him? What I mean is, ah, I don't know what I mean. I just want to make you happy. Oh man, this must sound so lame."

Annie hurried and took Bridger by the hands and looked directly into his eyes and thought. *How could I have not known that he was Robert?* Everything was so clear now. She could see the shy little boy who had walked past her at the swimming pool so many years ago, and she was filled with the same feelings she'd had then. All she wanted to do was protect him.

"Oh, Bridge, I am happy!"

After following Annie to her parents' house, Bridger made a quick stop before calling it a night. He was anxious to meet Lil and Barney in person. Annie's face glowed with happiness when she introduced him to her parents, and after a short visit, everyone agreed that they needed to get to bed so that they wouldn't be tired for the big day.

After placing a soft kiss upon his soon-to-be wife's cheek, Bridger told her one more time how much he loved her.

"I love you too, but can I ask you just one question about tomorrow?" Annie asked, smiling.

"OK, I guess you're allowed one question," Bridger answered back in a teasing tone.

"Well, I was just wondering what I was going to wear to my wedding."

"Crap, I knew I forgot something," Bridger answered and started rubbing his forehead with his hand. "What are we going to do?"

Annie's smiling face turned to worry, but within seconds she started thinking about how she could find a dress.

"Annie, I'm just teasing. I really don't know what you're wearing, but you don't have to worry, because that was on your mom and Karen's list of things to do," Bridger laughed before he gave Annie one last kiss goodnight.

"Oh, you are a funny guy, mister, but I want you to know there will be a payback!" Annie shot back.

As Bridger climbed into the car, he replied, "I figured." Then changing the subject, he said, "Hey, I was just thinking. You will be the most beautiful bride my Uncle Ray has ever seen twice."

Annie watched him drive away and then returned to the house. Lost in her dreams, she didn't even notice her father as he walked toward her.

"You really are happy, aren't you, sweetheart?" he asked before he took a drag of his cigarette and tossed it.

"I never thought it would be possible, Dad, but I am. I am so happy," Annie answered before she gave him a look of concern about his cigarette habit.

"Oh, don't worry. I'm quitting tomorrow. I don't need those things anymore," Barney answered as put his arm around his daughter's shoulder.

The wedding couldn't have been more beautiful. The little church that Annie had attended all of her life was filled with flowers, family, and friends, and as Bridger had predicted, Annie had looked just as beautiful on her second wedding day as she had her first. Karen and her mother had picked a simple white satin gown that fell slightly off her shoulders along with some fresh baby's breath for her hair.

Karen served as the matron of honor, and Ed Summers and Buddy shared the honor of being the best men. Buddy looked very handsome in his hand-tailored tuxedo that Bridger had custom ordered. Tradition usually calls for the best man to stand by the groom, but not this time. Buddy shared the honor of walking the bride down the aisle along with her father, and then he stood proudly by her side throughout the entire ceremony.

The sleepy little town of Milford would never forget the day Annie and Bridger were married. The wedding party and their guests were treated to an afternoon and evening of feasting and music. The little church seemed to

Finally

glow with happiness. After hours of celebrating their new marriage, Bridger thanked everyone for all their help, their love, and for sharing the happiest day of his life. Then he took his bride by the hand and led her to the limo that would take them to the Learjet, which was waiting to fly them to a honeymoon suite in Las Vegas. The following afternoon, they left for two weeks in Hawaii. Buddy headed back home with Mary and Flora on the other Learjet and waited patiently for his beloved Annie to return. Just as Barney had predicted, Buddy enjoyed the flight back in the jet with his own recliner, far more than his flight out in a dog carrier.

Chapter 20

Epilogue

Faith and Jacob's first birthday was celebrated in Milford, along with family, friends, and the entire community. As soon as the library, gym, and park were complete, Joe and Barney reminded Annie that they had asked her to dedicate them, and it just so happened that the twins' first birthday was the same day as the dedication. There had never been such a celebration to hit the little town. There were building dedications, a birthday party for two famous babies, a parade, a town barbecue, and a fireworks show like no other. Bridger had been asked to speak at the dedications, but he had declined, knowing that the celebration had nothing to do with his life or football. He was happy just to be with his wife and kids. And as he watched Annie speak at the dedication ceremony, the pride he felt that day surpassed any emotion a win at a Super Bowl could have ever given him.

At the dedication program, Annie announced that The Alex Davis Library had been built in memory of Alex and his love of children and education. She also told the crowd that each year at graduation, there would be two scholarships awarded to two graduating students from Milford High School. After sharing some of her special memories of her husband and how much he had loved his town of Milford, Annie moved on and announced that the new gymnasium would be named The Jack Davis Memorial Gym in honor of her son, Jack, who had lived the heart of a true athlete. She spoke fondly of her son and said that Jack always had the will to reach his next goal by practicing and using his strong determination to keep going, but his best qualities were those of patience and concern for his fellow teammates.

Annie turned and looked at Bridger when she said, "A wise man once said to me, 'Remember, it's just a game. In the end, it's the people that you love that are the most important.'"

She dedicated the park to her two daughters, Kara and Molly. Annie told the crowd that her daughters had taught her to make sure that she took the time to play and enjoy life, especially the simplest of moments. Annie looked over the audience when she said, "If there is anything I want you to remember about this day, it's that I want you to tell those you care about that you love them often, because one never knows what tomorrow will bring."

Jake Norton was the first to stand, and then the crowd followed, giving Annie a standing ovation.

Annie and Bridger's friends and family planned the birthday party for the twins. Everyone in the town had been invited. The new park was decorated like a circus. There was a petting zoo, along with pony rides, and there were one hundred decorated birthday cakes for the babies. The twins sat in highchairs on a small podium and were served birthday cake and ice cream while everyone joined together and sang "Happy Birthday." Everyone hooted and hollered as the twins took their first bite of birthday cake. Faith and Jake had a wonderful time and seemed to eat up all the attention.

Many of the same news reporters who had reported the accident over two years ago were there to finish their story. The photographers were captivated by the twins, and they snapped hundreds of photos of them as they gobbled up their birthday cakes.

The last night of the celebration included a dance at the city outdoor pavilion. Grandmas Lil and Gladys, and Grandpas Barney and Joe, insisted that they would baby-sit, and Bridger and Annie were to go to the dance and have fun. While they were at the dance, Annie had fun seeing all of her old friends, and Bridger enjoyed meeting new ones, though, Bridger had to admit he was a bit embarrassed when Annie introduced him to a lady named Stephanie. Luckily, Stephanie wasn't one to hold grudges. She even asked Bridger if he would pose for a picture with her and her family. While Bridger was getting his pictures taken, Jake Norton spotted Annie and asked her for a dance.

Walking hand in hand to the floor, Jake and Annie danced to a slow song.

Finally

"Annie, I'm so happy that things have worked out for you," Jake said as they danced.

"Thanks, Jake. Did you ever find your special girl?" Annie asked.

"Almost, but she married a guy named Davis and then one named Jones," he answered with a wink.

"Oh, Jake, we make better friends—always have and always will. You know, I named my son after you," Annie said smiling.

"When I heard his name was Jacob, I thought that you had just picked a good name, but I didn't know it was because of me," Jake replied, somewhat surprised and humbled.

"Jake, do you remember the day you almost ran over Buddy?" Annie asked.

"Did you have to remind me? I don't think I'll ever forget your face that day!" he answered and then added, "But I'm confused. How did my almost running over your beloved pup make you want to name your son after me?"

"That day and that experience finally caused me to let go of my pride and ask God to come back into my life. I really do believe in fate, and I am so grateful that it was you. Someone else could have reacted way differently than you did."

"Thanks Annie. That means a lot to me. I still miss Alex," Jake said and looked at the ground.

"I miss him too and I always will." Annie said, giving her old friend a hug.

Annie and Jake walked back to Bridger, who was now standing by Sherri.

Jake gave Annie one last hug and a kiss on the cheek and said, "Thank you for the dance and if you ever need a friend, you know where I am."

At that same moment, Annie looked over at Sherri and wondered if she and Jake had ever met.

"Jake, this is my good friend Sherri. Have you two met?" Annie asked the both of them.

"I don't believe so," Jake said with a huge smile.

Sherri reached to shake Jake's hand and with an even bigger smile said, "It's really nice to meet you, Jake."

Seconds later, Jake and Sherri were out on the floor dancing.

"Wife, are you playing matchmaker?" Bridger asked as he wrapped his arms around his wife.

"No, maybe just giving fate a little help." Annie answered.

Just then the lead singer of the band announced that the last slow song of the night was next. "How about one more dance before we head back and see how our babies are doing?"

"That sounds good to me," Bridger said as he led his wife back to the dance floor.

Both Annie and Bridger felt cold chills run up their spines when they realized what song the band was playing. It was the same song that Alex had dedicated to Annie, when he asked her to marry him, the night of the senior prom.

"I think an angel must have made a request to the band," Bridger whispered softly in his wife's ear. "I feel like I'm eighteen years old again but I guess this time, I had the courage to ask you to dance."

"That's amazing, I was thinking the same thing," Annie said and then she got a curious look on her face.

"What are you thinking about? You're squeezing your eyes together," Bridger asked with a curious smile.

"Maybe we shouldn't go home just yet. If you're feeling like you're eighteen, I was thinking maybe we should go and check out the stars or something like that," Annie answered and then gave her husband a mischievous smile.

"I love you," Bridger replied as he led his wife off the dance floor.

After the celebration, Annie and Bridger stayed a few extra days to visit with their family and friends. On the last day of their visit, just as they were about to leave town, Annie asked if they could make one last stop. She wanted to stop by the cemetery and take some flowers. After arriving at the cemetery, Annie showed Bridger the graves, and then he and Buddy watched the babies so that Annie could have some time for her thoughts.

Buddy had taken the role of watching the babies very seriously from the time they had brought them home from the hospital. Sometimes Annie had even teased him that he'd forgotten all about her. When the babies started to walk at eleven months, they had kept Buddy very busy. He would run to Faith and then to Jake, and then back to Faith and then to Jake again. He would make it just in time to either be there for them to grab onto or he'd act as a pillow softening their falls. Many times, he'd saved them from what could have been some pretty bad ouchies.

Finally

Bridger held Faith by the hand and Jacob and Buddy tagged along behind. After he and the kids had made the circle around the cemetery, he let go of Faith so that she could do some exploring on her own before they had to get back into the car. But instead of taking off on her own, she followed her daddy as he walked over to put his arm around his wife but when he stopped, she continued until she came to Molly's headstone. Once she was there, she patted the stone with her little hand.

Annie's eyes were filled with tears. "It just makes me sad that my children don't know each other. I just wish that Faith and Jake could somehow know them. I know it sounds weird, but I do," she said holding onto Bridger a bit tighter.

"Mawee," Faith said in baby talk. "Mawee."

"You know your sister, Molly, don't you, baby girl?" Bridger said. Then he looked at Annie, smiled and said, "Don't worry. They'll know all about Alex, Jack, Kara, and Molly. After all, they've got the world's best scrap booker as a mom."

Turning to face her husband, Annie nodded her head and gave him a smile.

After a moment or two in their own thoughts, Bridger asked, "Do you think they would have liked me?"

"No, Bridge, I know they love you!" Annie answered, reaching for his hand. "I guess it's time to hit the road. We've got a long drive ahead of us and I want to make sure we have time to have a cheeseburger with my favorite highway patrolman. I'll miss seeing Faye, but the last time we talked, she told me that she and the boys loved living in Tahoe."

"We aren't going to have to have any fire drills along the way, are we?" Bridger asked teasingly as he winked.

"You never know what's going to happen with me in your life," Annie answered with a smile.

Bridger and Annie loaded the babies back into their car seats, and then Buddy jumped in and took his place between them. Jake, Faith, and Buddy were asleep before they had even left town. Bridger steered the car west, and Annie took the moment to enjoy the desert morning. As they headed down off the Frisco Mountain and into the Wah Wah Valley, Annie took in the big, western sky that was filled with white, billowy clouds and once again, she caught sight of a herd of antelope running along the valley floor. Thinking quietly to herself, Annie came to realize that so many things in life seemed the same and at the same time so incredibly different. Sometimes the tragedy that took her family felt like it happened only yesterday and sometimes it felt like a whole other lifetime away. But once again, finally, Annie was headed for home.

Made in the USA
San Bernardino, CA
20 March 2014